A Turn of Cards

A Turn of Cards

Lowland Romance Book 3

Helen Susan Swift

Prelude

Even now I remember that evening. If I close my eyes I can hear the soft snick of cards on the polished walnut table and the sonorous ticking of the long-case clock. I can feel the gentle heat of the fire that crackled in the grate at my back and see the shifting shadow of the chandelier that swung slowly from the ceiling. It is a layered memory, for it is set in the middle of my life story, with the past behind it and my then-future in front, a hinge-day from which much sprung, yet also a day that reminded me of the steps that had brought me to such a pass.

There were eight of us present that October night in 1803. Emily Napier and her silent husband James, Elizabeth Campbell and the amiable Colin Campbell, young Marie Elliot and Gilbert, her intended, Mrs Bessie Faa, famous as Mother Faa and me, Dorothea Flockhart, *Miss* Dorothea Flockhart. You will notice that alone of the company, I had neither husband nor sweetheart. I was alone in this world of turmoil and tribulation and determined to remain in that state of solitude for I neither sought nor wished for anything to do with the sterner sex.

You may wonder at my disdain for men when much of our female world revolved around matrimony and much of the conversation of the unmarried centred on beaux and sweethearts and marrying greatly. Not only women discussed the opposite sex for in the male world, where business or the military or the running of an estate took up so much time, matrimony also figured in large part. A man needed an heir, and only a good wife could adequately provide such a thing. Why was I out of step with the tune that society played? I had my reasons and excellent reasons they were.

'Now pay attention.' Although Mother Faa spoke quietly, everybody in the room heard her. She shuffled the pack and spread the cards like a fan across the table. 'You all know what night it is.'

We nodded, one by one, some serious, most amused.

'It's the 31st October,' Emily said.

'It's Halloween,' Marie watched Mother Faa's multiple-ringed hands pass over the cards.

'It's Halloween,' Mother Faa lowered her voice, so I had to strain to hear her, 'the night of the year when witches and warlocks come out. The night of the year when the door to our world opens and the creatures of the supernatural enter.'

I would have snorted disbelief until I saw the expression on Mother Faa's face and the attention that Emily and Marie were paying. Colin and James exchanged amused glances while Gibbie Elliot poured himself another drink.

'We are five minutes short of midnight,' Mothers Faa continued, 'when the power is at its height.' She flicked the cards together again and lifted one finger. 'I will tell one fortune at that time. One only.' She looked at each of us in turn, her dark eyes unsettling.

We all exchanged glances. James smiled and squeezed Emily's arm. The Campbells looked serious, and Marie put a hand over her mouth, shaking her head.

'Whose?' Gibbie Elliot tapped a finger on the table. He was smiling, as if eager to be chosen.

'Whoever needs it most,' Mother Faa shuffled the pack. 'You must decide.' She smelled of wood-smoke and earth and the wild places of the world although I knew the rings that weighed down her ears were of pure gold. She did not belong in that urbane company, but there again, neither did I.

I kept my counsel as the others began to chatter. I could see Marie watching Gilbert. Her left hand stole across the table and touched his arm. I said nothing. It was none of my affair.

'No,' Gilbert said. 'You decide, Mother Faa.' He leaned back with a devil-damn-you smile on his face.

'Yes, do, Mother Faa,' Emily followed his lead. 'You must decide.'

I listened to the soft whirr and tick of the clock as Mother Faa ruffled the pack again. There is something quite ominous about the sound of a clock. From the instant that we are born, we have a limited time in this world, and every tick of the clock marks one second less in which to exist. I counted the seconds towards my own end and wondered what life was all about. The minute hand flicked forward and vibrated slightly; it was one minute short of midnight.

I did not care.

'Is that what you all wish?' Mother Faa asked.

'Yes, yes, get on with it,' Colin said at once, and the others nodded. I followed suit as Mother Faa fixed me with a stare. Her eyes were dark, bottomless pits in a face seamed by wrinkles. Yet despite her advanced years, they were bright with life while mine had long since lost their lustre.

Mother Faa gripped my hand. 'Touch the cards,' she said.

I started. I had not expected to be singled out. Then I shrugged; it did not matter.

'Touch the cards,' Mother Faa repeated.

When I did so, they were slightly warm with a sticky residue. Mother Faa pressed my fingers hard onto the pack. 'Say your name.'

'Dorothea Flockhart,' I tried to ease away from Mother Faa's eyes, but they held me fast. I could see nothing but her dark dilated pupils, sucking me inside her mind. I did not wish to travel there, to a place unknown.

'Now think about yourself.' Mother Faa's voice bored into my head. I did as she commanded, thinking about my life, past and present. It did not take long for I had no desire to linger in the dark rooms.

'Good,' Mother Faa released my fingers although her gaze did not relax. I was within her eyes, lost in her darkness that was so different from my own. 'Shuffle the pack.'

The cards stuck together as I shuffled. I handed them back. 'There you are.'

Mother Faa's fingers brushed the back of my hand as she recovered the pack. Her gaze remained fixed on me. I knew there were others in the room yet I could not see them. Nothing existed outside the duo of Mother Faa and me. 'Now cut seven times and place the chosen cards on the table.'

I did so, and Mothers Faa removed the top card of the seven little piles and placed it in front of her. I could not watch. I could not ease away from her eyes. I could only exist as the clock ticked again, mercifully shortening my life by another second.

'I have selected one card for the past, one for the present and the rest for your future.' Mother Faa looked down, and I felt the physical release as the power of her gaze ended. The clock continued to tick away my life. There was no other sound in that room.

'You have had a troubled past,' Mother Faa said. 'I see great distress there.'

I nodded. I knew my past and had no desire to return there. It waited to ambush me if I thought of it.

'You are not as happy as you could be in your present,' Mother Faa did not look up from her cards. 'You are lonely.'

'I am not lonely,' I denied. Mother Faa snorted.

Emily tapped me with her fan and whispered something. I did not hear the words. I had forgotten that she was there.

For the first time, I glanced down at the cards. Only two were face up, presumably the ones that signified my past and present. Mother Faa turned over the others, one by one.

The cards meant nothing to me. Two number cards and three face cards, a knave, a king and a queen. Mother Faa pored over them.

'What secrets are you hiding, Dorothea Flockhart?'

I shook my head. 'I have none that I wish to share.'

'That will not do, Dorothea Flockhart, the cards don't lie!' There was venom in Mother Faa's words. 'You are more secretive than open, and you hide more of you than you reveal.'

I said nothing, acutely aware that everyone was watching me. Marie started to comment but closed her mouth as Mother Faa continued.

'There is a man in your future.'

'That's good,' Marie was of too amiable a nature not to comment. 'Isn't that good, Dorothea?'

I said nothing. I did not need a man. They were unnecessary, insidious complications and I liked things to be clean and straightforward. I had done with men and their lies and deceits and … Other things. I shook away the memories, knowing they would return later.

'Of course, it's good,' Gilbert gave his approval. 'Every woman needs a man and every man needs a woman.' He exchanged smiles with Marie.

'He will wear a uniform,' Mrs Faa said.

'Oh, that's even better,' Marie enthused. 'He'll be an officer, Dorothea, a Colonel maybe, or a brave Captain of cavalry.'

I thought of the officers that swaggered around Edinburgh with their scarlet uniforms, side whiskers and gold braid. I did not wish to have anything to do with them. 'I don't wish a man to control my life.'

'Oh, they're not that bad,' Emily glanced at James. 'We know you're not on the catch and some men are trustworthy.'

James gave a little smile. 'Some.'

'Not many,' I knew that I was insulting three of my companions and withdrew the statement. 'I do not mean anybody at this table.'

'We all know that, Dorothea.' Marie was always first to spread oil over troubled waters. She was a treasure, that girl, and I hoped that Gibbie Elliot valued her as such.

'I see trouble around you,' Mother Faa had waited for the comments to subside. 'I see trouble and the draining of wealth.' When she looked up, I saw concern deep in her shadowed eyes. 'Take care, Dorothea Flockhart, and be careful of the horned beast that will bring death or happiness.'

'The horned beast?' I said. 'What does that mean?'

Mother Faa skiffed the cards together. 'I do not interpret what the cards tell me. I only tell you what I see.'

'How on earth can you see a horned beast?' I asked. 'There was nothing like that in the cards, only faces and figures.'

Mother Faa put her cards together. 'Your life is set to change.' Standing up, she walked out of the room, leaving me to my thoughts and the remorseless ticking of the clock. Talk of a possible future had awakened nightmares from my past.

'A man in a uniform,' Elizabeth Campbell said. 'How wonderful, Dorothea. You never know, we may have you married off before we pass another twelve-month.'

'Unless the horned beast comes for me,' I tried to make a jest of it. I did not feel like jesting. It was five minutes after midnight, and I wished I had never come that night.

Chapter One

I gasped as the coach jolted over a rut. 'I wish somebody would do something about these roads.'

Emily nodded. She peered out of the window. 'We're nearly there now.' She smiled. 'It's not like you to go to this sort of expedition, Dorothea. You must have taken Mother Faa's words to heart.'

'You mean I should search for a man with a uniform?' I shook my head. 'No, Emily, I only wish a distraction. I am not interested in finding a man.' No man would want to know me, once he discovered my past.

Emily frowned. 'Why not, Dorothea? You can't live alone all your life. Don't you wish a husband to look after you?'

'I don't need a man to look after me, thank you. I can look after myself very well.'

I must have sounded testy for Emily gave me a sideways look, softened with a small smile. 'There are other benefits of marriage.'

'You mean money?' I decided to be deliberately obtuse. 'I have sufficient for my needs.'

'I did not only mean money.' Emily said. 'I meant something quite different.' She lowered her voice, no doubt in case she shocked the driver or frightened the horses. 'I mean the physical side of things.'

'Oh, *that.*' I said. I knew too much about the *physical side of things.*

'Yes, that.' Emily touched my arm. 'It's comforting to have a man who loves you. It is quieting to have a man hold you at night.'

I nodded. 'I'm sure it is.' I closed that subject.

Emily peered at me across the width of the coach. 'Am I making you uncomfortable?'

I shook my head. 'No, Emily. I am quite all right.'

'Mother Faa was correct,' Emily said. 'You do have secrets. You never talk about yourself.' The carriage jolted again, throwing her against me. We disentangled ourselves, with Emily laughing. 'I declare that I will be one large bruise by the time we reach Portobello.'

'Travelling does have its discomforts,' I agreed and relapsed into my accustomed silence as we followed the road.

'Look!' Emily tapped her finger on the window. 'We're here.'

I looked outside where the long cold waves splintered into froth along the sand. A flotilla of seagulls paraded above, searching for prey under the grey clouds. Compared to the brilliant colours and heat of Bengal, this east coast of Scotland was a dismal place in early winter.

'This is where they will land.' Emily held onto my arm. 'Right here.' She indicated the long sweep of Portobello beach. 'Look!' A troop of cavalry practised their swordsmanship on a row of turnips set on stakes.

'They look the part,' I said. The cavalry wore splendid scarlet coats with blue collar and cuffs, silver breeches, black boots and helmets complete with leopard skin crest and white hackles. 'If ornamental uniforms could win wars Boney would take one look and surrender.'

Emily smiled. 'They are doing their best.'

One cavalryman made a galloping run and slashed at the nearest turnip. 'Cut them down, the villains, cut them down!' His sabre missed the vegetable by a wide margin.

'If that is an example of our defenders, Boney has little to concern himself with,' I said.

'That gentleman is the Quartermaster of the Royal Edinburgh Volunteer Light Dragoons,' Emily said after a moment's scrutiny. 'Walter Scott. He's an Edinburgh solicitor and a bit of a quiz.'

'I see,' I said, watching as the legal warrior dismounted and limped along the beach. 'I hope that our regular soldiers are more skilled than the Volunteers.'

Emily nodded. 'I don't believe you will be setting your cap at Mr Scott, then.'

'I don't believe I will,' I nearly rebuked Emily for using such a commonplace expression but forbore. It was not her fault that I was in a foul mood.

'The army will be waiting if the Frenchies come.' Emily was always forgiving. It was one reason I liked her.

I imagined the scene with the barges full of blue-coated soldiers approaching the bay, their bow-guns flaring orange as they fired at the defenders, the tricolour displayed at the stern and the hammer of artillery drowning the sound of the surf. 'Yes.' It was an inadequate response.

'It could be next month, or next week,' Emily gripped tighter. 'It could be tomorrow.' She looked out to sea as if the French fleet might rise from beneath the waves.

'That might be so.' I pulled the shawl tighter around my shoulders against the smirr of rain. 'Let's hope Nelson can keep them at bay. When does this thing start, Emily?'

'Soon. Look!' Emily pointed. 'Here are the ships!'

I saw them, ten single-masted gunboats creeping under sweeps across the chopped water of the Firth of Forth. Each had a white spume of spray at her bow and wore the Union Flag on her stern; presumably, in case we thought the French had indeed come to infest the Forth.

'Nelson would be proud,' I said.

'Or Admiral Duncan,' Emily waved her handkerchief to the gunboats.

'The army will be here soon, then,' I looked around. A crowd was beginning to gather along the beach, men and women and families come to watch the fun. A couple of collie dogs gambolled, furiously barking as they ran from person to person. A group of children ran to the waves and paddled while their mothers endeavoured to take them to drier ground. A less warlike scene would be hard to imagine.

Emily grabbed my arm. 'Listen!'

I heard the sweet trilling of fifes and the rhythmic tap of the drum. It is strange that the military makes such evocative melodies, pretty sounds to encourage men to march to their slaughter. The music accompanied the gaudy uniforms, both hiding the reality of warfare. I despised the senseless mass-murder as one group of rulers decided they wanted to control another group and all the people in that segment of land should expose themselves to agony and death on behalf of a coloured flag. All the same, I felt my toe tapping on the soft sand.

'Here they come.' I allowed Emily to show me a small group of mounted officers riding erect and proud above the crowd, closely followed by the Colours bouncing in military splendour. Behind them came a black column of shakoes, each resplendent with a blue plume, side by side with the barrels of muskets and the broad blades of pikes.

'That's the Third Battalion Midlothian Volunteers,' a knowledgeable man in a tall hat told his wife. 'They're to defend the beach against the Navy.'

'Oh, I see.' The wife looked bored. She pulled a child close to her and wiped its perfectly clean nose.

'Make way, there!' A tall red-faced major shouted and a host of sergeants reinforced his words, pushing at us with hard words and horizontal halberds until we backed away from the beach.

'I hope that's not your uniformed officer.' Emily said. 'He looks out of temper with the world.'

I smiled. 'I have no intention of finding an officer, whatever Mother Faa might say.' I watched the major hectoring a trio of junior officers with language that he should hesitate to use in front of ladies. I had no wish to ever meet such a man, let alone have him in my life.

'I have never heard so many oaths,' Emily said. 'That major is quite a card. He should be on stage.'

I nodded. 'He would draw a crowd for his language alone.'

Within a remarkably short period, the Volunteers had cleared us off the beach so they could practise fighting the French.

These sort of military Field Days were fairly common when we waited in daily expectation of Boney's Frenchmen invading. As well as giving the militia and the Volunteers the opportunity of improving their military skills, it provided free entertainment for crowds of people, a chance for some recruiting and plenty of purses for the busy pick-pockets to snatch.

The gunboats formed in line abreast half a mile off Portobello. Despite my dislike of wars, I could not help but watch. The boats were three cables-lengths apart and with a cluster of men around the six-pounder cannon in the bows. I saw the puff of smoke around each gun a second before I heard the crack of the shots.

'Oh, they're firing! How exciting!' Emily clapped her hands together, the white calfskin gloves making little sound against the rising clamour of the crowd.

The foul-mouthed major shouted more orders, and the Volunteers spread out to form two long red lines, the line in front carrying muskets and the one in the rear with the long pikes.

'Why don't they all carry muskets?' Emily asked. 'They could kill more Frenchmen then.'

'Oh, you bloodthirsty thing!' I rebuked her. 'I don't think they possess any more muskets. That's why they have pikes.'

'It's very mediaeval,' Emily said. I did not argue. It seemed strange that a nation as rich as Britain should arm its men with weapons similar to those used by Spartan hoplites or Wallace's freedom-fighters.

The gunboats were closer now so I could make out the faces of the crews, who cheered and shouted like madmen and waved cutlasses and muskets in the air. The cannons fired again, causing Emily to start.

'Oh, my goodness. I do hope nobody gets hurt.'

'They're only firing powder,' I reassured her. 'Not solid ball.'

'Do you think so?'

'I hope so,' I said. 'We've few enough men to defend the country without killing them off in Field Days.'

With white powder smoke adding to the rain, vision was unclear, so we only saw the left flank of the Volunteers, with the double scarlet line becoming more obscure as it stretched toward Joppa in the east. The gunboats were now a couple of hundred yards from the shore with the crews still bunching in the bows. The cannons roared again, echoed by the major's hectoring voice.

The front rank of Volunteers stepped smartly forward until they stood at the line of surf. The major strode along the line, while half a dozen other officers stood at regular distances.

'What about him?' Emily indicated a tall captain. 'He's handsome enough, surely.' She gave a sly smile. 'If I were not married to James I would give him a second look, and a third.'

'I'm not looking for an officer,' I said, 'whatever Mother Faa said.' I wished I had not gone to Emily's house that evening.

'He's a very handsome captain,' Emily insisted, turning her head to one side for a better look.

'You can have him, then,' I nudged her forward.

'I'm married!' Emily tried to look shocked.

'Then neither of us is interested.' I said.

The Volunteers stood at rigid attention until the major shouted again. The long brown muskets came up, the men aimed and then fired a rolling volley that sounded like hell's thunder.

'My! What a noise!' Emily clutched my arm in delight.

At the major's orders, the second line of Volunteers formed into four columns.

The volley of blanks failed to stop the gunboats, which ground onto the sand about fifty yards further out. The crews immediately jumped into the shallow water with a loud splashing and yelling and waving of cutlasses andboarding pikes.

'They're active enough but not quite Boney's Invincibles.' Emily crushed her handkerchief in both hands, her eyes bright. 'Isn't this exciting?'

The major gave an incomprehensible order, and the first Volunteer line fired another volley of blanks and then formed four great gaps through which the columns of pikemen charged. One unfortunate fellow slipped, jammed the point of his pike into the ground and came down in a tangle of scarlet jacket and white trousers. The others advanced at the run and jabbed at the seamen with their long pikes. For a moment the line of surf and gunboats became a mock-battlefield, although not all the strokes were in jest as warriors of the land and the sea threw more than a few shrewd blows in earnest.

Within a few moments, and possibly in a pre-determined outcome, the seamen turned around and pushed their boats back into deeper water. The sweeps frantically flailed as they withdrew.

'Well, that's Boney defeated again,' Emily sounded satisfied.

'I wish it were that easy.' I watched the Volunteers congratulate each other as the major passed around a silver flask to the officers. The handsome captain was smiling, his teeth white against a tanned face. I looked away without having to remind myself that I had no interest.

A civilian in a low-crowned hat as battered as his face, and old-fashioned knee breeches that had seen better days hurried through the Volunteers to help the fallen pikeman.

'There's another noble fellow there,' Emily nodded to a be-whiskered lieutenant who presented his profile to us. His chin was nearly as prominent as his nose.

'I don't believe I should like him.' I said. 'Come, Emily, the rain is getting heavy now.' I watched the battered civilian help the pikeman to his feet. His gentleness contrasted with the seeming indifference of the soldiers. The two men limped away together, with the civilian balancing the long pike on his left shoulder. Eventually, the tall captain strolled across and took the pike. I watched the other officers drinking and laughing together, and my opinion of them dropped even further. At least the captain had *tried to* help, I thought, grudgingly, albeit a little late.

With our parasols giving little protection from the increasingly heavy rain, we hurried to the carriage. Emily squealed as she stepped into a deep puddle, and we hunched our shoulders and tried to push through the crowd. When we first arrived the road had been comparatively quiet, but now our carriage stood in the middle of a whole row of chariots, carriages and country carts. The horses drooped under the rain, while the drivers sought what shelter they could and exchanged desultory conversation as they smoked their pipes. There were farmers in their best blue coats and broad-brimmed hats, with smart knee-breeches and shining brass buckles on their shoes; there were a scattering of hillmen with black-and-white collie dogs and a few ploughmen with clay on their boots and gay gaiters. Mainly though, there were city folk and townsfolk out to see the soldiers, white-faced clerks and their simpering wives, brewers and distillers, shop assistants, sharp-faced lawyers and solemn men from the university.

One mulberry coloured coach stood apart from the rest, with a handsome coachman sitting in front with his fancy hammercloth cape resplendent with lace and his tricorn hat dripping with water. On either side of the door, a liveried footman paraded his yellow uniform with a short jacket and breeches so tight I feared for the wearer should they ever have to bend.

The carriage door was open, and an elderly lady sat inside with her white well-coiled hair dry and her hands sparkling with rings.

'Good afternoon, your Ladyship' Emily gave a deep curtsey.

'Good evening Mrs Napier.'

'May I present my friend Miss Dorothea Flockhart?' Emily touched my arm.

'Good evening,' I gave a curtsey, wondering who this quiz may be.

'This is Lady Pluscarden.' Emily made the introduction.

'Most people just call me Pluscarden.' Her Ladyship's smile was warmer than I had expected as she leaned closer to me. 'You will see that I don't venture out of my chariot on wet days. Why should I, when I can sit here and admire two handsome men?' Her laugh could have come from a youth of seventeen rather than a woman who had probably passed her allotted three score years and ten. 'Take your pleasures where you find them, ladies, and don't stint.' She lowered her voice. 'Find a man with a broad chest and a shapely rump, and you are never short of entertainment.'

We curtsied again, but I could not help but liking Lady Pluscarden.

'Lady Pluscarden has her fancies,' Emily whispered with a twinkle in her eye. 'That's why the footmen have such tight breeches,'

'Mrs Napier,' I pretended to be scandalised. 'You are shocking.'

'I know,' Emily stopped, tipped her parasol to one side and peered around it at Lady Pluscarden's servants. 'I do appreciate her point, though. I prefer the man on the right. He has a delightful shape down there.'

'Emily!' I shook my head in mock despair. 'Poor James! Does he know what he has married?'

'That's one reason he married me,' Emily's smile was as smug as anything I had ever seen.

'Miss Flockhart,' Lady Pluscarden waved me back. 'Where have we met before?' Her eyes were shrewd as she lifted a glass to her lips.

My heart began to race. 'I don't believe we have, your Ladyship.'

Lady Pluscarden's eyes narrowed. 'Perhaps I know your mother?'

'My mother is dead, your Ladyship.'

'I'm sorry to hear that,' Lady Pluscarden said. 'Nevertheless, I am sure we have met.' She sipped at her drink. 'No matter, I'm sure it will come to me. Have a pleasant drive back.'

'Thank you, your Ladyship,' I gave another curtsey and hurriedly withdrew.

'That was strange,' Emily said. 'I said you were a mystery. Now, which carriage is ours? They all look the same to me.'

I was still shaking from Lady Pluscarden's question. 'You'd better not let James hear you say that, either. He is proud of his carriage.'

'Oh, one chariot looks much the same as another to me,' Emily tried to shake the mud and water off her left leg. 'Oh, there it is, it's the blue one with the gold trim. Now, where's Peter? Can you see our coachman, Dorothea?'

By that time an easterly wind had driven in the rain from the sea, and it fairly pelted down. We were sodden from bonnet to boots and would have been quite miserable had we not met Lady Pluscarden with her peculiarities and tight-breeched footmen. Emily opened the coach door, and we piled in, glad of the shelter.

'Is that you back then, Ma'am?' Peter, the coachman, appeared from somewhere, tucking his pipe inside his cloak. 'Are we set to go to Flotterstone?'

'Yes, please Peter,' Emily removed her bonnet and shook it to get rid of the worst of the wet. 'Take Miss Flockhart home first. We can't have her walking in this.'

'Yes, Ma'am.' Peter was a middle-aged man with quiet eyes. 'Will that be Thistle Street, Ma'am?'

'Yes, please, Peter,' I said. At that minute the prospect of being safely home was most desirable. I could not think why I had adventured so far out of town at all. Yet the memory of Lady Pluscarden's bright eyes was worth remembering, and I wished that I could be as lively and interested at her age.

'It might take some time for all this to clear, Ma'am.' Peter indicated the queues of carriages and carts.

'Oh, just get us home, Peter!' Emily was beginning to get a little testy.

'Yes, Ma'am.' Peter touched a hand to his hat and climbed onto the driver's seat.

Driving through congested traffic is never easy. Driving through congested traffic in what was now a torrential downpour must have been a nightmare for poor Peter. To judge by the snarls and out-bursts of colourful language, the other drivers thought the same. We jolted away from Portobello in a confusion of horses and grinding wheels, with the occasional bump as one coachman jostled past another, although fortunately, Peter was efficiently skilled or sufficiently fortunate, to avoid scraping James's prize coach.

'Will we never get out of this?' Emily said, and then, 'Oh, here we are now,' as Peter eased us past the worst of the crowd and cracked his whip. The horses responded with a will, stretching their legs to pull us along at a much more suitable pace.

As you may know, the road from Portobello to Edinburgh passes through some bleak and unpopulated countryside before it reaches Jock's Lodge and the cavalry barracks at Piershill. At one time this area had been the haunt of footpads and sorners and such like un-desirables so when Peter began to slow down we were naturally perturbed.

'Peter!' Emily rapped on the ceiling of the carriage. 'What are you doing now? Why are we slowing?'

'Sorry, Ma'am. There is a problem with the wheel.'

'Oh, dear God! Will you get us home *today*, Peter?'

'I can try, Ma'am.' Peter sounded doubtful.

'Get as far as you can.' Emily said. 'We might be able to hire a post-chaise from a stable somewhere.' She looked out of the window at the drear countryside and said quietly, 'if they have such a thing in this forlorn place.'

However, it was only five minutes later that the coach gave a tremendous lurch to the side. Emily screamed and grabbed me for support as we slewed to a grinding halt. We ended up pressed against the door in a clutching tangle of cloaks and bonnets and dresses. I heard the horses neighing and Peter swearing as he quietened them down.

'Are you all right?' I took hold of Emily.

'Yes, thank you.' She looked up, straightening her clothes, 'what's happened?'

I looked out of the window. 'We've lost a wheel,' I said. 'We won't be going any further until it's fixed.'

'How are the horses? How is Peter? Is anybody hurt?' That was Emily at her best, and I warmed to her anew.

Peter had left his perch to tend to the horses. 'No,' I said. 'Everybody's fine.'

I raised my voice. 'Peter! Is there a stable nearby?'

'There's one at Jock's Lodge,' Peter said at once. 'About two miles ahead. Shall I go and find a wheelwright?'

'Yes, Peter. You do that.' Emily sighed. 'And be as quick as you can, mind.'

'Yes, Ma'am.' Peter looked in on us for a moment. 'You ladies sit tight here, and I'll be back soon.'

I saw Peter tramp head down into the driving rain. 'We can do nothing but wait,' I said to Emily, 'so we may as well make ourselves as comfortable as possible.'

I looked around. Dusk was already falling and together with the rain made the countryside even more dismal and lonely. I sighed; this was not how I had expected the day would go.

'I hope there are no footpads around,' Emily nearly voiced my thoughts. 'It's getting dark.'

Putting my hand within my travelling cloak, I touched the smooth walnut butt of the pistol. I knew it would not let me down, for Joseph Manton, the best gunsmith of the age, had made it for me. I was not scared of footpads, although I carried the pistol for quite another man. A man I hoped never to meet again. I closed my eyes, imagining the bark and kick of the piece under my hand, the orange spurt of flame and the cloud of acrid white smoke. His unhealthy white face haunted my thoughts.

'It will be all right, Emily,' I said.

'It's very dark.'

'It will be all right. I promise you.' I gripped the butt of my Joseph Manton again. Part of me desperately hoped that some footpad would come so I could shoot him. I pushed that thought away. I would not descend to that level; I could not for I might never crawl back up again.

We were in a dip of the road with a couple of wind-tortured hawthorn trees sagging under the rain and potholes rapidly filling with water. What I could see of the surroundings appeared monotonous, a dreary wasteland with scattered sad bushes.

Emily cleared a circle of condensation from the window and peered outside. 'How horrid,' she said. 'There could even be dragons out there.' She forced a smile. 'Marie would keep as amused if she were here. She has such a sweet peculiarity of manner.'

'She's getting married next week,' I reminded. 'Distract yourself by thinking of that.'

'It feels as if we will never get away from here.' Emily smeared the condensation from another section of the window. 'I swear that rain is getting heavier. Maybe James will come looking for us.'

'We have his chariot,' I reminded. 'He will find it hard to come this distance on foot.'

'He's got Jessica, his horse.'

I nodded, and we relapsed into silence, listening to the drum-beat of the rain on the carriage roof and the whine of wind through the coarse grass. I do not know how much time passed before I heard the soft clop of hooves in the mud. I curled my hand around the pistol butt as my heart-beat increased.

'Halloa!' The voice echoed hollowly in the dark.

I looked at Emily. 'That's not Peter.' I placed my thumb on the hammer of the pistol.

'Halloa! In the coach there!'

Keeping my hand on the pistol, I opened the door and peered outside. A lone horseman was negotiating the slope to the carriage. Surely a highwayman would not announce himself?

'Halloa yourself,' I called. 'Who are you?'

'George Rogers' the reply was quick and clear. 'Do you need help?'

'Yes,' Emily replied for me as she thrust her head out of the open door. 'Yes, we do.'

The horseman reined up beside us. He sat tall in the saddle, with a dark cloak covering him from neck to heels yet there was no disguising his military bearing.

George Rogers dismounted and nodded to the broken wheel. 'Has your driver gone for help?'

'He's gone to Jock's Lodge to find a stable.' I confirmed.

'How long ago?' George Rogers was pleasingly direct.

'He's been about two hours as far as I can judge.' I resolved to buy a watch as soon as I could.

Rogers nodded. 'He'll have arrived long ago. He should be back within an hour unless you wish me to ride ahead and hurry him up?'

'Oh, no, please stay with us,' Emily spoke quickly. 'There may be footpads around.'

Rogers examined the wheel and grunted. 'There may be,' he said, 'and a stranded coach with a broken wheel and two wet lady passengers would be a tempting target indeed.' He glanced at us. 'Two *very* wet lady passengers.' Unfastening his cloak, he revealed the splendid uniform of a captain in the Volunteers. 'You are both shivering, but I only have one cloak.'

'Mrs Napier feels the cold more acutely than I do.' I said.

'Then Mrs Napier shall have my cloak,' Captain Rogers said.

I acknowledged the chivalry with a brief curtsey. 'I know you,' I said. 'You were at the Field Day.'

'I was indeed.' Captain George Rogers said. 'I saw you watching us.'

He was the tall and handsome captain who had carried the injured soldier's pike.

Emily wrapped Rogers' cloak around her. 'Thank you.'

'I hope you are not too cold,' Captain Rogers said to me.

I thanked him for his concern and turned away. I had no desire for anything more than a casual acquaintanceship, even if the captain was handsome, or perhaps *especially* if the captain was handsome.

Emily had no such inhibitions. 'Where are your men, Captain Rogers?'

'The major is marching them back to the Castle' Rogers said, 'and I have you two to myself.'

I was not sure if Captain Rogers' presence made things easier or harder. Emily undoubtedly felt safer with a tall soldier in our company, while the cloak helped keep her warmer. I, however, was uncomfortable in his presence, as I was uneasy in the presence of any single man, and most married men. I moved slightly further away from him and stared into the dark.

'Hurry up, Peter,' I muttered, too loudly, for Rogers heard me.

'He'll be here in good time,' the captain said.

'I'm sure you're right.' I watched the rain teeming down and listened as one of the horses whinnied.

'I'll be back directly,' Rogers said and stepped out of the coach and spoke to each horse in turn.

'The captain is good with the horses,' Emily said.

'Many men prefer horses to women,' I watched the captain stand in the driving rain for quite some time before he returned to the shelter of the coach. 'And some men think that both women and horses are merely beasts for the convenience of themselves.'

'Somebody is coming,' Captain Rogers called out. 'You ladies remain here until I investigate.' He launched himself onto his horse, touched a hand to the hilt of his sabre, kicked in his heels and rode off in a shower of spray and mud.

'How gallant,' Emily said. 'Don't you agree, Dorothea?'

I watched Emily's gallant captain mount the slope and disappear into the dark. 'He makes a fine show,' I said.

There was the sound of rough voices, a low laugh and then Peter was with us together with a group of half-shaved men and a barouche that had seen better days. 'This is the best I could get,' Peter patted the body of the barouche as if it was a living creature rather than an elderly carriage. 'It will get us back home, and these lads say they'll fix our wheel and return the coach first thing in the morning.'

'Oh, Peter, you are a saint,' Emily shouted. 'You are the rock on which we all depend.'

'I hope you were all right out here in the wilds,' Peter said. 'I took longer than I expected.'

'We were fine,' I said. 'You did well, Peter.'

'We had a white knight,' Emily said. A gallant captain of cavalry was here to protect us from sorners, blackguards, Frenchmen, footpads, Highwaymen and dragons.'

'Fortunately, not one member of that formidable list appeared,' our white knight said. 'If I was able to set your minds at rest, ladies, then I am glad of it. Now I must get back to the regiment in case they list me as a deserter.' Lifting his hand in farewell, he kicked in his spurs and set off at an impressive trot, and that was the end of that damp little adventure. I neither expected nor desired to see the captain again, gallant though he may have been.

Chapter Two

I must have attended fifty weddings in my life, and most merge into my memory as a confusion of swirling gowns and long speeches, handsome men gradually succumbing to an excess of alcohol and weary-eyed women reminiscing quietly of their youth. The marriage of Marie to Gilbert Elliot was not quite of that ilk.

It was 15th November 1803, dull and dismal but thankfully not wet. I had to hire a post-chaise and driver, for Marie and Gibbie had chosen to marry at the church at Crichton, about fourteen miles south of Edinburgh. Perhaps you know Edinburgh, but if not, then pray forgive me while I explain something of the geography of my native city as it was back then.

Nature and history combined to divide the city into two halves, the ancient Old Town, or *Auld Toon* as the good neighbours of the burgh would have it, an immensely crowded city that straggled from the castle on its rock down to the neglected royal Palace of Holyroodhouse. The Old Town comprised the High Street, which connected to the Lawnmarket at the west end and the Canongait at the east end, and a warren of interwoven lanes known as wynds or closes. Running parallel to the High Street and to the south was the Cowgait, or South Back, into which respectable people did not enter at the risk of their reputation or their purse, or worse. Once it was the home of the city elite as well as the lower orders, but by 1803 the Old Town was becoming the refuge of labourers and beggars, the poor and the unfortunate. A few of the older lords and ladies remained, shining pearls among the drabness of mediocrity who filled the picturesque and crumbling houses. To the north of the Old Town and separated by a steep valley in which the remains of the North Loch was rapidly becoming a muddy marsh, was the New Town.

As obnoxious as the Old Town was, the New Town was its polar opposite, a selection of streets and squares of grandeur and elegance, where ladies and gentlemen could walk in perfect security and respectable society continued unruffled and serene. At least on the surface, for some beautiful houses contained men and women who were neither elegant nor genteel in any sense of the word.

The environs of this, Scotland's capital city, contained a score or more of little villages and hamlets, each with a storied past. Nowhere else in Scotland will one find in such a limited space so many castles and mansion-houses tucked away in the most picturesque and romantic countryside imaginable. There are the massive palaces of the very rich, such as Dalkeith Palace within its park that contains a fragment of the ancient Caledonian Forest, and Dalhousie Castle, nearly as grand. Other castles such as Borthwick stand alone in splendour, and there are places where castles and villages exist in proximity, such as Roslin, with its famous castle and the mysterious chapel. Another was Crichton, with the castle on its eminence about the river and its church nearby.

The journey from Edinburgh to Crichton took me over two hours, and I stepped out of the chaise without enthusiasm, eased my cramped limbs and looked around. The church was as solid and unpretentious as I remembered, with the decorations for Marie's wedding adding brightness to what otherwise would have been a dull scene. Skeletal trees stretched naked branches upward to a grey sky, while a trio of rooks croaked and cawed in a dismal chorus.

'Hello, Dorothea,' Maria was trembling with excitement as she ran to meet me. 'I'm getting married today.'

'I know,' I said. 'You look lovely.' She did not. Her yellow dress clashed with her auburn hair and the muddy ground had already soiled the silver embroidery at the bottom of her skirt. Her manteaux was fine, silver tissue lined with yellow satin, with embroidery matching the Greek key design on her dress, all fastened in front with the most enormous diamond I had ever seen.

My cynical side wondered if the jewel was genuine.

'Gibbie is not here yet,' Maria took hold of my arm. 'Do you think...?'

'He'll be here,' I squeezed her hand. 'He would never be anywhere else.'

'Yes,' Marie smiled. I could see that she had been crying.

That was one reason I did not like weddings. They were too emotional, with too many people weeping over broken dreams, too many people recalling old memories, too many false hopes and insincere promises. I pushed aside my past. 'Do you wish to talk?'

'No,' Marie shook her head. 'No, I have to see my mother.' She smiled before she turned and I watched her run back inside the church.

'I'm glad you could make it,' Emily and James alighted from their coach and walked arm-in-arm toward me.

'I could not let Marie down,' I watched the mulberry coloured coach draw up and hoped I could avoid the sharp Lady Pluscarden. I had not known Marie had invited her.

'Shall we go inside?' James indicated the church.

'Not yet,' I said. 'You go ahead, and I'll join you both later.' I walked away with the memories bitter in my mind. I heard the quick footsteps behind me and was not surprised when Emily slipped her arm under mine.

'Why the Friday face, Dorothea? This is Marie's wedding day. I hope you are happy for her.'

'I am happy if she is happy,' I gave a deliberately cryptic reply and kept walking. 'James will be looking for you.'

'James is my husband and a grown man,' Emily said. 'He will survive without me for a few moments.' She squeezed my arm. 'You need me more.'

I blinked away my surprise, unused to loyalty or friendship and glad that Emily had such a sensible attitude to her marriage. 'I am all right.'

We walked on with our feet making little sound on the damp, muddy grass. After a while, I stopped as Crichton Castle spread before us in all its ruined glory. Rain had dampened the cold grey walls, and grass grew on the shattered battlements and the sills of the windows yet there was no mistaking the power that had once existed here. I could imagine the music here and see the flitting shapes of women in long dresses and men in formal clothing. Long-gone voices floated across to me, and the memory of events that had once been.

'Crichton Castle,' I said. 'There was a battle here in 1337 when Sir Andrew Murray stopped an English invading force.'

'How do you know that?' Emily's gaze was more penetrating than comfortable.

'I've been here before,' I said.

'Oh?' Emily's arm tightened around mine. 'Do tell, lady of mystery.'

'It was a long time ago,' I said.

'What was a long time ago?' Persistent Emily asked.

'It was a long time ago since I was here.' I turned the question into a statement and closed the conversation.

'What were you doing?'

'I was at another wedding,' I said. 'Come on; we have to support Marie.' I did not say that the wedding did not take place; Emily did not deserve such an odious statement at such a time.

Crichton Church is historic but small, and while carriages and horses crowded the outside while men and women packed the interior. I escorted Emily to James' side and searched for a seat somewhere at the back, as far from Lady Pluscarden as possible.

'Miss Flockhart!'

I started. Captain Rogers raised himself from one of the polished pews and gestured beside him. 'You may have my seat if you wish.'

'I can't do that,' I said.

'A gentleman cannot sit while a lady stands,' Captain Rogers was splendid in his full regimentals.

I gave a small curtsey. Not all gentlemen adhered to their self-imposed code. 'Thank you,' I looked around desperately and in vain for an alternative place.

'It's all right,' Captain Rogers said. 'I'll move elsewhere.' He gave a little bow. 'You will not need to suffer my company.'

'Your company, sir, does not make me suffer.' The response came too quickly as I regressed to the amiable girl I had once been.

Captain Rogers' smile seemed genuine. 'That is a capital piece of news.' He stepped past me without the least contact and moved to the back of the church. Ignoring my guilt at having deprived the good captain of his pew, I sat down and waited for the ceremony to begin. I could not stop nausea from rising in my throat.

These occasions are very similar, so I will not write a minute by minute description of Marie's wedding. I will say that Gilbert arrived on time, dressed in the very height of fashion, smiled as he strolled up the aisle and said all the right things at all the right times. What else can one say about a wedding? The guests behaved themselves, the minister was long-winded, and after the ceremony, we all repaired to nearby Tynebridge Hall for the wedding breakfast. I always thought that 'breakfast was a strange name to call celebrations that began in the middle of the afternoon and continued well into the next day. I watched Lady Pluscarden's coachman like a rabbit cowering from a stoat and noted the two footmen in their oh-so-tight breeches. I wondered how many other women were also watching.

'Does Gilbert own this place?' Elizabeth Campbell stood outside the splendid Georgian mansion with her head craned back to admire the many windows and Adams architecture.

'I believe not,' Colin told her. 'He leased it for a year through some Edinburgh solicitor.'

'Marie is fortunate in having such a rich husband.' Elizabeth nudged him. 'Perhaps I made the wrong choice.'

Colin smiled. 'I made the right choice.'

I stepped further away to allow them privacy and to ease my heartache.

'You and I appear to be alone here,' Captain Rogers joined me outside the house. 'Everybody else is in pairs.'

'That seems to be true,' I said.

'Would my company offend you?' He tipped his shako as he smiled.

Again the answer came before I had time to think. 'Not in the slightest.'

'Then shall we go inside?' Captain Rogers indicated the stairs that swept to the pillared front door.

I did not wish to enter that house. If I had known that Gilbert Elliot had leased Tynebridge Hall, I would have found some excuse not to attend Marie's wedding. I stood outside, feeling sick. 'Not yet,' I temporised.

I knew people were watching me. I could feel their eyes and wondered what they were thinking. I saw Lady Pluscarden sitting at the door of her chariot, sipping at a glass as her bright eyes surveyed everybody and everything.

'Dorothea?' That was Emily, of course. 'Are you all right?'

Was I all right? No, I was anything but all right. I forced a smile. 'Captain Rogers is taking good care of me.'

Emily's approval was in her eyes. She dropped in a curtsey. 'I wish you luck, Captain Rogers. Our Miss Flockhart is no lover of male company, or of talking about herself.'

Did she have to say that? My frown dissipated when I realised that Emily was trying to help. By hinting that I disliked all men, she was removing any personal antagonism I may have held towards the captain.

'Thank you for the warning,' Captain Rogers gave Emily a short bow.

I took a deep breath. I did not like to be the centre of attention. I did not want people to pay attention to me at all, and I was more exposed to scrutiny out here. 'Shall we go inside? Poor Marie will be wondering what has happened to her guests.'

We were fortunate that Gilbert and Marie did not insist on formality, so there was no precedence as we entered the Hall. We each walked in as it suited us without an announcement of our names, and mingled with no regard to rank. The click of my shoes on the steps sounded like the ticking of the clock when Mother Faa told my fortune, regular, sharp and inexorable.

The main door led to an outer hall, and it was there that my nerves failed me. I felt myself begin to shake as soon as I stepped in, and the perspiration started from my forehead. *Oh, dear God I can't do this.*

'Dorothea?' I heard Emily's voice as if from a long distance. 'Dorothea? Are you all right?'

Somebody wrapped a strong arm around me as I fell. 'Give her air!' That was Captain Rogers' voice, barking orders. 'Move aside, there!'

I can't recall much about the next few moments except a confusion of faces and a blur of movement. I know I was perched on a heavy wooden chair in the inner hall under an old portrait of a stern-faced matriarch, with Captain Rogers on his knees at my side and Emily fanning me and making anxious enquiries.

'I'm sorry to make such a fuss,' I tried to rise, only for Captain Rogers to put a gentle hand on my arm.

'Give yourself a minute to recover.'

'I'm all right now,' I said.

Somebody put a glass to my mouth, and I drank, spluttering when I tasted brandy where I expected cool water.

'That's the way,' Emily said. 'Drink it down, Dorothea. It will help.'

'I'd rather not,' I began, and she tilted back the glass, and I had the choice of swallow or splutter and choke. I swallowed, and the liquid burned my throat and exploded inside my stomach.

'What's happening? Oh, Lord is that Dorothea?'

I heard Marie's voice and looked up. 'I had a little turn,' I said. 'It must have been the excitement of the day.'

'Are you all right now?' Marie asked.

'I'll look after her,' Captain Rogers said. 'It was only a little dizzy spell.'

Emily smiled. 'Yes, Dorothea, you allow Captain Rogers look after you.'

Feeling more like a burden rather than my usual self, I did as Emily suggested. Closing my eyes, I sat there for a few moments while the turmoil inside my head subsided and I could breathe again. When I opened my eyes, Captain Rogers was still there, holding a brandy glass.

'Do you wish to try and stand?'

I nodded, feeling very foolish. 'Yes, thank you.'

'May I?' He offered his arm.

It was some time since I had accepted an arm from a man and this house was not the best place to start. Taking a deep breath, I placed my hand on the crook of his elbow and rose.

'Take your time,' Captain Rogers gave a sudden smile. 'I'm sure Mr and Mrs Elliot are too engrossed with each other to think about us.'

'I am sure they are.' There were so many memories in Tynebridge Hall that I had to block them out and think only of the present. 'Thank you,' I said again and meant it. I was genuinely grateful for Captain Rogers' help.

The reception breakfast was held on the first floor, in a vast room with three tall multi-paned windows adding natural light to the twin chandeliers above. The tables were set out in a T formation, with the bride, groom and their close families at the head of the T and us lesser mortals in the leg. As befitting my humble status as a mere friend of the bride, I sat where the left ankle would be. The room was a-swirl with scarlet of course, as every man and his brother was either in the Militia or the Volunteers, depending on whether they genuinely wanted to fight Boney or merely wished to appear eager to do so. I had hoped to be near somebody that I knew, but Emily and James and Elizabeth and Colin were both around the thigh, as longstanding friends of the bride. Even Captain Rogers was higher up the table, so I sat in passive silence as the conversation washed around me, like the tide around a lonely rock. I watched Marie and Gilbert at the head of the table, envying them their happiness and hoping that it lasted. Lady Pluscarden, by virtue of rank and title, also sat at the head of the table. I kept my head down and hoped she would not notice me.

'You are very quiet.'

The speaker had to repeat himself twice before I realised that he was talking to me. I looked up with a slight start. 'Oh, yes, I am, rather.' I frowned, wondering where I had seen this man before.

He was a civilian, I was glad to see, with smart clothes that had seen better days, and long fingers. You can tell a lot about a man by his fingers, from the broad, calloused fingers of a man who lived by honest toil to the pampered and soft digits of a fop. This man's fingers were neither calloused nor pampered, they were long but powerful, graceful but also used to work.

'May I introduce myself?' The owner of the fingers gave a formal little bow. 'I am Mungo Hetherington, Dr Mungo Hetherington, the family physician to Mrs Marie Elliot, and now to Mr Elliot as well.'

'How do you do?' I half stood up and gave a little curtsey. 'I am Dorothea Flockhart, a minor friend of Mrs Elliot, through her friendship with Emily Napier.'

Doctor Hetherington. I remembered where I had seen him before; he was the civilian who had helped the fallen pikeman during the Field Day at Portobello.

'Shall we sit down? We are making a bit of a spectacle of ourselves bobbing up and down across the table.'

'That is uncommonly sensible of you,' Dr Hetherington said.

We sat down simultaneously, and I wondered what to say next. I wished I had not come to this wedding; I wished I had not come back to this house.

'You are still very quiet,' Dr Hetherington said.

'I am not much of a conversationalist,' I wished the amiable doctor would leave me alone in my misery.

'Then you must permit me to converse for two,' the amiable doctor seemed to have no intention of leaving me alone. I tried to convince myself that it was better having him talk to me than for me to sit in solitary silence. At least he was a harmless sort of fellow and with a broad chin and misshapen nose, as ugly as sin.

I forced what I hoped looked like a smile. 'Thank you, Doctor.'

'That's settled then,' the good doctor said. 'I could ask many questions about you, Miss Flockhart, yet I fear your replies would be eloquently silent.' His smile was far more effective than mine, 'so instead, I think you shall have to endure my observations about the present company.'

I nodded, trying to appear more sociable than I felt.

'There, now!' Doctor Hetherington said. 'We have a response! That was all the encouragement I seek. Do you like to observe people?'

I had to reply to what was a direct question. 'I prefer to avoid them,' I said.

'And yet here you are at this most happy and convivial of gatherings.' Doctor Hetherington said. 'I believed that I knew all Mrs Elliot's acquaintances, so you must be a newcomer to her circle.' He continued without affording me the opportunity of replying.

I nodded again. 'I have known Mrs Elliot for less than a twelvemonth.'

'Excellent!' Dr Hetherington beamed. 'There you, you see? We are getting on like a house on fire.'

I ducked my head as Lady Pluscarden scanned the tables. It was a long time since I had felt as uncomfortable as I did at that wedding. The doctor was watching me, perhaps with his professional interest aroused, possibly out of compassion. I searched my mind for something to distract him.

'Are you a local man, Doctor?'

'I live just outside the policies of the Hall,' Doctor Hetherington seemed pleased to talk about himself.

'Have you been here long?'

'Eight years,' the doctor gave a sudden smile. 'Another ten and people will nearly begin to accept me as a local.'

'It will take longer than that,' I did not have to search for the words. 'Country people find it hard to accept strangers.'

'Oh?' The doctor's eyebrows rose, and he neatly passed the topic back to me. 'Are you familiar with the country then? Or are you a lady of the town?'

'I live in Edinburgh.' I closed the question as something far more important imposed on my mind. 'I do have one question for you, Doctor.'

Doctor Hetherington's smile could not have been broader. 'Ask away my dear Miss Flockhart, ask away.'

'That minister,' I indicated the elderly churchman who had married Marie to Gibbie. 'Is he also local?'

'The Reverend Brown has been here for the past five years,' Doctor Hetherington's words eased away one of my worries.

'Thank you,' I relapsed into silence again.

The doctor smiled, waiting to hear why I had asked such a question. I did not enlighten him. Fortunately, the meal began then, and we were too busy with soup and meat to have time to talk, which I hope saved me from the necessity of making any further disclosures to this garrulous and observant man. Wedding feasts are much the same, so suffice to say that the cooks did not disgrace themselves and the servants did not throw food into anybody's lap. Unfortunately, even a wedding feast of 1803 had a limit to the amount of food it applied to its guests, and when the servants had cleared the last course away and produced the glasses for the inevitable rounds of toasts, Doctor Hetherington was still there. I searched the table for sanctuary from his probing mind but, like Johnny Armstrong, I sought grace from a graceless face and there was none.

Emily and James were deep in conversation with the Campbells, and Captain Rogers appeared to have forgotten about me as he laughed and joked with his scarlet-jacketed colleagues. I did not look in the direction of Lady Pluscarden in case she recalled my face. I could only thank the Lord that this gathering did not retain the custom of keeping a chamber pot within the sideboard for the men's use during the meal. Like horses one can no longer ride, some habits of the good old days are best put out to grass.

The first toast was inevitable, given we were at war and Boney's mighty army was poised to invade: 'The King, God bless him.'

We all had to stand for that and drink back the red claret, imported from France by devious means and Leith smugglers.

'Confusion to the French' was next, and we all agreed to that.

'How strange,' Dr Hetherington observed. 'Drinking confusion to the country all the best families acknowledge as the cultural centre of the world and whose fashions most at this table are sporting.' He spoke in French, a language that everybody at the wedding would understand to some degree. I admired his cynicism and replied in the same tongue.

'The world is a strange place, Doctor.'

He raised his glass and eyebrows to me.

The toasts continued. 'To the bride and groom.' We all drank that one with enthusiasm, and then, as the claret began to affect heads, the accents broadened as the native voices overcame learned attitudes and imposed mannerisms. As Doctor Hetherington observed, 'the native Scot is coming through.'

'Thumpin' luck and fat weans'

'When we're gaun up the hill o' fortune, may we ne'er meet a friend coming down.'

By that time I merely sipped at my glass and did not indulge myself in the deep draughts that others did. I had no desire to end up drunk and incapable, especially in this house. Heavy drinking was another tradition that was best left in the past.

I heard Colin's voice growing louder higher up the table and saw Elizabeth put her hand across the mouth of his glass. I nodded; *well done Mrs Campbell. Keep control.*

Doctor Hetherington had also seen Elizabeth's action. 'There'll be trouble in paradise soon unless this night ends,' he said. 'Colin is a man with a temper when the wine gets in.'

I nodded, watching Gibbie Elliot, who seemed flushed as well. Marie was laughing at his side. I caught her eye and gave a small wave with my fingers. She responded happily, grinning down the table.

Other snippets of conversation came to me as the wine bit deep and chased away sense and decorum.

'Here's a lark!' I heard the words and thought that Gilbert Elliot spoke them although in the general hubbub I could not be sure. 'We can visit one of the low pubs in Whisky Row and mix with the lower orders.'

There was loud laughter after that, with some of the Volunteer officers drumming their glasses on the table-top until the crockery rattled and the silver wear sang. One gangly, ginger-haired scoundrel was especially demonstrative as he nearly clambered onto the table in his enthusiasm.

'Who is that?' I already guessed the answer.

'The Honourable Hector McAra,' the doctor said. 'The friend of everybody who he might need to advance his connections and a bad enemy for those he dislikes. He has powerful connections but few true friends.'

I nodded and said nothing. I had met the like before and thought of them with nothing but contempt. I had my reasons, especially for a man who shared the name McAra. This so-called 'honourable' shared the family shape and colouring. I watched as he sauntered across to talk to Lady Pluscarden, and tried to shrink into invisibility.

Lady Pluscarden pushed McAra away. 'That's surely great nonsense, sir!' Her voice was clear above the hubbub.

Well said, my Lady.

And still, the toasts continued.

'Here's health to the sick, stilts to the lame, claes to the back and brose to the wame.'

I was no longer even pretending to drink now and covered my glass as the claret made its inexorable rounds. I watched the men at the table and knew that the doctor was watching me. I wondered again if he saw me as a potential patient. Did I have some symptoms that interested him?

'Mair sense and mair siller,' came the next call.

'They call for mair sense while drinking themselves into insensibility,' Doctor Hetherington observed, 'and toast to more silver while spending their wealth on more claret in one night than a poor country doctor could afford in a month.'

I agreed with him. Despite myself, I was growing to like this garrulous man. 'Are country doctors so poor then, Doctor Hetherington?'

'As church mice,' Doctor Hetherington said sadly. 'If I had the funds, there is so much good I could do and so many people I could help.'

I studied him across the width of the table, wondering how genuine his words were or if he was only saying what he thought I wished to hear. He was about 30, I judged, the same age as me, and anything but handsome, with that short, broken nose above a wide mouth and a broad chin, while his forehead was unusually smooth. Except for that pugnacious nose, the doctor looked young for his years, while I felt immensely old.

I had not had much time to analyse Doctor Hetherington's words before the dancing started. I had been a famous dancer in my youth, but events had dulled my enthusiasm, and now I sat on the sidelines and watched as a host of busy servants cleared away the tables around me.

A four-piece orchestra appeared at the head of the room, and within a few moments, the floor was a bouncing array of men and women dancing together. Gowns flared around legs and boots thumped on the polished floorboards in synchronised unison as partners made their way up and down the line. Naturally, Marie was the leading lady, while I decided to remain seated. I saw a servant scurry up to Doctor Hetherington and hand over a slip of paper.

The doctor leaned towards me. 'You will excuse me, I know,' he said. 'One of my patients is near her time. I must go to her.' He showed me the note. It read:

'*Come out here directly. I have got something to do. I have got to die.*'

'Yes, of course,' I did not know why he showed me what his patient had written as we were no more than casual acquaintances. I watched him hurry away, and sat tight, planning how long I had to remain here before I could make my excuses and escape back home to Edinburgh. I calculated another hour would be sufficient for politeness and by that time the dancing should be taking up everybody's attention, and nobody would notice my absence.

Damn.

A uniformed man strode toward me, and I steeled myself to talk again.

'Would you care to accompany me onto the floor, Miss Flockhart?' Captain Rogers bowed most elegantly.

'I fear my dancing will be clumsy at best,' I said.

'Then we will be well matched for a pair of carthorses,' Captain Rogers extended a hand in invitation.

We did not touch of course. At that period before the scandalous introduction of the waltz, men and women did not have physical contact on the dance floor. In 1803 we were respectable in public, if not always behind closed doors. There were two worlds then, as there are now and one was the mirror image of the other, yet the reverse was as dark as the obverse was light, and bitter where the obverse was sweet.

As I had warned, my dancing was clumsy when I stepped onto the floor, with my feet forgetting where they should go despite the messages from my weary brain. It was more than ten years since I had last stood opposite a man in such surroundings, in the same room in the same house and on the same type of occasion.

The memories returned, more powerful than before so I had to fight away the prickle of the tears I thought I had drained from my soul over the past decade. I remembered the charming smiles, the oh-so-fashionable clothes, and loud laughter. I remembered the pale face as well, and the staring eyes, and my dreams of a future of bright promise that stretched before us.

'Come along, Miss Flockhart,' Captain Rogers stretched out a hand to steady me as I tripped over my laggard feet.

'Thank you,' I jerked back to the present.

'It's a Scotch reel next,' Captain Rogers said.

At one time, the Scotch reel had been a speciality of mine, with its alternate heying and setting, with the short four-line of dancers. That day I had to concentrate to remember the intricacies of the steps and the sequence of moves. I drifted again, back and forth in time as I allowed my feet to remember how to perform and pushed away the bad memories to concentrate on Captain Rogers, who had never done me any harm. It was unfair to punish him, even silently, for a past of which he could have no notion.

'You dance uncommonly well for a carthorse,' I forced out the words.

'I am endeavouring to keep up with a thoroughbred,' my gallant captain replied. 'I fear the next dance may show me to be a true clodhopper though.'

'And why is that, pray?'

'It is an eightsome reel,' Captain Rogers said.

I smiled at him. I could not remember the last time I had smiled. 'That makes it all the more interesting.'

For the first time in a long time, I began to enjoy myself, facing the challenge of an eightsome reel in company I did not know well. The ten years since I had last danced slid away as we bounced around that oh-so-familiar room and for a moment, for a few moments, for a precious, delectable agonising space, I was happy within my own limited world. I heard the skirling of the dancers and the rhythmic clatter of hard shoes on the wooden floor. I saw the swirl of gowns, and the gleam of candlelight on bare shoulders and gold braid and I allowed myself the luxury of forgetting.

By the time the eightsome ended, the passage of years was catching up with me, and my breath was coming in short gasps. I was glad to seek the sanctuary of a seat and discreetly fanned myself to calm the glow.

'May I join you?' My gallant captain asked. I consented at once for, in the wake of so many glasses of claret, he seemed a fine, brave soldier. We sat in companionable silence for a while as the chatter and light laughter drifted around us.

'Oh, heavens,' I said at last. 'You must think me all sorts of oafs for neglecting you after your earlier kindness.' I raked through my mind for something to ask him although in truth it was so long since I had last attempted to speak to a gentleman that I was rather at a loss. My questions to Doctor Hetherington would not be suitable for a military man, so I relied on the old standby.

'What sort of literature do you read?' I finally asked. 'No, don't tell me. Military manuals and the history of great generals, I'll be bound.'

'You won't be bound then,' Captain Rogers said. 'I've never read a military manual in my life.' He grinned. 'I follow orders on the battlefield and hope that my fellows follow mine.'

'How do you intend to defeat Boney then, if you don't know the theory of your profession?' That was a genuine question although I asked it in a flippant tone. The thought of Bonaparte's massive army poised to invade was never far from our thoughts.

'I leave the tactics to the generals,' Captain Rogers said, and I knew by the shadows in his eyes that his answer was serious. 'I only have two lieutenants, a double-brace of ensigns and a company of rank and file under my command.' He was not smiling. 'My only tactics are the ambush and the bald-headed charge.'

'Bald headed?' I was cooling down now and lowered my fan.

'There was a famous general named the Marquis of Granby. He lost his wig during a mad cavalry charge and ever since we've used the term to go at it bald-headed, meaning to charge in full force.'

I did not know if that little anecdote was true, but it certainly made me smile. 'Have you ever been in battle?' I already guessed the answer. It was in the shadows in his eyes when he was not smiling and the way he walked. I could not describe it except to say Captain Rogers had an awareness, perhaps, but so much removed from the pointless arrogance of other men I had known in this same room.

'I have.' There was no humour in my captain's face now as his eyes darkened with memory. 'I have been in a battle or two and some outpost skirmishes.'

I took hold of his arm. It was hard as granite. 'You are a brave man,' I told him. I was neither praising nor exaggerating. Despite my best intentions, I was beginning to rather like this man.

He was not listening to me. Just looking at him I knew he was back in action in Flanders or Egypt or wherever it had been, marching the bitter winter fields or standing on burning sands, hearing the thunder of the French cannonade and the hoarse yells of cuirassiers, witnessing the carnage and courage of battle. It was a place we could never share.

'Do you wish to talk about it?' I kept my voice gentle so as not to break his mood. I wanted to know all about this apparently flippant man, not just the outward politeness but also the inner darkness, the fears and thoughts and experiences.

'Warfare is not all glory and bravery,' Captain Rogers spoke quietly, as though from very far away. 'Oh, there is plenty of that as the men stand under the flapping Colours and the white powder-smoke drifts past, now revealing, now concealing. Then you hear the French with their *pas-de-charge*, the most sinister drumbeat in the world, and their shouts '*Vive la France*' and our boys respond with three barking cheers. The Highland pipes scream out then, thin and high, raising the hairs on the back of your head.'

I was there with him, holding my sword as I stood at Captain Rogers' side, facing the French. Perhaps I had drunk more claret than I realised, or maybe my nerves were reacting from their earlier strain by pushing me in the opposite direction. I do not know. I only know how I responded to Captain Rogers' words.

'The cannon fire increases, sending their iron balls bounding toward us and then we see the French advancing, huge blue columns backed by artillery and cavalry. Our men shiver, stamp their feet and spit tobacco juice onto the ground. And we wait for orders, and we wait, and wait as they come closer.'

'Oh, give the order,' I could nearly smell the Frenchmen as they marched towards the British lines. I gripped the captain's arm until my knuckles were white and my fingers ached. 'Give the order, do.'

'We can see the moustaches on the infantry's faces; we see the braided hair and shining breastplates of the cuirassiers. Our men are falling as the enemy artillery plays among us, blood and death and pain and raw courage. And still, we wait the order to fire.'

I gripped ever tighter, trying to lend my strength to my captain. 'Oh, give the order, please, before the French overrun us.'

The scene was plain in my mind, the thin red British lines and the dense blue columns of the French, the men falling in agony and the steady hands gripping the Brown Bess muskets.

'They are eighty paces away with the skirmishers in front, lithe, active little fellows aiming and firing at our men, picking off the officers. And still, we wait for the order.'

By now I was in an agony of suspense. 'Oh, order us to fire.'

'Present!' Captain Rogers' bark made me jump. 'Aim! Fire!'

'Hurrah!' I cheered at the order as if I had been there. Luckily there was so much noise in that room that nobody heard me, or if they did they were too polite to take notice. It must have been ten years since I had experienced that level of excitement.

'The muskets crack in a long volley, and the first three ranks of the French column disappear, shot flat. But still they come on, brave Frenchmen who expect another victory.'

'Oh, no.' Captain Rogers' forearm was like iron. I leaned closer across the table.

'Load!' Captain Rogers snapped. 'Ram! Present! Aim!'

'Fire!' I shouted for him.

'Not yet, damn it!' Captain Rogers said. 'Let them anticipate first; let them feel the fear, so they shiver and quake. Let them come closer so we can fell more of them with every shot.'

'Yes indeed,' I said, quite carried away by his words. 'Let them come close, the scoundrels, the Republican blackguards, the French devils!'

'Fire!'

'Fire,' I repeated.

'See? They are running!' Captain Rogers was on his feet, pointing to the window. With one movement he drew his sabre, 'bayonets, lads and after them!'

I was also standing, visualising the scene as we charged at the French in that upper room where Marie was celebrating her marriage, and the prancing, happy ladies were displaying all their splendour despite the battle the captain and I fought around them.

'So that's what it's like,' Captain Rogers replaced his sword where it belonged after putting the chandelier in grave danger. 'Fear and gore and blood.'

'And glory,' I said, momentarily all eager to be part of the captain's life. 'And bravery.'

Captain Rogers screwed up his face. 'You don't feel brave, Miss Flockhart. You only feel that you have your duty to do and you don't wish to let down your men.'

We were silent for a few moments. A coal slipped in the grate, and a quiet servant picked up the tongs and added more fuel to the fire. The music continued, and the dancing. Captain Rogers massaged his arm. 'You have a strong grip' he said, smiling.

'Not as strong as yours, I think,' I said.

The music stopped, and the flushed dancers returned to their seats. For one moment the noise dipped, just as there was a sharp rapping at the door. I watched as a servant slid silently away, and a few moments later a travel-dishevelled ensign stepped into the room. He approached the senior major, saluted and whispered a few words. The major called over Captain Rogers, and within minutes all the Volunteer and Militia officers were slipping away.

'Captain Rogers,' I stopped him before he reached the door. 'Pray tell me what's to do?'

'Now don't you fret,' Captain Rogers spoke calmly. 'This is just a precaution. There has been a report that the warning beacons were seen alight on the coast, so we are mustering to ensure Boney does not land.'

'The French?' I looked at the officers as they filed from the room; a few moments before they had been smiling with their dance-partners, now they were grim-faced and professional.

'I think not, but we must muster and see.' He lowered his voice. 'I'll send you a message when this is over, Miss Flockhart; I have taken quite a liking to your company.' He held my gaze. 'Unless you have an objection?'

I curtseyed, 'Captain.' I was not sure I wished to see my gallant captain again. The notion was not completely unpleasant. If nothing else, Captain Rogers was a passable dancer and an entertaining raconteur. I had to agree that I did not dislike the man, and that was a major admission. 'Thank you, Captain Rogers. I have no objection.'

'Enjoy the rest of the evening, ladies and gentlemen,' Captain Rogers's roar completely drowned any other sound in the room. 'If Boney is here, the Edinburgh Volunteers will soon send him packing back to France with his tail between his frogs' legs.'

'Oh!' Elizabeth Campbell covered her mouth. 'Oh, Colin!'

Colin put his arms around her. 'It's only a precaution, as the captain said. It'll be a false alarm.'

I stepped back as Lady Pluscarden stood up, her face furrowed into a frown. 'Take care, gentlemen,' she called.

'Oh, gentlemen and ladies,' the senior major paused at the door. 'Given the possible urgency of the situation, I have decided to requisition your carriages and coaches. I have sent an express to raise the local Volunteers, and we shall travel with them to their rendezvous point. I know that you will understand. I trust you will all make your way home in safety.' Lifting his shako, he departed, leaving the room a-buzz with speculation and alarm.

Only then did I recall that the Volunteers did not serve abroad. My gallant Captain's war story could not have happened unless he had been in a regular regiment, and if so, why had he left?

I shook my head. I was not the only person present who was hiding the past.

False alarm or a mass invasion by the French, either way, the ensign's arrival effectively ended Marie's wedding ceremony. When the officers left, the heart went out of the night. Although the orchestra tried their best to reinstall some joviality, the men and women preferred to congregate in anxious little groups to discuss what they should do.

I heard McAra voice his thoughts. 'If it is Boney,' he said, standing at the head of the table, 'then we had better hope the regulars come quickly. These Volunteers won't stand for a single volley.'

'That is surely great nonsense, sir.' Lady Pluscarden had to lean backwards to face McAra. 'These men will fight. If you had the courage to don a uniform, I would think better of you.'

Giving a high-pitched laugh, McAra stalked away. I watched with the hatred strong inside me. I had never met the man, but he was too similar to another with the same surname and the same appearance.

Unable to stop myself, I curtseyed to Lady Pluscarden, who inclined her head in return and beckoned me forward.

'Miss Flockhart,' she said, 'I have been watching you.'

'Yes, your ladyship.'

'I do know you, I am sure.' She peered closer at me. 'Were you at the Great Northern Ball in Inverness last year?'

'No, your Ladyship,' I said. 'I have been overseas for some time.'

'I'll work it out,' Lady Pluscarden said. 'Now our host is talking.'

'You'll all stay the night here,' Gibbie insisted loudly. 'There are sufficient rooms for everybody and stabling for any horses and servants that the army may not require.'

With neither the desire nor intention to remain the night in Tynebridge Hall, I felt something flutter inside me and recognised the beginning of panic. 'Excuse me,' I sought a chair and took deep breaths, hoping that Emily or Elizabeth would happen along. Not Marie; she would be too flustered with this sudden influx of guests into her new house on the first night of married life. Poor woman; life could be so unfair sometimes.

'Miss Flockhart?' The voice was soft. 'Miss Dorothea Flockhart is it not?'

The man's smile stretched his thin face as he dragged a chair across the floor to my side. 'I thought I heard Lady Pluscarden call you that.'

I gave my coldest of nods. 'You may have done so.'

'That is interesting,' the thin-faced man sat beside me without by-your-leave or introduction. 'I also heard Lady Pluscarden say she had met you before.'

'Indeed?' I raised my eyebrows, wishing this odious fellow would leave me in peace.

'I am sure I have also met you before.'

I felt the suddenly increased hammering of my heart. I tried to edge further away. 'I do not believe I know you, sir.'

'William Turnbull.' My thin-faced companion gave a half bow that was more mockery than politeness.

'Mr Turnbull,' I acknowledged his presence with another nod.

'And you are Miss Dorothea Flockhart,' Turnbull mused, 'or so you say.'

I looked around in vain for somebody to rescue me from this man. A French invasion would have been welcome at that moment. 'I am not sure I understand you, sir.'

'Oh, I think you do,' Turnbull said. 'I think you understand me very well indeed.' Turnbull's smile contained as much humour as a cat at a mouse-hole. 'You are no stranger to this district at all, Miss Flockhart. I wonder why you wish to be known by that cognomen.' He continued to smile, stretching his legs out in front of him as he sat at my side. 'I really do.'

'If you'll excuse me, sir,' I said, 'I find this discussion most tiresome.'

'I do believe that you do,' Turnbull said. 'Yet others in this room may be extremely interested to hear that the shy Miss Flockhart is not all she appears. You do have a reason for your reticence.'

'I am sure my affairs would be of little interest to anybody.' I prepared to stand up and leave this unpleasant fellow to his own devices, yet he held me fast.

Turnbull's smile did not falter one whit. 'In which case, Miss Flockhart, you will have no objections to me announcing my knowledge to others in this room? The garrulous Mrs Elliot will certainly be interested in hearing about her new friend, or Mr Colin Campbell, perhaps? Even Mrs Emily Napier, your most particular companion who accompanied you to the Field Day so recently, will be delighted to learn you have deceived her.'

I stared at Turnbull. 'Have you been spying on me, sir?'

He laughed. 'Spying is such an ugly word, Miss Flockhart. Let us say I was ensuring that I knew you better before approaching.'

'And is there a purpose to your approach, sir?' Again I looked around in desperate hope for somebody to come along and interrupt this most unpleasant conversation.

'You have a secret you don't wish to be known,' Turnbull said, 'and I have a slight problem with finances.'

'Money?' I stared at this obnoxious fellow. 'You want me to give you money?'

'That's the ticket,' Turnbull faced me openly. 'That way I keep my silence and you keep your little secret, and we are both happy.'

'The devil!' I stared at Turnbull, revolted at the audacity of the man. 'How dare you, sir!' Yet I knew there was little I could do to retaliate. I did have a secret, and it seemed that Turnbull knew what it was. His next words confirmed my fears.

Turnbull's smile was unwavering. 'You are not quite who you appear, Miss Flockhart, and I am sure you have an excellent reason for keeping that to yourself. I would have no reason for disclosing my intelligence if my financial affairs were more comfortable.'

'Damn you, sir!' I hissed, searching frantically for some way out. 'You are no gentleman!'

'Perhaps not,' Turnbull said, 'but that is not the question. My reputation is beyond repair, you see, Miss Flockhart and can hardly be further damaged. Yours, on the other hand, is barely known.'

I stood up, seeking some air and space in which to think.

'Yes, you think about it,' Turnbull uncoiled at my side, tall and sinewy and basilisk-eyed. 'Think about the consequences and the small price that is all you have to pay to avoid them.'

'The small price?' I felt dirty even talking to this man.

'Oh, yes Miss Flockhart. I am not asking for a great deal. Shall we say £100?' He gave another little bow, turned on his heel and stalked away, the very picture of sordid elegance. After three steps he turned around. 'Don't concern yourself with finding me, Miss Flockhart, I am well aware of your Thistle Street address, and I will call round by-and-by to make the arrangements.'

I felt sick. The trepidation with which I had returned to this house had been well founded, and in a way that even I could not have expected. I could not stay here. I must get away and seek fresh air. Making my stumbling excuses to poor Marie, who appeared flustered enough with all the coming-and-going on her wedding day, I grabbed my cloak and rushed out of the house into the damp coolness of the November night.

Chapter Three

A Scottish winter is not kind to a woman in distress, and within ten minutes I was shivering like as aspen leaf. The night closed around me, damp and chill. It penetrated my light cloak and the thin material of my gown and reminded me that it was only comparatively recently that I had returned from a much more welcoming climate. I halted my heedless rush into the policies and looked around, listening to the wind roaring through the stark branches and the surge of the nearby River Tyne.

I used to be very familiar with the grounds of Tynebridge Hall and recalled an old Summer House where I could find a modicum of shelter. It was less than five hundred yards from the Hall, yet in the decade since I had last been here the paths had become overgrown and the trees more tangled. Even the undergrowth had grown denser so I tripped and stumbled as I moved across the once familiar ground. The memories returned, bitter and savage with the passage of years and onset of my maturity. I stopped in the partial shelter of a rowan tree.

'Beware the horned beast,' Mother Faa had warned me, and sure enough, a horned beast had appeared. Turnbull. What better name could there be for such a man? A bull was a horned beast, and he had shown himself to be dangerous and thoroughly unpleasant. If that part of Mother Faa's prediction had come true, were her words about a man in uniform equally accurate?

I took a deep breath and knew I needed space and time to think. I would generally return to my sanctuary of Thistle Street, but Turnbull had polluted that by his knowledge. I had nowhere else except the windy spaces of the hills. They would have to wait. At present I needed the shelter of the summer house or I would catch my death of cold out here. I had to concentrate on tonight and leave the future to look after itself.

My feet found the path despite the dark, and I saw the structure ahead. In keeping with the main building, it was neo-classical, with Doric columns around the walls and a dominant pediment cutting into the stars above. Thankful that the door was open, I nearly fell inside and lay on the stone-flagged floor, gasping in relief. The place may have been stark, but the walls kept out the wind and the roof provided shelter from the rain.

I do not know how long I lay there. It may have been minutes; it could have been hours. I only moved when the cold was numbing, and my teeth were chattering a tempo faster than any of the dances that already seemed so long ago. I dragged myself to my feet and stumbled in the dark, knowing there was a stone seat along the wall, with a beautiful summer view over the estate and the castle of Crichton. That night there was no view, and the unglazed windows allowed the rain to chill my face.

The door creaked, and somebody entered, with the soft glow of a lantern casting a pool of yellow light. Was there no peace in this world? I sat still, hoping to be left alone.

'Who's there? I know somebody's there.' The voice was Doctor Hetherington's, pleasant and familiar. 'Come now, there's no need to hide from me, whoever you are. I won't hurt you.'

The light eased in my direction and settled on my face.

'Why, Miss Flockhart! Whatever are you doing here at this time of night?' Doctor Hetherington lifted his lantern higher. 'And you're soaked to the skin, woman. Get you back inside now, before you catch a pneumonic infection.'

The sound of his concerned voice was just too much for me after Turnbull's threats, and I began to cry.

'Oh, now, whatever is the matter,' Doctor Hetherington was at my side in seconds with one arm around my cringing shoulders and his voice comforting in my ear. 'Shall I take you back to the Hall?'

I shook my head, unwilling and unable to speak.

'All right then.' Removing his cloak, he placed it on me. The extra layer of warmth was welcome against the chill. 'We will sit here together a while, and I will talk to you.'

I took deep whooping breaths of the damp air and said nothing.

'I often come to this spot,' Dr Hetherington spoke conversationally, as if to an old friend or the family dog. 'It is where I think things out. It's better in daylight when I can see half of Midlothian spread out before me and listen to the birds singing. Nothing eases the heart like birdsong.'

I nodded through my tears, for in all the long years of my exile abroad the one thing that I missed most was the song of the blackbird. Overseas birds are all very colourful and exotic, but not one of them comes close to the melancholic beauty of a blackbird in the evening. People may talk about the sound of bagpipes, but the call of a blackbird is the authentic music of Scotland.

'You're shivering,' Doctor Hetherington said. 'Come on. If you don't wish to return to the Hall, you can come home with me. I don't have a grand house but God knows it's warmer than out here and we can get you out of these wet clothes.'

I followed him like the proverbial sacrificial lamb as he picked his way along a half-seen path to the southern edge of the policies. I heard the rush of the River Tyne and a tiny part of me thought about stepping in and allowing the cold water to usher me to a more peaceful place.

'It's all right.' Misunderstanding the reason for my shudder, Doctor Hetherington comforted me. 'We don't have to ford the river.

There an ancient bridge over the Tyne, the Royal Union Bridge they call it because it dates from 1603, the same year as the Union of the Crowns.' His arm was firm around my shoulder. 'There's no danger, Miss Flockhart.'

It was not the danger that concerned me. Doctor Hetherington talked me over that hump-backed bridge where there was no parapet to prevent the unwary from falling into the foaming brown water below. 'If it were daylight I would show you the coat of arms with the lion of England and the unicorn of Scotland. It's worn now with age yet still clear, and that's us over, and there's the main road ahead and my home on the left. We've only hundred yards to walk and we're safe and in the warmth.'

'This is an old road.' My mind was wandering after the tribulations of the day. 'Did Jeremiah not say that?'

Doctor Hetherington nodded and quoted from the Bible. 'Thus saith the Lord. Stand ye in the ways, and see, and ask for the old paths, where is the good way.'

I completed the quote. 'And walk therein, and ye shall find rest for your souls.'

We exchanged looks, and he smiled, and I did not. Even so, I felt we had made some contact although I was unsure if it was for better or for worse or not for anything at all. I did not matter; I would not find rest for my soul on this path or any other.

Before I knew it, we were outside the doctor's dwelling, a modest two-storey building with a red pantiled roof, all set within a small vegetable garden of perhaps a fifth of an acre.

'In you come, Miss Flockhart and don't be concerned about your reputation. I am known as an eccentric, and I often bring my patients home with me.' Doctor Hetherington smiled, 'just not often in the middle of the night.' He used the flame in the lantern to light a couple of candles and led me in.

'Come into my parlour, said the spider to the miserably wet lady.' The doctor's parlour was a dishevelled room warmed by the dying embers of a fire and furnished with worn but serviceable furniture.

'Sit down, sit down,' he ushered me into the only armed chair while he fussed over the fire until the flames revived and threw light and warmth into the room. 'Now you sit there while I find you something to eat. There's nothing like warm broth to set you to rights on a night like this.'

I did as the doctor ordered and allowed him to take my cloak off and rub the circulation back into my hands. His broth was reheated from the day before if I was any judge but nourishing and restored life to me.

'You've been crying,' Dr Hetherington said.

'Yes.' I agreed.

'Heavens, woman!' The doctor put a hand on my arm, and then on my shoulder. 'You're soaked through and through. Quickly now, get out of these wet things, or it's pneumonic fever for you. Now no arguments! Off with them.'

I hesitated. 'I can't,' I said.

'Oh, stuff and nonsense,' Dr Hetherington said. 'I'm a doctor.' He sighed as he tried to understand my fears. 'It's all right, Miss Flock-hart, I'll leave the room.' He rummaged in a battered sea- chest that squatted under the small window. 'Here; put these on until we get your clothes dry. They're not stylish, but they'll cover you, and they're warmer than what you're wearing now.' The white duck trousers and canvas shirt that he handed me were worn but spot-lessly clean. I thanked him as he left the room.

Despite Doctor Hetherington's reassurances, I stood with my back to the door as I hurriedly changed and slipped on the dry clothes, folding up the shirt sleeves and trouser legs so they at least approximately fitted. Unsure what to do, I sat back down, closed my eyes and allowed the warmth from the fire to seep into my body as a hundred images crowded through my mind.

Past and present combined in a confusion of memories, where Captain Rogers fought the French while Lady Pluscarden fixed me with her gimlet gaze and William Turnbull proffered a grasping hand. I wriggled and writhed to escape as other, older and worse horrors surfaced, with terror coming to the fore and always an underlying knowledge of sickening loss.

When I woke up, I was tucked into a bed in an unfamiliar room with grey light struggling through a tiny square window. The wall opposite me was decorated with three slightly faded prints of wild birds and an incongruous whaling harpoon.

'Welcome back,' Doctor Hetherington must have heard me stir. He peered through the open door. 'You must have needed that sleep. You've been out for hours.'

I quickly checked to make sure I was still dressed and then the memory of Turnbull's blackmail threat returned. 'I have to get home.'

'I'll get you home,' Doctor Hetherington said. 'Calm yourself, and don't worry about the French. The invasion was a fudge so there's no danger. Some overzealous look-out thought he saw a signal that was not there.' He shrugged, 'oh, well. Better safe than sorry and if he had seen a signal and ignored it we would be under the heels of Boney in no time.'

I did not admit that I had forgotten all about the invasion scare. Sliding sideways out of bed, I remained sitting as my head cleared of the nightmares. 'How can I thank you for your hospitality, Doctor?'

Doctor Hetherington smiled. 'You can allow me the pleasure of your company for the journey into Edinburgh.'

'You are too kind,' I glanced down at my current state of dress. 'I had better wear my own clothes first, Doctor. I would raise a few eyebrows leaving Edinburgh in a gown and returning in a pair of sailor's trousers.'

'I think they are very fetching,' Doctor Hetherington said, 'yet they would invoke comments.'

'They are hardly fetching,' I caught a glimpse of myself in the pier-glass, saw how tightly the breeches hugged my hips and felt the colour rise to my face. 'Could you fetch my own clothes please, Doctor?'

'They are on the chair opposite the bed.'

'And all washed and ironed,' I noted. 'You would make some woman a fine wife, Doctor, except for the décor.' I nodded toward the harpoon. 'She might ask you to remove that.'

'A souvenir of my one-and-only sea voyage,' Doctor Hetherington touched the shaft of the harpoon. 'I was a student raising funds to continue my studies.' He stepped to the door. 'I'll leave you to get changed.'

Doctor Hetherington's finances did not stretch as far as a coach and pair, so it was in an open dog-cart that we trotted out of the village, over the Royal Union Bridge and onto the Edinburgh road. I held my travelling cloak close to my shoulders against the chill and allowed my mind to drift.

'If ever I had a secret to tell,' Doctor Hetherington said as we rolled past the ploughed fields and tiny collier villages of Midlothian, 'I would confide in you. You are the most close-mouthed woman I have ever met. No, you are the most close-mouthed *person*, woman *or* man, I have ever met.'

'Thank you.' My mind was set on William Turnbull, so I fear I quite neglected poor Doctor Hetherington despite all his kindness. What did that man Turnbull know and how had he obtained the intelligence?

'I am not sure I deserve to be thanked for that particular observation,' Doctor Hetherington negotiated the steep descent of Toll Brae, paid with good humour at the barrier and turned to the right, where the ancient settlement of Newbattle soon clustered before us. The one-time abbey rose above the trees, serene and lovely despite the dull skies.

'The truth should always come out, welcome or not,' I said.

Doctor Hetherington looked over his shoulder at me. 'You were scared last night,' he said, 'and it looked very much as if you had been running from someone or something.'

'Was that how it looked?' I tried to close that conversation.

'One can only run so far,' Dr Hetherington slowed down as a group of round-shouldered miners crossed the road in front of us, men and women and children all bowed with weariness and un-remitting labour. One looked around, her eyes sunk deep in a face seamed with coal dust and scars. Compared to these collier's every-day lives, I had no worries at all. 'And then it is time to make a stand.'

I was silent as we rattled through Newbattle and into Eskbank. 'Thank you,' I could not think of anything else to say.

'It can be hard to stand alone,' Doctor Hetherington continued the second I spoke. 'If you find yourself in that position, a sympathetic doctor could be helpful, a shoulder to lean on.'

I nodded, wondering if I could trust this man. My life's experi-ence suggested that whatever his promises just now, he would be notably lacking when I needed him most. I thanked him yet again and allowed him to prattle on the remainder of the weary road to my home.

It was strange that after years when I avoided the company of single men, I had spoken to three in two days. One was a gallant captain with a twinkling eye and a storyteller's skill at entertain-ing. One was a serious-minded doctor with compassionate eyes and a battered face, and the third was the gaunt-faced Turnbull, who planned to rob me. Of the three, Turnbull was the man who I be-lieved most typical of the sex.

It was a relief to have Doctor Hetherington pull up in front of my little house in Thistle Street, one of the lesser streets in Edinburgh's New Town. I climbed out, easing cramped limbs and wishing des-perately to rub parts of me that one ought not to even think about, let alone touch in a public place. Hard dog-cart seats tend to do un-pleasant things to the more ample portions of the female anatomy.

I tried not to notice the man who lounged in a doorway on the opposite side of the street. I could not cope with Doctor Hether-ington and Turnbull at the same time. I could feel Turnbull's gaze following me into the house and hoped he did not come to the door while Dr Hetherington was inside. Somehow I knew he would not; creatures such as Turnbull often avoided the company of real men. All the same, I spent an uncomfortable hour entertaining the good doctor and worrying about Turnbull outside. I noticed Mrs Macfarlane, my housekeeper, watching me and knew she was harbouring a hundred questions.

When at last Doctor Hetherington said he had better be making his way back to Crichton I could have sobbed with relief.

'Thank you again,' Doctor I said. 'I don't know how I would have coped if you had not happened along.'

Doctor Hetherington bowed. 'It was my pleasure, Miss Flockhart.'

'Now he was a gentleman,' Mrs Macfarlane said as Doctor Hetherington cracked his whip for the long drive back to Crichton. 'Not like the last person who called.' Mrs Macfarlane was a middle-aged, efficient woman with the burr of the Highlands in her throat and wisdom in her eyes.

'Yes, Doctor Hetherington seems like a gentleman. Was the last person tall and thin?'

'That he was,' Mrs Macfarlane said. 'Tall and thin and with Satan's smile on his face.'

As we spoke, there was a knock at the door. 'Please see this man in, Mrs Macfarlane, and best leave us alone.'

Mrs Macfarlane frowned. 'If that's the same person that last called, Miss Flockhart, I'd prefer you're not alone with him.'

'Do as I say, please, Mrs Macfarlane.' I tried to sound commanding.

'Yes, Miss Flockhart,' Mrs Macfarlane put just sufficient inflexion in her words to show her displeasure. 'You be careful now.'

'Show him in.'

Turnbull had retained his insincere smile as Mrs Macfarlane ushered him into the withdrawing room. 'Your maid does not like me,' he sat down without an invitation.

'She has good taste,' I said. 'I don't like you either.'

'Oh, come now, Miss Flockhart, I could have revealed your secret and given you real cause for dislike.' Turnbull leaned back in the chair and stretched his legs. 'Aren't you going to offer your guest a drink?'

I sat opposite him, taking care there was space between us. 'No. Speak.'

'One hundred guineas, a mere hundred golden boys and your secret is safe.' Turnbull's smile did not waver.

'I will never see you again,' I tried to control my rising anger.

Turnbull spread his hands in a gesture more French than Scottish. 'I cannot say. I may have a desire for your company, Miss Flockhart. It would depend on my financial situation.'

'You have gambling debts,' I wanted to hurt this odious man.

'I may soon have gambling *profits*,' Turnbull said. 'Do you have the money with you?'

'I do not,' I said. 'I don't keep that sort of sum in the house in case of burglars, house-breakers or visits by unpleasant blackguards.'

'Will you have my funds tomorrow, then?' Turnbull's smile wavered slightly.

'A week today,' I had decided that, although I had no choice but to pay the piper, I would not rush to put my money into his avaricious hands.

'I can't wait that long.' Turnbull said.

'Then do your damndest,' I tapped my fingers on my knee. 'And not one brass farthing will you see from me.' As Doctor Hetherington had said, the time for running was finished, yet I was not quite ready to make a stand.

'One week today,' Turnbull rose and clapped his tall hat on his head. 'And you'd better have my money.'

'Show yourself out,' I said, 'for I'm sure I won't.' I heard the door slam as he left.

Chapter Four

'I said he was no gentleman, Miss Flockhart.' Mrs Macfarlane entered the room before the echoes of the slammed door had time to fade. 'Blackmail is it?'

'Were you listening at the door?'

'Yes,' Mrs Macfarlane nodded without a trace of shame. 'I don't know what hold he has on you, Miss Flockhart, and it's not my business.' She paused, obviously waiting for enlightenment that I was not inclined to give. 'I can help you.'

'There's nothing you can do,' I said.

'Macfarlane can help,' Mrs Macfarlane folded her arms and stood beside me in my drawing room. About fifty years old, not much over five foot tall, she looked as immobile as the granite of Ben Lomond, the mountain that overlooked her birthplace.

'Macfarlane?' I queried the name.

'My husband, Macfarlane.' Mrs Macfarlane had not budged a fraction of an inch.

'How can your husband possibly help?'

'Macfarlane knows people,' Mrs Macfarlane could be as obscure as Highland peat when it suited her. 'And he has his unique methods.'

'Thank you, Mrs Macfarlane, but I must pay the man Turnbull and hope he goes away.'

'Men like Turnbull never go away,' Mrs Macfarlane said. 'They crawl into your life and suck you dry. Macfarlane can help.'

'You seem to know a lot about this sort of business.' I tried to dominate the conversation while nausea rose within me.

'The moon is Macfarlane's lantern,' Mrs Macfarlane's reply was even more cryptic.

Ignoring Mrs Macfarlane's protests, I dismissed her to the kitchen, stood up and began to pace up and down the drawing room, trying to work out a way out of my dilemma. The only one that I could think of was to disappear again, book passage back to India and vanish in that immense place. No. I had decided to stop running. Doctor Hetherington was correct; it was time to make a stand.

What sort of stand? What could I do? I sighed; I would pay Turnbull and hope he was successful with the cards so that I would never see him again. It was a slender hope, yet any hope was better than none.

Moving to the window, I stared into the narrow gulley that was Thistle Street, where the ashlar buildings blocked the light and tradesmen's carts were more common than stylish carriages. I could afford better but had no intention of drawing more attention to myself. Why had I not remained in India? And then I remembered Captain Rogers open smile. There was some hope in this world. Now I had to see my solicitor about money.

That was tomorrow. Tonight I would eat, go to bed and hope the nightmares did not return. Tomorrow I would visit Mr Pryde.

The clerk looked me up and down as if I had no business to trouble him. 'May I have your name, Madam?'

'Please tell your master that Miss Dorothea Flockhart is here,' I said.

The clerk was a young man with hair as long as his nose and a high, ill-fitting collar. 'Is Mr Pryde expecting you?'

'Mr Pryde knows I am coming,' I said and waited while the clerk stamped away. I inhaled the smell of dust and age in this room that I had only visited twice before.

Mr Charles Pryde looked the same as he had the previous year, if a little bit greyer and with the lines around his eyes and mouth a little more defined. He bowed as he approached and ushered me past the counter and into his inner sanctum. 'Have a seat, do, Miss Flockhart.'

Mr Pryde's desk was piled high with ledgers and buff-coloured files, with his inkwell brimming full and his goose-wing quills standing to attention at the side. A pen-knife lay beside his blotter.

I glanced around the room. Glass-fronted bookcases covered two walls, with a deep-set window allowing in a modicum of grey light in the third. All was ordered and safe. Mr Pryde was not a man to take chances.

'Is it a year since you were last here?' Mr Pryde waited until I sat down before he slid down onto his hard chair. 'Time passes so quickly now. Why, it seems no time at all since your father sat on that very chair.' He shook his head. 'Well, well.'

When Mr Pryde rang the brass bell that stood beside his inkwell the clerk appeared at once.

'Bring me Miss Flockhart's file,' Mr Pryde said.

'Yes, sir.' The clerk bowed and disappeared.

'Do you wish some refreshment, Miss Flockhart?' Mr Pryde fussed with his ledgers. 'It does not seem correct to call you that.'

'Miss Flockhart is the name I use, Mr Pryde,' I said. 'Or Dorothea, if you wish. After all, you have known me since before I was born.'

'And your father and mother before you,' Mr Pryde said with a smile. 'Miss Flockhart it shall be.' He looked up as the clerk returned with a buff folder tied with linen thread and sealed with a blue wafer. 'Now, Miss Flockhart, to business.'

I fixed the clerk with as evil a look as I could to encourage him to leave. Mr Pryde took the hint and waved him away before breaking the wafer.

'I have of course kept in touch with your investments,' Mr Pryde placed half a dozen documents in front of him. 'You have shares in these ships,' he read out the names and continued. 'They are two whaling ships, two Baltic traders, one East Indiaman and one West Indiaman.'

'I have been watching their progress in the shipping columns,' I said.

Mr Pryde looked up. 'You have been fortunate that all have made good voyages, given the current state of hostilities with France.'

'Perhaps less good fortune than good masters in the ships,' I said.

'Shall we agree on a mixture of both?' Mr Pryde passed a sheet of paper over to me. 'Here are this year's figures, Miss Flockhart.'

I nodded as I scrutinised the columns and the final figures. 'The war certainly raises the profit margins for the vessels that get through.'

'Unfortunately, it also raises insurance premiums,' Mr Pryde said.

'Have the insurance premiums been taken from these figures?'

'Yes, Miss Flockhart. The figures are net.' Mr Pryde pointed out the entry with his thin finger and waited until I had absorbed the totals. 'As you see, the profits are quite substantial. And your other assets,' he lifted another buff folder, 'are all in here.' He handed it over in its entirety.

I hesitated before I opened the file. As always, the name at the top made me shiver. 'I'm glad to see you're putting it to good use,' I said. 'Although I don't know if I intend to retain this particular asset.'

Mr Pryde grunted. 'It is a regular source of income,' he advised, 'whatever your personal feelings may be.'

'There are occasions that I just want to be rid of the whole thing.'

'I do understand that Miss Flockhart,' Mr Pryde said. 'It was a horrible episode in your life, yet practicalities are practicalities, and everyone needs an income.'

'I have the shipping shares,' I reminded.

'If even one of the ships sinks or the French capture it, your income from that source diminishes. Take the whaling ship, for instance, every year about one in every twenty whaling ships sinks in the ice, so that year by year, the chances of your vessels safe return reduces. And this new French war has just started. The last one lasted eight years; God only knows how long this war will continue.'

I nodded. Mr Pryde's facts were unpalatable but undeniable. 'I understand, Mr Pryde. You advise that I keep hold of that asset at present rather than exchanging it for its present cash value.'

'Exactly so, Miss Flockhart. A bird in the hand is better than two in the bush and anything that generates wealth in these uncertain times is worth retaining. When this present emergency subsides, and the world settles down, then you may wish to reconsider your position. At present I would advise you to hold tight and bite down your memories, however bitter.'

I nodded. It was not pleasant to hear, but there was little point in employing a solicitor if I did not take heed of his advice. I tried to push away the faces and memories that hovered at the fringes of my mind.

'One last thing,' I said. 'I will need an extra cash withdrawal. An unexpected expense has occurred.'

'Such things happen,' Mr Pryde agreed. 'How much?'

'One hundred pounds.'

'In gold or a bank draft?' Mr Pryde did not turn a hair at the figure.

'In gold, please, and could you make that a hundred and ten?' I had a sudden desire for some luxuries for myself, or perhaps a small contribution to Doctor Hetherington's practice. He had seemed a dedicated man and had undoubtedly helped me in my time of need.

'My clerk will do the needful.' Mr Pryde said.

Winter dusk was already upon us when I left the office, and I was thankful to clamber into the waiting post-chaise. 'Back to Thistle Street,' I ordered Alexander, my driver. I was glad that my trip to Mr Pryde was complete for another year. He was a pleasant enough fellow and adequately kept my affairs in order, but I preferred to keep solicitors and such like people at arms' length. I glanced at the barracks of Queensberry House across the street, wondered if Captain Rogers had ever been in there and shook my head. I should not think such things. My future would and could not contain a husband, and I would never countenance any other form of male relationship.

Alexander whipped up, and we moved away, with the wheels rolling and grinding over the granite setts and the tall tenements sliding past on either side. I always thought that driving through Edinburgh's Old Town was like passing between two walls of a canyon with the cliff-like buildings pierced with a thousand small windows from which watchful eyes peered.

'There's trouble ahead, Ma'am,' Alexander shouted back to me and pulled the coach to a halt.

'What's happening?' I tried to peer out of the coach window, saw nothing, opened the door and stepped outside. A horse had fallen, spilling a cartload of coal to block the Canongait. Traffic was already beginning to build up, with tradesmen's carts predominant and much commonplace language. 'Can you get us out of here, Alexander?'

'We can go by the Cowgait,' the driver said at once. 'Best keep the blinds down on the windows.'

Many years ago the Cowgait had been a prosperous area but now was rapidly filling up with immigrant Irish labourers. Once grand houses were now divided and sub-divided into smaller homes, and whole families lived in single rooms.

'I've seen worse,' I said, although I knew that the more deprived areas of Edinburgh could be odious at best and horrendous at worst.

'Hold on then, Ma'am,' the driver said.

It could not have been easy to turn the chaise in that narrow street, but Alexander was a man of skill. Ignoring the curses and waving fists of the other drivers, he had us trotting back down the slope of the Canongait within a few moments. We passed the old Palace of Holyroodhouse and headed into the dark depths of the Cowgait. Here, the road was even narrower than the Canongait, and only the intermittent flicker of tallow candles glimmered from broken-paned windows on the crowding tenements.

Despite Alexander's advice, I kept the blinds up and looked with some curiosity at this notorious quarter of the city. Crowds filled the streets, dissolute and wretched labourers with broad faces and heavy boots together with slatternly looking women. Hordes of filthy, bare-foot children erupted from every crevice and dirty close to stare at this coach passing by. It was hard to believe that we were in the Modern Athens, home to the Scottish Enlightenment and the most civilised and educated city in the world.

'Move aside there!' I heard Alexander's shout and craned my neck to look ahead. A mob of people had congregated in the road ahead, staring insolently at the chaise. Somebody threw a stone that rattled from the bodywork, and then the driver lashed out with his whip, cracking it above their heads. 'Get out of the way!'

I saw the crowd part slightly, and the driver slashed his whip sideways. 'Move away there, you blackguards!' He aimed at the legs of the most stubborn, forcing them to jump aside, creating a slight gap. Alexander drove straight forward, and the mob parted like the Red Sea under Moses's staff. I had a momentary glimpse of predatory faces with open mouths, and then we were past. 'Thank you, driver,' I shouted, determined that I would give this man far more than the statutory fare the minute he got me safely home.

We slowed again as a drunk woman reeled from one of the many hole-in-the-wall public houses in which the denizens of these sordid closes spent their time and money. Positioned at the bottom of a wynd that thrust upward into a dark morass of interlocking closes and alleyways, the pub door was closed, no doubt concealing all manners of horror and unrecognised sin. As we passed, a group of people burst out of the pub, men and women arm-in-arm and all were shouting or singing loudly.

Central to the group was an elderly man with a long nose and a sharp chin. I recognised him with a cold shiver: Old Q, the Duke of Queensberry, one of the most notorious rakes and gamblers in the country. He had a semi-dressed woman on his right, with her dress cut so low that her breasts were exposed nearly to the nipples. On his left was a tall, gangly man in gaudy clothes that looked out of place in this dismal place. His flame-red hair was instantly recognisable. That was Hector McAra, who had been so vocal at Marie's wedding. He had wrapped his arm around the waist of a gaudily-dressed woman, who had her hand thrust into the waistband of his breeches. I would have expected nothing more from McAra. The third man, with a woman on both arms, was Gilbert Elliot.

I leaned back quickly in case Gilbert would catch a glimpse of me, and then we were passed, and the driver was making good time along the gloomy cavern of the Cowgait.

Oh dear God, not again, I thought, not again. With Old Q involved, Gibbie Elliot would be dragged along the path of the rake, and poor Marie would suffer. Whatever Gibbie wanted to happen, he would be taken deeper into the world of gamblers and rakes, deeper and darker into the lair of prostitutes and cynical, dissolute men. I could not allow it.

But how could I prevent it?

The memories were never far away, and now they returned in a confused jumble of emotions and images. I no longer saw the tall tenements of the Cowgait but relived my past. I recalled the momentary surge of happiness and hope as we entered the romantic ruins of Crichton Castle and the sickening disbelief as I faced reality and then the horror of the later events. I remembered the panic of that run through the grounds, the bite and sting of thorns and nettles, the fear as the hounds bayed behind me and the high-pitched laughter of the huntsmen echoing through the trees. I jerked my eyes open, trying to escape, unable to face what happened next.

Perspiration dampened me as I tried to fight free of these events of a decade ago. I shook my head. I may be mistaken; perhaps McAra had inveigled Gibbie into going out? And then I remembered Gibbie's comment at the wedding. What had he said? 'We can visit one of the low pubs in Whisky Row and mix with the lower orders.' No, it was no mistake. Gibbie knew what he was doing. Oh, God, I could not allow Marie to go through such things. But how could I help her? I was only a lone woman with sufficient troubles of my own.

I closed my eyes and wept.

Chapter Five

'Halloa there!' I heard the rich voice as I stood at the head of the Earthen Mound, looking down on the gracious streets and squares of the New Town. It was a view of which I never tired, this spreading beauty of our capital city with the classic grace that spoke of order, culture and the laws of architecture. It was Edinburgh that had called me back from India; I had missed the city. There were other reasons; legal matters, the call of a blackbird, the desire for a Scottish spring, the feel of cool rain, but Edinburgh's grace had been paramount.

'Halloa there, Miss Flockhart,' the voice sounded again.

Not used to being accosted in public, I did not turn and continued to enjoy the view.

'Miss Flockhart!'

I looked around slowly and felt a surge of relief that was nearly pleasure. 'Why Captain Rogers,' I said. 'I did not expect to see you here. I thought you would be fighting the French, or at least exercising your troops.'

'My troops have seen enough of me for one morning,' Captain Rogers said. 'And the French appear to be content to remain on the Continent rather than chancing the sea, Admiral Nelson and the Edinburgh Volunteers.'

'I cannot fault them for that,' I said. 'In my experience, the sea is a very boisterous element while Admiral Nelson has a reputation for destroying French hopes and French ships.' I shook my head, 'and the whole world knows the quality of the Edinburgh Volunteers.'

Captain Rogers raised immaculate eyebrows as he fixed onto the first part of my conversation. 'I was unaware you were a seafarer.'

I cursed my wayward tongue. 'I have been on a voyage or two.' I admitted.

'You intrigue me.' Captain Rogers stepped to my side and bowed. 'To where did you sail?'

'Bengal,' I told the bald truth. 'And then back again.'

'Were you accompanied?'

'I was alone,' I said, rather sharply and forestalled his next thought, if not his next question. 'And I was not part of the fishing fleet.'

'I could not see you as one of these women who venture all the way to India to try and catch an eligible bachelor.' Captain Rogers smiled, as though the very idea amused him. Perhaps he was hinting that no eligible bachelor would be interested in me and if so he was correct. 'You will have had your reasons, no doubt.'

'I had my reasons,' I agreed.

Captain Rogers laughed openly. 'You give very little away, Miss Flockhart.'

I tried to change the subject. 'It is a bracing day.'

'And here you are, walking abroad quite alone,' Captain Rogers said.

'I was visiting the poor, as any charitable Christian ought to do.' I thought the man deserved some explanation. He had never shown anything but kindness to me and here I was, spurning his innocent questions as if he were a leper. I took another look at the captain, trying to see past the bold uniform to the man beneath.

In truth, he would be reckoned a handsome enough fellow by those who took an interest in such shallow measurements of man's accomplishments. He was indeed tall and dark, with groomed whiskers and a long Scottish nose that jutted most imperiously from a face of regular features without blemish or fault. Or rather, he did have one flaw, a small scar that marred the smooth perfection of his chin, on the left side. Was that imperfection a flaw? Or did it merely highlight the handsomeness of his other attributes?

For a moment I wondered how he came by that scar, picturing the captain in the cut-and-thrust of the Battle of Alexandria where brave General Abercrombie defeated the French, and the bayonets of the Royal Highlanders destroyed Bonaparte's Invincibles. Perhaps it had been at Serangipatam when General Baird had taken Tippoo Sahib's mighty fortress. I remembered the captain's story-telling at Marie's wedding; maybe he had not been pulling the long-bow but had told the truth.

'Helping the poor is a very laudable object,' Captain Rogers' words brought me back to the present, 'Although I would advise you to hire a carriage next time, or even a sedan. There are some unpleasant fellows among the lower orders who would not appreciate your help as much as they would your purse.'

I curtseyed to acknowledge his advice. I did not tell him that in Hindustan I had ventured alone among far more desperate fellows than the poor in Edinburgh's Old Town. Or, remembering the mob who had tried to stop my post-chaise in the Cowgait, perhaps they were only equally desperate.

'I do not like to think of a gentlewoman putting herself in danger with such people.' Captain Rogers continued as I grabbed my bonnet before a gust of wind flicked it away. I had visions of my hat flying across to the castle ramparts or playing helter-skelter among the promenading couples of Princes Street.

'I was in no danger,' I said.

'You are a very intriguing woman,' Captain Rogers repeated. 'Now I am afraid I must leave you. Duty requires me.' He lifted his shako and hesitated. 'I would like to call on you, Miss Flockhart, if you do not find my company offensive.'

I was not sure what to say. I remembered Mother Faa's words about a man with a uniform, yet I was not seeking a man at all. Not even this amiable gallant.

Captain Rogers raised his eyebrows and smiled, waiting for an answer.

'I do not find your company offensive, Captain,' I had already told him that.

'That is an excellent start,' Captain Rogers said. 'I will not rush you. I will be in touch.' He bowed again. 'If you ever need a military escort, Miss Flockhart, send for me.'

I thanked him. 'I shall remember that,' I could think of no situation where I would require such a thing.

Once more bowing, Captain Rogers marched away. I watched him for a few moments with my eyes straying with conscious thought to his long shapely legs. I jerked my gaze away quickly, in case … in case of what? In case I began to enjoy the captain's company? I remembered Lady Pluscarden's liking for handsome young men and frowned. There was no need to remind myself why I could not become too companionable with a man, any man.

Chapter Six

I lined up my shot and chipped for the hole. The ball rose high, floated for a moment above the green and fell to the ground. It bounced once, twice, three times and rolled past the hole and on for another three yards. I watched it with some pleasure.

'Good effort,' Doctor Hetherington said. 'Let's see if I can beat it.' He chose a niblick from his tattered golf bag, took a practice swing and hit the ball sweet as a nut.

The ball barely rose above ground level as it soared toward the green. It landed a foot from the hole, bounced over the top and came to rest an inch from my own.

'Not as good as I had hoped,' Doctor Hetherington admitted.

'Most men would not care to play golf against a woman.' I eyed the distance between my ball and the hole and selected my putter. 'In case the woman wins and disgraces them.'

Bruntsfield Links was quiet at this time in the morning, with the winter sun sending long shadows over the undulating course and the lights of the surrounding buildings mere candle-flicks of hope. Women and men had played golf here for centuries, I knew, although it was more usual for each sex to keep to their own. I took a deep breath of the chill air and looked around. With the click of club on ball and groups of players and observers scattered around the Links, this was a place of peace.

'Most men would not care to play with me anyway,' Doctor Hetherington said. 'My game can be erratic.'

I tapped the ball home and heard the satisfying rattle as it sunk into the hole.

'Good shot,' Doctor Hetherington said. He followed suit, with his ball rolling sweet and true. 'Did you know that Mary, Queen of Scots used to play golf?'

'I knew that,' I said. 'And the fishwives of Musselburgh are famous golfers.'

We walked a few yards and dropped our balls on the springy grass. We both selected a play club, and I prepared to strike for the next hole.

'You did not merely come here for a round of golf,' Doctor Hetherington was smiling.

'No.' I lined up my shot and let drive. There is nothing quite as gratifying as the sound of a well-hit golf ball followed by the sight of the white orb soaring across the ancient links. I savoured the moment.

Doctor Hetherington's ball closely pursued mine and we watched the dual flight. Both landed within a few feet of each other and rolled frustratingly into a damp hollow. We walked toward them with our steps sounding hollow in the cusp of the morning and our breath clouding around our faces. Golf in an Edinburgh winter morning is an exquisite pleasure, a combination of skill and exercise suitable to set the blood pounding and wake one up for the day ahead.

The doctor took out his brassie next and eyed the distance to the hole. A couple of young lads were behind us, shouting as they swung, and laughing at each other's misfortunes. Golf is still like that, thank goodness, a game played by all classes on Edinburgh's ancient links and other places around the Scottish countryside. If it ever becomes the pastime of the spoiled rich, it will lose both its character and appeal.

I preferred a spoon to a brassie and scooped the ball skyward to endeavour the green. The boys behind us cheered and clapped as my ball soared well past the hole and landed in a patch of rough. I acknowledged the boys' laughter by lifting my club. All the same, the lantern glow of the Golf Hotel was very welcoming as a haar crept across the course. I failed to hide my shiver, and the doctor tucked my cloak closer around my neck.

'You have decided to make your stand then,' Doctor Hetherington waited until a couple of stray dogs barked past before he made his shot. His ball also flew wide, landing well clear of his intended target. I nodded, corrected my stance to allow for the westerly breeze that drove in the haar and hit the ball.

'Good shot,' Doctor Hetherington said as my ball lofted, hung in the air for a heart-stopping moment and then fell straight onto the green.

'I have decided to make my stand.' I did not mention Turnbull.

We walked together to the doctor's ball, eyed its lie and pondered the doctor's next shot. The two dogs splashed through a puddle nearby, still barking.

'Do you wish my support?' Doctor Hetherington continued with his brassie, slicing the shot, so it nearly smacked into one of the two dogs. The two boys grinned and nudged each other.

'I may wish your advice, doctor.' That was hard to say. I had not asked for a man's help for a decade.

We watched the doctor's ball land on a slight slope and roll damply toward the green. 'That was fortunate.' Doctor Hetherington said.

'Or you have more skill than you admit.' I said as his ball rested two feet from the hole.

'The devil looks after his own.' Doctor Hetherington accompanied me to my ball. 'You can knock this one right into the hole now, Miss Flockhart.'

My putting was good that day. I holed the ball. 'Marie Elliot could be in serious trouble,' I did not say more.

'Tell me over a bowl of punch,' Doctor Hetherington did not conceal his shiver. 'We have had sufficient exercise for one morning.'

I did not object, scooping up my ball and heading for the hotel with my skirt snapping against my calves and the clubs under my arm.

Alexander McKellar ran the Golf Hotel, or more accurately Mrs McKellar ran the hotel while McKellar spent much of his life on the Links as Cock o' the Green. We were fortunate that morning as McKellar had been playing the short holes by lantern-light the previous night and Mrs McKellar had called him to account. Now McKellar was behind the counter with his shirt sleeves rolled up and his golf clubs leaning against the far wall, ready for instant use.

'By the Lord Harry!' McKellar greeted us as we entered his inn, 'you're the keen ones. How are the greens this morning?' He beamed at me from above his hooked nose.

'Slow with the dampness,' Doctor Hetherington responded. 'But true. We are after a golfing breakfast Alex, and a bowl of steaming punch.'

We sat at a crowded table as other early golfers came in and the talk was of niblicks and spoons and brassies and how poorly everyone had played that day. In a golfing tavern, nobody mentioned the war. Far more critical matters occupied their minds. Doctor Hetherington allowed me time to settle down before he began his gentle probing.

'Tell me about Marie's problems,' he invited.

I told him what I had seen in the Cowgait. He listened without interruption, nodding at all the correct places.

'Do you wish me to talk to Mr Elliot?' Doctor Hetherington's gaze had not strayed from my face. 'I could perhaps warn him about infections and how they could affect Mrs Elliot, but with all due regard, Miss Flockhart, I am his doctor and not his moral guide.'

'I know that Doctor,' I said. 'I am not sure that I expect you to do anything. I just wanted to tell somebody what I saw.' I wished to unburden myself of the memories I had carried for ten years. I did not know how.

Doctor Hetherington looked away. 'It is a difficult thing to see a friend go wrong,' he spoke slowly. 'Or when you think a friend is going wrong. You only saw him leaving a public with two other men and some women. You do not know if any impropriety took place.'

I clutched at that straw, desperate for some shred of hope. 'Gilbert was arm-in-arm with another woman,' I pointed out.

'Does he not have a sister?' Doctor Hetherington asked.

'I do not know,' I said.

'He has two,' Doctor Hetherington drank more of the steaming punch. 'The younger still lives with their parents, and the elder is in Edinburgh.'

'Oh,' I wondered, hopefully, if it had been the older Elliot sister that Gibbie had been with that evening. If so she required some strong maternal advice as to the kind of company she was keeping.

Doctor Hetherington smiled. 'Now, Miss Flockhart, I am not saying that you are mistaken. I am saying that you had a brief glimpse of Mr Elliot, at night, from the window of a moving chariot in a dark street and in the rain. Are you certain that you saw what you think you saw?'

I reconsidered, bringing every detail to mind. 'I also saw Old Q with Gibbie, that unpleasant McAra fellow and a group of women.'

The doctor nodded. 'All right,' he said. 'I will have a wee word with Mr Elliot. Please remember that, given our respective social conditions, he has every right to tell me to mind my own business.'

I flinched. Social standing was one of the biggest curses in Scotland. Everything one did and said and every person with whom one associated was class-dependent. I liked Doctor Hetherington, but he was only that, a country doctor, while Gilbert was a scion of the nobility, one of society's privileged. 'I see,' I said. And I did see. Doctor Hetherington was scared to step outside the limits of his class. For all his friendliness, he could not help me. I was, once again, on my own. It was a situation I was used to, but one that did not get easier with time. I sighed and wished I had never mentioned the subject.

'Thank you, Doctor,' I thought I hid my disappointment. 'I'd better be getting back to Thistle Street now.'

'I'll take you in my dog-cart,' the doctor offered.

'Thank you, Doctor, I can walk.' I dismissed the dismay on Doctor Hetherington's face as unimportant.

The knock at the door took me by surprise. I heard Mrs Macfarlane patter to answer and the low rumble of a male voice.

'It's that man again,' Mrs Macfarlane entered the drawing room. 'The obnoxious one.'

I felt sick. 'Mr Turnbull,' I put down my book.

'That's him,' Mrs Macfarlane said. 'Shall I put a flea in his ear?'

'No, bring him in.'

'I thought we had seen the last of you,' I did not pretend politeness as Turnbull slithered into my drawing room. 'I gave you what you asked for last time, now state your business and get out.'

'Oh, if life were only that simple,' Turnbull looked slightly the worse for wear, with a stain down the sleeve of his jacket and his breath foul with recent drinking. 'If the cards ran sweet and my faces did not meet other's aces, I would never trouble you again, but alas, fate does not smile kindly on me.'

I glared at him. 'I'm not going to fund your gambling habit any further. Please leave.'

'Yes, Miss Flockhart.' Turnbull sank into a chair and then laughed. 'Oh, what fun it will be when everybody finds out the truth and who you are. I will invite everybody to watch when I make the announcement.'

I knew when to fold my hand. 'How much do you want?' I asked.

'Only another hundred guineas,' Mr Turnbull said. He looked around the room. 'That should not be hard for you, why the contents of this room alone must be worth ten times that. That picture there,' he indicated the portrait above the fireplace. 'That would sell for a few hundred. Who is the gentleman?' Uncoiling from his seat like the snake he was, Turnbull stepped to the portrait. 'Why, it's...'

'I have a hundred,' I said. I had no desire to hear Turnbull's tongue befoul the name of anything or anybody in my house. 'I will get it for you, and you can hand it to your damned creditors.'

Turnbull patted the portrait. 'My damned creditors will be most happy and very surprised if they learned the source of my blunt.'

I could only glare at him. A few days ago I had hoped to make a stand and improve my life; now I felt as if I was sliding back into an abyss. Between Turnbull's blackmail and Gibbie Elliot's misbehaviour, I was not sure where to turn. I could not ask Captain Rogers for help without revealing more than I wished and Doctor Hetherington had proved less practical than I had hoped. I did consider informing Emily or Elizabeth, but they had known Marie and Gibbie longer than I had. They might not wish a relative newcomer to their circle to interfere. I was indeed alone again.

Mrs Macfarlane was standing on the landing as I stepped upstairs to my office to retrieve the money from my bureau. She said nothing while the expression in her eyes spoke volumes. 'Haven't you got work to do, Mrs Macfarlane?'

'Yes, Miss Flockhart,' Mrs Macfarlane said. 'And not the devil's work in which you are involved.' Mrs Macfarlane was not a woman to shirk from the truth as she saw it.

'Then please attend to it.' I snapped. I liked Mrs Macfarlane and knew she would understand I was not directing my temper at her.

'We'd be better attending to that Turnbull creature,' Mrs Macfarlane stomped away to show her displeasure.

When Turnbull left with my hundred guineas, I knew that I had to make some decisions. I could not make them in the Thistle Street house, not with Mrs Macfarlane growling her disapproval every time I moved or made a statement. I needed space and clean air and the freedom of solitariness. In the hills, I could think with more clarity.

I was fortunate that I am not afraid of my own company, and doubly fortunate that I was on good terms with Willie Anderson, the proprietor of the local stable. I procured a horse in short order and, giving Mrs Macfarlane instructions to keep the house secure for the next couple of days, I packed food, warm clothes and a few necessities into saddlebags and headed west.

If you know Midlothian or Edinburgh, you will be familiar with the Pentland Hills, Edinburgh's guardian range. They are not high, as hills go, with the tallest not reaching 2000 feet, nor are they rocky or romantically precipitous, yet within the twenty- odd miles that they stretch there are some lonely places where Man barely sets foot. Much water had passed beneath many bridges since I had last visited those hills and I found my humour improving as I approached.

An early ploughman lifted a hand in greeting as I approached. His plough gear slackened and rattled as he scrutinised me, and he spoke to his horse in some local dialect that only ploughmen and horses understood.

'Aye, it's a grand day for it,' he said and continued ploughing, with the earth turning over to the hiss of the blade.

I agreed and walked on. I had passed whatever test the ploughman had set me, for these men of the soil have standards that gentlemen, ladies and those who require silk beneath their well-cushioned posteriors would never understand.

'Watch yourself,' the ploughman grunted over his shoulder. 'It's the season for peat reek.'

Waving my thanks, I walked my horse on. Although peat reek was one name for illicitly distilled whisky, I could think of no reason why any whisky smuggler should concern me.

It was pleasurable to return to the hills I had known so well. I followed the old trails once used by Border cattle reivers and now, more legally, by Highland drovers, and rode into the heart of the hills, with the heather slopes swelling brown and cool and austerely stark on either side and the air perfumed and clear. There were few people here, a scattering of sheep picking their way carefully over the thin soil and overhead a skein of geese dragging winter on their outstretched wings. I heard the bleat of sheep and the distant trilling of the curved-beaked whaup, the whistling of plovers and the rau-cous call of seagulls and allowed the deceptive peace of nature to settle into my soul.

In a way, I was more at home here than in any city street, with no humans, no play-acting or deceiving, and no well-bred men to fawn and lie to me. The hills were austere and clean, and a significant part of me wished I could set up house here all alone, live my life and ignore the passage of the world. The idea was tempting, yet I knew I could never be a hermit. For a limited time, yes, but I would soon miss the shouts of children and the coy laughter of lovers, the bustle of the streets and the grand architecture of the city. I was a woman of many parts, and only one side wished solitude. That was what made my present situation so intolerable and why I continually longed for company, female or even, God-willing, an honest male.

'Do you like this place?' I whispered into the ears of Mercury, my misnamed plodder of a horse, 'do you like the smells?'

Mercury responded with a faint snicker, and we walked on, slowly and carefully along the track that wound through the pass. I took a deep breath, savouring the peace. Unusually, there was no wind to stir the vegetation, and the Lord had withheld the rain, so we walked dry-shod as the sky altered from amethyst blue to fine grey, the gloaming bringing sweet melancholy to the close of day.

'This is another old path,' I told Mercury, 'like the path over the Royal Union Bridge.' And again I quoted the Bible 'ask for the old ways and walk therein and ye shall find rest for your souls.'

I sought rest here as much as I had ever sought rest anywhere.

The sunset took me by surprise. I had expected the gloaming to fade into winter night, but nature stored a surprise for me. I do not know from where it came, but a slender dark blue stratum of sky eased along the horizon as the sun made its final descent. For one glorious minute golden light suffused across every hill, every curve and every ripple of the dry-stane dykes that snaked across the heather miles. I stopped Mercury to wonder at this reminder of nature's blessing that puts all our infinitesimal troubles into focus, and then, as suddenly as it burst free, the radiant light snuffed out. The darkness was all the more intense for the splendour it replaced yet it was no less welcome. The sun had done its job, and I was as relaxed as I had been for some years.

Pulling Mercury from the main track, I dismounted and led him up the slopes of the Cairn Hill, where small burns had worn a path in the heather flanks and night animals were beginning their circle of life. I knew where I was headed and did not care what else was abroad that night.

It is not just the paths that are old in these hills. There are places where things happened in the dimness of history, places that have retained the atmosphere of ancient knowledge and forgotten wisdom. The pile of grey-granite rocks where I stopped is one such. We knew it as the Borestone. Here, in this lonely place a scant hundred yards from the pass, with no company except Mercury and the wind, I hoped to find a solution to the problems that beset me. Here, with nobody nearby and no distractions, I had space to think.

I had brought a canvas sheet as shelter against wind and rain, sufficient food to last me two days and kindling and tinder to start a fire. Some may think me eccentric to camp out in the hills on a Scottish winter night, and they may be correct. If I was and am eccentric, then the world has made me so. Spreading the sheet at an angle between two rocks, I weighed down the corners and soon collected enough wood to start a fire. Out here in the Scottish hills, wind and cold are the only enemies. In India, I would have been afraid of badmashes, snakes and the wild creatures of the night. Of the two countries, Scotland was by far the safer. All the same, I kept Joe Manton to hand.

The flames were cheerful in the dark, and I relaxed with my back to the Borestone and the dark a comfortable blanket keeping people away.

So what was best to do?

I spoke out my problems one by one.

The first was Turnbull and his blackmailing. As well as the constant drain on my finances there was the unsettling knowledge that Turnbull was aware of my past. One drunken slip and he could tell the world, with God only knew what consequences.

The second was Gibbie Elliot and his unsavoury companions. I had only known Marie for fourteen months or so, yet she had welcomed me into her circle with open hands. Friendship was too precious a commodity to treat lightly, and I did not wish her to suffer what I had once endured.

There was my past that I now knew I could never run away from and must confront sometime. Doctor Hetherington had advised that I stop running, and he was right, but how did I stop when there were so many problems to overcome?

With the brisk air of the hills refreshing my tired brain, I allowed the problems to ease into my mind, and then I thought of a solution to one of them. Although I could do nothing about my past and had no idea how to deal with Turnbull, I could at least discover if Gibbie was the rake I suspected. To do that I would have to spy on him or send somebody, I trusted to do so.

The idea was so novel that I nearly shocked myself. Unable to sit while the unprecedented thoughts raged through my head, I stood up and began to pace back and forward around the ragged clump of the Borestone. At times I recoiled from my own daring, and in between, I felt the cold grip of fear at the possible consequences.

While in India I had adopted native dress and wandered among the local people. There was nothing sinister about my actions; I merely found that the people responded better to me when I looked less alien. As I was naturally dark-haired and took to the sun without burning, my Indian disguise was soon complete. Now I considered doing something similar in Edinburgh.

The sudden desire to act was overpowering. Since my return to Edinburgh, I had allowed life to use me as it would, and I had been knocked back and forth like a shuttlecock. No longer. Now my decision was made I worked out the details. Should I go alone? I thought of McAra's face, Turnbull's false smile, and recalled other, older and more vicious memories. No, I would not, could not, go alone into such a den of thieves; I would bring an escort if he were willing to accompany me.

I heard the soft thud of hooves in the dark and smelled a whiff of tobacco. Somebody was coming down the pass, and when the low rumble of voices came to me, I knew there was more than one person. Touching the butt of my pistol, I settled down beside the fire and waited. Let them come to me.

'Halloa! Over there by the fire!' The voice floated through the dark.

'Halloa!' I shouted back. 'The soup is heating, and you're welcome to join me.'

Although I was quite aware of the possible threat from wandering gypsies and sorners, in my experience men who shouted out greetings in the dark were less likely to do me harm than oh-so-polite gentlemen in immaculate clothes.

There were two of them, middle-sized, middle-aged men with hirsute faces and broad Scotch bonnets slanted low over wrinkled foreheads. At their back was a convoy of a dozen Highland garrons, each laden with six panniers. I guessed their occupation and kept the knowledge to myself.

The men crouched at my side, touching their bonnets in greeting. 'Your face is not known to me.' The older spoke in a pleasant Highland accent.

'I am Miss Dorothea Flockhart,' I introduced myself and waited for the response.

The man bobbed his head. 'Thank you for the welcome, Miss Flockhart, and we won't ask what is not our business.' The cudgel in his hand looked a formidable weapon, while his companion carried an old Highland pistol thrust through his belt.

'And I won't tell what is best not said,' I nodded to the train of Highland garrons. 'You'll be staying to eat?'

'Your hospitality is all the more welcome for being unexpected.' The Highlander said.

I did not hear the third man until he emerged from the slopes of Cairn Hill and into the circle of firelight. 'She's alone.' He said.

'I am.' I agreed. 'Did you think otherwise?'

The spokesman's smile was slow and genuine. 'It's best to make sure about these things.' He looked around beyond the circle of light from my fire. 'There is better shelter at the Hoolet's Wa's.'

'I know of it.' The Hoolet's Wa's was a small, long abandoned cottage high up in one of the gulleys that seamed the side of the Cairn Hill. 'I am fine here at the Borestone.'

The spokesman sipped at his soup. 'As you wish. If it is solitude you wish, Hoolet's Wa's would be quieter.'

'Then I would have missed your company,' I said. Joe Manton rested heavily inside my cloak, easy of access.

'Are you not afraid to be alone in these hills?' The third man was harder of face, with the same Gaelic twist to his words.

'I am not alone,' I pointed out. 'I have three sturdy Highland men with me.'

The men exchanged glances, and two of them laughed. 'You have that,' the spokesman said. 'You have that.' He finished the soup and handed back the empty bowl. 'Thank you and may the Lord bless your camp and all in it.'

'May the Lord bless your journey,' I gave the expected answer and watched as the three men returned to their convoy of garrons, each with its load of illicit whisky. They could be nothing else but whisky smugglers, the peat-reekers of whom the ploughman had warned me. They had not bothered me, and I had no reason to inform anybody of their existence.

The darkness closed around me as the hoof beats of the garrons faded into the night. I sat beside the fire, enjoying the peace and the soft whine of the wind as I formulated my plans. It was not long since Captain Rogers had offered his help; it was time to see if he was genuine or merely another man who made false promises when it suited them. I stood up, allowing the wind to caress my face. I would prefer to have his company in the expedition I had in mind, yet if he proved fickle, I would work alone. Gripping the butt of Joe Manton, I resolved that my time for running and hiding had passed. With or without Captain Rogers, I would make my stand and begin to fight back.

Perhaps because my mind was resolved on something, or maybe through the pure hill air, I slept better that night than I had for a long time. I woke up cold but happy and wondered how to contact Captain Rogers. I need not have worried. His card was waiting for me when I returned to Thistle Street, together with a sealed letter that I opened with some anticipation.

My dear Miss Flockhart

I hope I do not inconvenience you by leaving you my card. If it is not offensive to you, I would be obliged if you could receive me at your address this evening at seven. I shall send my man around two hours before for your reply. I assure you that I shall not detain you for long.

Your friend

Captain George Rogers.

That was convenient. Perhaps fate had finally blessed me with a smile. When a dapper corporal tapped politely on my door at five that evening, I was able to hand him a small wafer-sealed note of acceptance, and I prepared to launch the first of my counter-offensives into operation. While the generals and admirals got ready to receive the French, I was forming my plans for a more limited but to me just as important offensive.

Should I wear formal attire to meet the captain? Or should I dress casually, as one would do to receive an old friend? I was not at all expert in matters of etiquette and doubted if Mrs Macfarlane would be any better. In the end, I decided to wear something formal to show how important I thought Captain Rogers' company, and to greet him informally, to prove my friendship.

Not sure if I was deceiving the gallant captain, or if he was playing some devious game of his own with me, I had Mrs Macfarlane show him into the drawing room, where I sat sewing in an attempt to appear calm.

'A gentleman to see you, Miss Flockhart,' I could tell by the tone of Mrs Macfarlane's voice that she approved. 'Captain Rogers of the Volunteers.' She lowered her voice, 'and looking very handsome too.'

Mrs Macfarlane was correct. Captain Rogers looked exceedingly handsome in his regimentals, with his whiskers newly trimmed and that small scar on his chin gleaming white under the light. He bowed as if he had never seen me before and I gave a lower curtsey than usual, much to Mrs Macfarlane's approval.

'Thank you, Mrs Macfarlane,' I said, and she left, although I guessed she was listening outside the door. Servants can be a bit precocious when they choose.

'I will not keep you long,' Captain Rogers stood awkwardly with his shako under his arm. 'I merely wished to ask how you were and to apologise for any inconvenience I caused you when we met on the Earthen Mound the other day. I should not have approached you in so direct a manner.'

'I am very well,' I said. 'Thank you for your concern, and I assure you I was not inconvenienced in the slightest.'

Captain Rogers smiled and bowed again. 'Thank you, Miss Flockhart. If I may say so, you are a most intriguing lady. Indeed I have never met anybody quite like you before.'

Not sure how to respond, I gave another brief curtsey. 'Would you care for a drink, Captain Rogers?' Once again, I was unsure of the current etiquette. 'I have brandy and claret, and some fine Ferintosh that Mrs Macfarlane obtained for me from sources unknown.'

The captain smiled again. 'Whisky would be excellent, Miss Flockhart, but only if you join me.'

I needed the liquid courage for the favour I had to ask, so poured the captain a sizeable Ferintosh and myself a glass of brandy. We toasted each other's health with the firelight catching the cut of the crystal and sending a hundred glistening sparks around the contents.

'I know nothing about you,' Captain Rogers said.

'Oh, sit down, do,' I said and returned to my seat by the fire. 'I am not interesting, Captain. I have never faced the French.'

'You must be wondering how I fought the French when Volunteers never venture outside the country,' Captain Rogers settled himself comfortably in the chair. 'The answer is simple, Miss Flockhart. I was not a Volunteer at the time.'

'Oh,' I said. 'That clears up that little mystery. Did you transfer?'

'In a manner of speaking, Miss Flockhart.' Captain Rogers looked into the fire as if gathering his courage.

'I do not mean to pry,' I said. 'There is no need for you to tell me anything that you do not wish to. Goodness knows that I never discuss my past, so I have no right to question yours.'

'I was in the Guards in the Low Country,' Captain Rogers continued as if I had never spoken. 'I am the youngest son of four, with no prospects, so my father packed me off to the army.'

I nodded, listening. 'I see.'

'My oldest brother died in a hunting accident. He fell off his horse and broke his neck. Then the next in line celebrated his good fortune, caught a fever and died in bed. That left David and me, and David ran off with a maidservant and was disinherited, leaving only me.'

'He was disinherited?' I said.

'Yes indeed. Our family will not tolerate anything with the slightest hint of impropriety. Of course, father needs an heir, so he bought me out of the army.'

'I see.' It was interesting how easy it was to get men to talk about themselves.

Captain Rogers finished his whisky, and I topped up his glass.

'Thank you,' he looked up at me, his face serious. 'I did not wish the life of a landowner,' he said. 'I did not wish the endless social gatherings and the meetings with tenants and the hunting parties. I had tasted the excitement of the Army, and I liked it; the life was hard but worthwhile, and I ran away.' He tossed back the whisky as if it had been water.

'I see,' I said for the third time.

'And then I came back.' Captain Rogers gave a twisted smile. 'My father died, and somebody had to look after things.' He stood up. 'And that is my story, Miss Flockhart, the story of a man who tried to run away from his duty.'

'The story of a man who was not afraid to put his life in danger,' I countered. 'And the life of a man who returned to do his duty and still join the Volunteers.'

Captain Rogers put his glass on the table. 'Thank you for the whisky. I am sure you no longer wish my company.'

'On the contrary,' I poured more whisky into his glass, feeling closer to Captain Rogers than I had to any man for years. 'I cannot think of any man whose company I would prefer.' Men were strange with their notions of honour and duty; what made them think that we care about such things? We understand them, but do not treat them with equal importance.

Captain Rogers looked genuinely grateful that I did not order him out of my house for his terrible crime of not wishing to tie himself down to the life of a landowner. 'You do not ask me which lands I own,' he said.

'I don't care,' I said honestly. 'Lands and titles and such matters don't interest me.'

'You don't look to marry greatly?' Captain Rogers asked. I may explain here that 'to marry greatly' meant to marry above one's social class and therefore to rise in the world. It was the ambition of many women to marry a title.

'I don't.' I said.

'Then you are even more of an enigma than I had thought,' Captain Rogers had found his smile again.

'This enigma has a favour to ask,' I could not hold off any longer.

'Anything,' Captain Rogers said. 'Any lady who accepts me despite my attempt to evade my duty, and who has no interest in lands and fortune is too intriguing to turn down.'

I wondered how to start and then plunged in. 'I think Gibbie Elliot is in with a bad lot,' I said and explained where I had seen him. The captain listened without interrupting.

'How can I help?' Captain Rogers asked, and I wished to kiss him there and then. I closed my eyes at the thought. Kiss him? Kiss a man? I had not thought of that for the past ten years.

'Thank you,' I said.

'Don't thank me until I've done something,' Captain Rogers said. 'What do you wish me to do?'

'I want to find where Gibbie Elliot spends his time and see what he does,' I said.

'As soon as he sees you,' Captain Rogers pointed out, 'he will leave.'

I poured us both another drink. 'I will go in disguise.'

'It will have to be a damned good disguise,' Captain Rogers shook his head. 'You're a brave woman to even think of doing this for a friend.'

I remembered the howling of the hounds and the white, predatory faced through the trees. I remembered the pain and the humiliation and the later deep, terrible sorrow. I remembered the guilt that I suffered every day and every night of my life. 'I'm not as brave as you may imagine.' About to tell him that I also ran away, I thought it better to refrain. 'I have wrongs to put right.'

Captain Rogers stroked his immaculate whiskers. 'Where do I come into this?'

'I know nothing about Edinburgh's gambling world or the sort of places Gibbie Elliot might go. I hoped you might know more than me.' The brandy was less powerful now, its bite less potent. 'I also hoped you might accompany me.'

Captain Rogers' smile could have charmed bees from a honeycomb. 'I hoped for nothing less,' he said, 'for I'm damned if I would allow you to go alone.'

I do not know if I kissed him, or if he kissed me. I only know that we kissed and his lips were sweet on mine. I had not kissed a man for ten years and I nearly, very nearly, put my arms around him. But I could not. I could not and I would not.

Chapter Seven

While dressing down to walk around Hindustan had been relatively easy, deciding what to wear to infiltrate an Edinburgh gambling hell was well outside my experience and I was glad to take Captain Rogers' advice.

'You must look the part,' he said. 'You must appear attractive to the type of man who frequents such a place, and you must be willing to be pleasant to him.'

'I am grateful for your help,' I said and added curiously, 'have you ever attended such an establishment?'

When Captain Rogers laughed, that interesting little scar elongated across his chin. 'As a younger man, I did many things of which I am not proud.'

I nodded. Young men were often foolish and grew out of it. Respectable young women had less opportunity for waywardness. 'Do you know where these places might be?'

'Some of my younger colleagues were helpful when I asked.' Captain Rogers said. 'Your Gibbie Elliot has been seen in Weir's Inn more than once.'

'Should we go there?'

'Weir's Inn is well known for harbouring gaming tables,' Captain Rogers spoke quietly.

'Then that is where we shall go.' Part of me felt as if I was betraying Gibbie. Another stronger, part was wild to help Marie.

I hired a chaise and parked outside some of the more notorious places in Edinburgh, watching the kind of people who entered and left. I did not see Gibbie, but I did find out that my wardrobe of clothes did not extend to the gaudy articles that seemed to be preferred by the women who frequented gambling halls.

'The best place to purchase them will be in pawnshops,' Captain Rogers leaned back in my chair and crossed his elegant legs. He seemed quite at home in my drawing room, much to Mrs Macfarlane's satisfaction. 'Have you ever visited a pawnshop, Miss Flockhart?'

'I have not.'

'Would you prefer me to accompany you?'

'I would.' I swirled the brandy in the bottom of my glass. 'I would be very grateful for your company, Captain Rogers.'

'Is it not time we were a little less formal?' Captain Rogers smiled over the rim of his glass. 'My Christian name is George.'

I hesitated for only a moment. 'I am Dorothea.'

'That is a lovely name,' Captain Rogers said.

We shook hands as if we had only just met and then George grinned. 'There now, that wasn't too hard, was it?'

'It was not hard at all.'

'It was not hard at all, *George*,' George prompted.

'It was not hard at all, George,' I said.

'I am on duty tomorrow,' George was smiling now. 'If you are free on Friday we can shop for your new creations.'

'Thank you,' I said again.

'I haven't done anything yet,' George said.

'Thank you for not letting me down.' This time there was no doubt who kissed whom. There was slight stubble around the scar on his chin, sufficient to be interesting on my lips.

'I will have to watch you, Miss Flockhart,' George said.

'Dorothea,' I reminded.

'Dorothea,' George said.

Passing through the streets of Edinburgh in a chaise and shopping elbow-to-elbow with the good neighbours are two vastly different experiences. In the former one is something of an observer, watching the people as they work and play. In the latter one is part of things, a participator in life's events, mixing with the shifting, noisy, emotional mass of the population who live and breathe and work in one of the most crowded and historical cities in Europe.

I was glad that Captain Rogers was at my side when I visited half a dozen of the pawn shops, each one of which seemed to be less salubrious than its neighbour. Each shop had shifty-eyed men and women behind the counter and a selection of ragged clothing, tawdry jewellery and possessions in drawers and glass-fronted boxes. They all smelled of damp clothes and cheap tobacco, with guttering candles pooling sufficient yellow light for the proprietors to see the customers yet not enough light for the customers to accurately assess the goods.

'We are looking for clothes for a fancy-dress show,' George lied easily and took over the buying with an aplomb that I could only admire. There was much about this man that I still had to learn.

The pawnshop proprietors eyed Captain Rogers' uniform and the hilt of his sword, looked at my unsmiling and unfashionably suntanned face and decided they would best oblige us. I am sure they had as much honesty as that class of person could find. I found it comforting being so close to a man who commanded such instant respect as my gallant captain. Once or twice I looked up at him and wondered if Mother Faa could have been correct. And then my memories crowded into the front of my mind, and I knew I was destined to be alone.

I felt grubby handling the gaudy clothing and wondered what sort of people had worn these clothes. Had they been clean? Or had they neglected to wash, and what kind of lifestyles had they? I wondered at the personalities and experiences as I chose the most outrageous clothes I could find and parted with small amounts of money for each. Twice I was about to pay the first amount the proprietors demanded, and each time George shook his head.

'You're not cheating us,' George said to the shop woman. 'If you try I'll have my men mount a picket around your shop and chase away your customers.'

The proprietors had spread their hands in innocence and immediately dropped their price.

'I could afford the first price,' I told George.

'Money is a finite commodity,' George said. 'If you can afford it, give it to the poor, not to these leeches. They live by sucking money from people who have nothing.'

'You're a good man, George.' I squeezed his hand, liking this soldier more each time we met.

Fortunately, I had the foresight to bring a canvas sea-bag into which I crammed each article without concerning myself over their condition. I would ensure these clothes were adequately scrubbed before donning them. When George saw the bag, he reached across and took it from me.

'A gentleman should never allow a lady to carry a bag when his hands are empty,' he said.

'You're an officer,' I saw him swing the bag across his right shoulder. 'It's not fitting.'

'Who's going to complain?' George touched the hilt of his sword. For a second I saw the shadows return to his eyes and wondered what darkness they indicated. I suspected that Captain Rogers could be a very dangerous man.

The wig was in the fifth pawn shop we entered. I lifted it without thought and held it at arms' length. I had seen men wearing wigs of course, for they had been quite fashionable in my youth and some elderly men still sported them. Turning it this way and that, I wondered how it would feel and how I would look.

'That will alter your appearance,' Captain Rogers said, and with those few words, I made my decision. The long, curled blonde hair was human, and I guessed that some poverty-smitten person had parted with her treasured locks to feed her children.

'I'll take it,' I said.

George grinned. 'You'll look a picture,' he said. 'I find myself anticipating our little trip with great pleasure.'

I felt the same, although I did not like to admit it. I was becoming used to Captain Rogers' company. He was proving himself a man of resource and surprises.

I should have asked Mrs Macfarlane to wash my new acquisitions, after all, that was why I employed her, but either embarrassment or shame forced me to scrub them myself. It was many years since I had stooped to such a task, for Mrs Macfarlane was the most efficient of housekeepers while in India I had an army of busy servants waiting for my word.

'What on earth are you doing, Miss Flockhart?' Mrs Macfarlane's voice made me start as I delved to my elbows in warm water and soap-suds. 'It's hardly your place to be washing clothes.' She looked at the strange assortment in the washing tub, 'especially not clothes like that.'

'It's for a sort of masked ball,' I tried to excuse myself as if it mattered a damn what a servant thought.

'Is it now?' Mrs Macfarlane said. 'Well, it must be the strangest sort of ball when you wear this.' She held up a dripping dress that was all flounces and bright colours, yet would leave my ankles exposed to public view. She peered closer at me. 'You take great care, Miss Flockhart. I don't know what sort of thing you are planning, but I know that it's a dangerous game. I hope that Turnbull creature is not involved.'

I shook my head although in truth I did not know who might be involved. 'It's quite all right, Mrs Macfarlane.'

Dropping the clothes back in the washing-tub, Mrs Macfarlane put both hands on my shoulders. 'Now, listen, Miss Flockhart. You are a good mistress, you never rail like some of the others and you pay well. I have taken a liking to you, and I know you are in some trouble. If you need help, then don't be shy to ask.'

'I am all right.' I was unused to people offering me help.

'I'm not sure that you are,' Mrs Macfarlane was not a woman to be easily deflected. 'My husband is a handy man to know. He's a hackney-sedan chairman, down by Canonmills Bridge.'

I nodded, although for the life of me I could not see how a sedan chairman could be of use to me. Chairmen were some of the invisible labourers whom one passed in the street without noticing, an unseen face in the mass. 'Thank you, Mrs Macfarlane.'

'Well, that's my offer made,' Mrs Macfarlane said, 'and it stands as long as I am in your employ. My Macfarlane is a handy man to know.' She held my gaze as if allowing her words to sink in. 'Now step aside and allow me to wash these clothes, and that wig. God only knows who wore it last and what sort of crawling creatures ran about their scalp.'

'Thank you, Mrs Macfarlane,' I repeated. I was not sure if I was thanking her for washing the clothes or for her offer of help. Or rather, I was sure. I was thanking her for her friendship. Good friends are one of the rarest commodities in the world, and I seemed to be collecting them that winter.

Despite all my preparations, I was extremely nervous when we stepped into the hired coach for the short journey to the Grassmarket.

'I'm glad Captain Rogers is with you,' Mrs Macfarlane gave her parting wisdom as we rattled away.

'Your servant approves,' George said, and I nodded.

'I agree with her.'

George leaned back in the leather seat. 'You look different like that,' he said. 'I would hardly recognise you in the wig.'

I may have smiled to hide my sick nervousness.

Weir's Inn advertised itself as a purveyor of fine wines and ales as well as having rooms to let. It sat near a corner, three storeys of sin and with men and women entering and leaving in an irregular rush.

I heard the raucous laughter coming through an open window and tried to push my fears away. The red and blue dress I had selected was short in the leg and left my neck hideously exposed, while the wig was hot and uncomfortable. I wriggled, adjusting the fit and wished I had never thought of this ploy.

The coach driver gave me an odd look as I alighted in a flurry of waving ribbons. 'You be careful in there,' he said, apparently recognising that I was not a natural denizen of such places. That did not bode well for my attempt to merge into the company.

'Thank you, my man,' Captain Rogers tipped him handsomely. 'There is no need to wait. When I leave here, I will be able to purchase a coach and four, and the house and grounds to go with it.'

'Aye, that'll be right,' the uncouth fellow responded. 'You mind your back, sir, and you, Ma'am. There's queer things go on in Weir's and not always for the benefit of the players.' Touching a finger to his broad-brimmed hat, he whipped on, and the coach jolted over the greasy cobbles.

I stood outside the inn with its gaudily painted sign showing Major Weir, the Captain of the City Guard who was executed for witchcraft and incest.

'Are you all right, Dorothea?' George's voice was quiet as he touched my arm.

I nodded, nerving myself to step inside. Now that the time had come I was not so sure of my idea.

'Then let us play the game.' George winked and smiled, with his little scar crinkling across his chin. 'Life is all a game Dorothea, God's chess game and we are the pawns, knights and rooks.'

I had a last look around before I entered. The Grassmarket was busy that evening, as it usually was. Situated right at the foot of the Castle Rock, and where the West Bow and the Cowgait debouched into relatively open ground, tall tenements surrounded the market space, with the site of one of Edinburgh's execution spots to add sordid memories. With the Grassmarket being so close to the garrison, there were a sprinkling of scarlet jackets among the fustian of the labourers, and more than a few brightly clad Cypriots eyeing me as a possible rival as they vied for the attention of any man who wished to avail themselves of their sordid services.

'Shall we enter?' Captain Rogers offered me his arm. 'Now, you must trust me in here, Miss Flockhart. This will be different to anything you have seen before. A certain type of gentlemen thinks it a lark to frequent such low inns and mix with the lower orders.'

I nodded, aware that George was giving me time to collect my nerves and hoping that my intelligence was faulty. I desperately did not wish to find Gibbie Elliot inside Weir's Inn. 'I will keep close to you.' George's arm was firm, a rock on which to depend.

'Even if Mr Elliot is present, it does not mean he is a wrong 'un. Only that he has temporarily gone astray.'

'Yes, George.' I squeezed his forearm as a thank you, extracted ten guineas from my pocket and pressed it into his hand.

'It is not right that you should gamble with your own money as a favour to me,' I whispered.

'Nor is it right that a gentleman should take money from a lady,' George pushed the gold back. 'I win or lose on my own merits, and I chose to come here.' He leaned closer to me. 'You are a woman of character,' he said.

I do not think I have ever had a more sincere compliment. We stepped forward.

I had not expected the two beefy porters who lounged just inside the door, or the hard looks they threw at me.

'Might I have your name, sir?' The accent was Highland and the 'sir' more like a sneer than a title.

'I am Captain George Rogers of the First Royal Edinburgh Volunteers,' George said. 'And this lady is Marion Blairgowrie, my companion.'

I had not thought to give myself a new name and marvelled at George's powers of instant invention.'

'I don't know you,' one said.

'Nor I you,' I responded, wondering what would happen if I slapped his insolent face. Hard.

'I thought I knew all the wantons,' he said. 'No matter, who looks at the mantelpiece when he's stoking the fire.' He shrugged and addressed George. 'Are you here for the play?'

'We are, my friend,' Captain Rogers hitched up his sword and smiled. He guided me past the porter, perhaps sensing my dislike.

'It's through that door and upstairs, Captain and the best of luck to you.'

The porters ushered us through a heavy door and into a crowded den where crowds of people surrounded small tables. Jugs of whisky and porter occupied the centre of each table and drinking as quickly as possible seemed to be the prime recreation. That and making hideous noises while leering at each other's faces. Busy servants kept the jugs topped up and relieved the patrons of their money.

George lifted the first whisky jug, threw a coin at one of the servants and poured himself a small glass. He tasted it and screwed up his face. 'Kill-me-deadly rot-gut' he said. 'God knows what that would do to your stomach.'

I was thankful to leave that den. Another burly porter allowed us through an iron-studded door onto a turnpike staircase that wound around a worn stone column on its journey upward. Naked flames provided harsh light that only highlighted the scars and scrapes of the stonework, and I wondered what dark deeds had been performed here over the past many centuries. This inn was as far as one could get from the gracious squares and terraces of the New Town, or the pastoral beauty of Midlothian. Weir's Inn was Edinburgh in the raw, battered and dangerous. I could nearly feel the history sharpening its claws on the coarse stonework as it waited to coil around us.

At the head of the turnpike, a wide door opened into a room that surprised me with its grace and opulence. After the sordid saloon downstairs I had expected a grimy lair of unwashed floorboards and filthy chairs. Instead, I walked into a large room with elegant lace-trimmed green curtains framing three tall windows that looked down on the Grassmarket. Two crystal chandeliers cast sparkling light onto a long oval mahogany table around which sat half a dozen players.

On the outside of the room, four women sat in silence, watching as they sipped from crystal glasses, and each one over-dressed in a profusion of ribbons, feathers and sham-finery. I was glad that I had sought Captain Rogers' advice because my attire fitted them exactly.

'Is there anyone you know?' Captain Roger murmured.

I looked at the men who sat around the table. They were strangers. I was not sure whether to feel relieved or disappointed.

At the head of the table, nearest the windows, a tall, lean gallant with a face ravaged by care or disappointment looked up on our arrival. Three unopened packs of cards sat at his side.

'We are just completing this game, Captain. Please remain quiet until all the cards have fallen. Have a drink.' He returned his concentration to the game.

Captain Rogers lifted his hand in acknowledgement and guided me to a seat at the far side of the room where the light was dim, and I could hide in near shadow. Pouring me a drink from a ship's decanter, he handed over the glass. 'Watch and say nothing,' he whispered.

Aware that all four women had transferred their attention from the table to us, I avoided their stares and watched the fall of cards.

That game lasted another ten minutes, and the gamesters were silent until the very last hand, when the youngest man at the table, a mere boy who could not yet have reached his majority, threw his cards on the table in a sudden frenzy and began to cry.

'I'm cleaned out,' he said. 'I can't pay.' His voice rose on the last word.

'We'll need your IOU,' the ravaged man at the head of the table spoke quietly.

'I can't get any more,' the boy was sobbing.

'You'll find it,' the ravaged man produced a pen, inkwell and a small pile of paper from a hidden drawer. 'Write out an IOU for every man here and one for the house.'

'I'm ruined,' the boy looked up as the other men crowded around him.

I sat in shaking silence as the boy wrote. George sipped at his drink. The other women watched without expression, and I guessed they had witnessed similar scenes before.

The ravaged man checked the IOUs and nodded to the door. 'Take him away.'

Within minutes the room was empty except for us, the four women and the ravaged man, who collected all the loose cards and threw them into the fire.

'We always use new packs for each game,' he explained. 'This is a straight house. No cheating, no mirrors and no marked cards.'

'You have a good reputation,' Captain Rogers said.

'That young boy,' I asked as the four women looked at me with mild interest. 'What will happen to him?'

The ravaged man shrugged. 'He gambled his all and lost. His creditors own everything he has and everything he will ever make now. It is up to them. Even if he puts a period to his existence, his family will have to pay his debts.'

I nodded, feeling sick.

'Your name, sir? I did not catch it.' Captain Rogers did not appear perturbed at the fate of the unfortunate young gambler.

'I did not give it,' the ravaged man said. 'You may call me Charon.'

Charon, I knew, was the ferryman who took dead souls across the River Styx. It was a name well-suited to this place where men entered with hope and left in despair.

'When will the next party arrive, Charon?' George asked.

'Very soon,' Charon straightened up the chairs and opened the windows to allow fresh air to enter. I heard the noise from the street below. Somebody was laughing and somebody else singing, the words wild and Gaelic as they echoed from the surrounding buildings. They seemed honest compared to this room of subtle evil.

'Your whisky is good,' George said. 'Better than you serve downstairs.'

'I would not know,' Charon said. 'I don't drink.'

I heard the patter of feet on the turnpike, and then the door opened. Captain Rogers put a heavy hand on my shoulder as I made to rise.

'Sit still, watch and say nothing,' he said. 'Whatever happens, and whoever comes in, say nothing, Marion.'

I cowered into my disguise. I was Marion Blairgowrie and had to act the part. Leaning back in the chair, I crossed my legs and allowed my skirt to slide up slightly, exposing my right ankle. My face was in shadow and my insides in turmoil.

When George nodded approval, I adjusted my skirt, only a fraction, sufficient for the hem to rise to my lower calf. Perhaps I was a respectable lady from a good background, but I was also a woman with natural skills to attract a man. I wriggled my foot and watched as the door opened.

All my bravado vanished as Hector McAra entered with his ginger hair and pale face sinister under the chandelier's bright glow. He took a seat at the foot of the table and snapped his fingers. One of the girls ran to serve him, saying nothing as his hand drifted along her arm.

I cringed inside my wig and hoped he would not recognise me. That man scared me.

Next to enter was Turnbull, complete with the sycophantic smile and long, bony fingers. His eyes darted around the room, passed over me and away again as one of the girls handed him a glass. I hoped that my disguise was sufficient, although there was no reason for Turnbull to expect the respectable Miss Flockhart to come to such a place. I shifted my chair deeper into the shadows and tossed my head, so the long hair of the wig partially concealed my face.

'I'm not drinking anymore,' George declined the invitation of one of the women. 'I prefer a clear head to count the cards.'

'Wise man,' Charon said.

Gibbie Elliot was next, looking nervous as he accepted a glass of brandy and tossed it back with a single swallow. In his fancy pearl-buttoned vest and yellow coat, he looked more like a dandy than I had seen before while his white breeches hugged his legs. Marie had chosen a well-shaped man, I saw and wished she had found one with a stronger character.

'Would you care to join us, Captain?' Charon asked.

'My pleasure, Charon.' George removed his jacket and handed it to me. 'Pray look after that, Marion.'

Turnbull glanced at me and away. McAra did not look around.

'And the sword belt, Captain, if you please,' Charon said. 'We don't want any hasty actions here that may bring the house into disrepute.'

'Forgive me,' Captain Roger unfastened his sword belt and hung it on a hook beside the fireplace. He sauntered across to the table.

'Good evening gentlemen,' he said.

'Good evening Captain Rogers.' Turnbull gave a low bow. 'I have not seen you in here before.'

'I've never been before,' George said. 'Do I know you, sir?'

'I am William Turnbull.'

'You know me, George,' Gibbie said with a smile.

'I certainly do,' George said and, bless him, added. 'And I know your lady wife. I'm surprised that you're inclined to the cards so soon after your wedding.'

Gibbie's grin was so innocent I wondered if he knew what he was doing. 'Oh, once the inclination bites, Captain, one must follow. I'm sure you feel the same. Anyway, I have the chance of increasing my slim fortune.'

George smiled. 'Not at my expense, I hope.'

'Are we playing cards or having a social gathering?' McAra tapped his fingers on the table.

Charon waited until they were all seated before putting the three unopened packs of cards in front of him. I was scared of being recognised, although by the intensity of the players' expressions the last thing they were concerned about was a stray woman watching them.

'Faro? Whist, Loo? Piquet?' Charon did not look like a Captain Sharp as he surveyed the table. 'You may choose, gentlemen and the house will oblige.'

'I'd prefer *vingt-et-un*.' Gibbie said quickly. 'If that suits the rest of the company?'

'It suits me,' Turnbull said at once. 'It is an opportunity to regain my losses from last time.'

'I am surprised that you managed to find credit so quickly,' McAra said. 'You were quite cleaned out, Turnbull.'

Turnbull's laugh was high-pitched and unpleasant. 'I have found a milch-cow' he said.

I was disappointed that Gibbie laughed as loudly as Turnbull and McAra. I tried to remain expressionless as Charon offered his three packs of cards.

'Would one of these packs suit, gentlemen?'

'Yes, yes, get on with it, man,' McAra glanced at Captain Rogers. 'Good evening, Captain. I did not think you followed the cards.'

'I am not normally a gambling man,' George said. 'However, I do not object to allowing Chance to rule my life from time to time.'

'Here!' McAra gestured to the nearest woman. 'Brandy!'

The woman filled his glass, rubbing her hip against his shoulder. Gibbie watched with his mouth slightly open.

'How is Marie?' George asked.

'Very well, thank you,' Gibbie said, and again I blessed Captain Rogers.

Charon dealt with a swift flowing movement that saw one card float across the table to land in a shimmering blur face down in front of each person. 'House will act as banker,' he said. 'House rules;

first hand has an upper limit of fifty sovs, and after that, the players decide the limit.'

I shifted in my seat, hoping that I had not involved Captain Roger in a game that was too rich for his purse. He sat back as the second card flicked across the table to join the first.

You will know *vingt-et-un*, I am sure, or twenty-one or pontoon, which are all different names for the same game. The idea is to get to the total of 21 with the fewest number of cards, although a five-card-trick is also worth having. It is probably the most simple of all gambling games. If the house had a hand equal to any of the players, the house won, giving them a slight advantage.

The second cards had been dealt face up, so each player could see one of his opponent's cards. Gibbie had the six of spades, George the eight of diamonds and Turnbull the three of diamonds. McAra had slapped a hand on top of his card, hiding it. Charon had the seven of clubs.

'Move your hand please, Mr McAra,' Charon said. 'Rules of the house.'

McAra glared at him and moved his hand, revealing the two of spades.

'We'll start with five sovereigns,' Charon slid the gold into the centre of the table, and the others followed. I watched Turnbull add his coins and knew that they had recently belonged in my purse.

'Another card,' Gibbie said at once and smiled when Charon flicked across the four of spades. 'I'll raise the pot another five sovs.'

I sat back, hoping that Gibbie knew what he was doing as the pile of gold in the centre of the table increased. Forty sovereigns sat there, as much as a skilled man earned in nine months or a soldier in three years, and the betting had barely started.

There was another round of gambling that increased the pot to eighty sovereigns before a jubilant Gibbie announced that he would see everybody's cards and revealed his first card to be the knave of spades. Sitting on twenty, he waited for the others to show their hand.

'Too strong for me, Elliot.' George folded at once.

'And for the house.' Charon also tossed in his hand.

McAra swore and showed he had nineteen while Turnbull gave a loud whoop.

'*Vingt-et-un* old boy!' He said. 'The cards have spoken, my luck is in, and fortune favours the turning bull.' He scooped up the shimmering pile of gold.

I met Captain Rogers' gaze and read nothing there.

'First blood to Mr Turnbull,' Charon shuffled the pack. 'Are you gentlemen prepared to continue?'

'Yes, deal the cards, damn it.' Gilbert did not hide his frustration.

The next round went to George and Charon scooped the one after that, with Gibbie and McAra both losing heavily. No longer smiling, Gibbie emptied the last of his purse onto the table and snatched at the cards as they fell in front of him.

'If the table's too rich, Mr Elliot, perhaps you should withdraw from the game,' George suggested.

'You're not forcing me away, damn you!' Gibbie scribbled a note on a scrap of paper. 'There's my IOU.'

I half rose, until George motioned me back down with a frown and a shake of his head.

Sitting at the back, I was the only person present to see McAra lift a finger to the women. The youngest, shapeliest and prettiest slipped out of her seat and crouched at Gibbie's side, pressing herself against him in a manner that Marie would have found most unsettling. I felt the increase of my heartbeat and wondered what was best to do.

'Fortunes change,' the woman whispered. 'And luck favours the brave.' She placed his hand on his thigh and allowed it to drift upward.

I opened my mouth to protest. At that moment I hated Gibbie more than anybody in the world. I had seen enough; Gibbie was as innocent as Lucifer. About to walk out, I caught George's eye.

'If you could ask your lady friend to move, Elliot,' George spoke calmly, 'we can continue with the game.'

Turnbull laughed as Gibbie placed his hands on the woman's shoulders. 'Deal the cards,' Turnbull said, ran a hand over the pile of gold in front of him, and slapped the woman's swaying backside as she passed him. Not hard enough, in my opinion, despite her little yelp.

When George met my gaze, I saw the sympathy in his eyes. He was hurting for me.

'Gentlemen,' Charon said quietly. 'We'll continue when you are ready.'

The cards continued to fall unkindly for Gibbie. He lost that round, with McAra scooping the pot, and the House won the next, with George folding early each time, so he retained at least some of his earlier winnings. Gibbie's luck altered and he won two games in a row, with Turnbull betting and losing heavily. The woman returned to Gibbie's side, perching on his lap and helping him drink.

'When you are ready, Mr Elliot,' Charon said.

After that, there was a run when each player in succession won, except Gibbie and Turnbull, who were now the most significant losers.

'Damn you!' Gibbie swore again when he gambled on a three-card twenty-one, only to lose to Charon's ace and face. 'You'll have to take my IOU.'

'You can't have much left,' George glanced at the figures on Gibbie's IOUs. 'I know you lease your property and as the youngest son you've little to inherit.'

'Bad form to discuss personal affairs, old man,' McAra said.

'Mr McAra is correct,' Charon's voice was grave. 'House rules state that every player is responsible for his own finances.'

Perspiration glistened on Gibbie's face as he drank deeply from the glass the shapely woman handed him. 'I've my gold watch and the clothes on my back,' he said.

'We'll take them,' McAra said. 'If you're willing to put them on the table.'

I wondered if he was joking until I saw the leer on Turnbull's face. 'We'll send you out naked as the day you were born, Elliot.' He thought that a great laugh.

'There's no need for that old man.' My gallant Captain Rogers said. 'I'll gladly lend you a hundred sovs to see you through. Think of that lovely new wife of yours eh? Best take my hundred and fold for the night.'

'I'm damned if I will,' Gibbie said. 'I can still win it all back and more.'

'Don't be a fool man!' Captain Rogers said. 'Quit while you still can. My offer stands.'

Charon gave a little nod, and the shapely woman pressed closer to Gibbie, slid onto his knee and put a brandy glass to his lips.

I watched in increasing agitation as Gibbie drained the glass, took hold of the woman and gave her a resounding kiss.

'There now!' Gibbie nearly shouted. 'And another for luck.' Pushing the woman off, he called across to Charon. 'Deal the cards, Charon!'

I felt my nails digging into the palms of my hands as Charon again passed out the cards. I am not much given to praying outside a church, but I admit that I closed my eyes tight and begged the Lord to allow the cards to fall sweetly for my friend and Marie's husband Gilbert. However on that day either the Lord closed his ears or decided not to interfere with the Devil's work, for Gibbie's unfortunate run continued.

By the end of the night, Charon and McAra had divided the evening's winnings between them, with Captain Roger and Turnbull having minor losses and Gibbie as the major loser.

'You gambled the clothes off your back,' McAra reminded. 'Let's have them.'

'Come on, Elliot,' Turnbull said. 'A gentleman must always keep his word.'

I saw the dismay on Gibbie's face and had a momentary vision of him walking stark naked through Edinburgh. I bowed my head at the ritual humiliation as Gilbert stripped off his coat and handed it over.

'And the rest,' Turnbull said. 'One must pay one's dues.'

'There's no help for it, Elliot, unless you wish the world to view you as a man with no honour.' McAra watched with a small smile on his face as poor Gibbie bowed his head and peeled off his boots and breeches. I was glad to see that he wore drawers beneath. Three of the other women watched without expression while the shapely one was smiling, her gaze running up and down Gibbie's slim body.

Gibbie stood in his underwear, scarlet with mortification. 'Damn it, man, leave me some dignity.'

'All your clothes,' McAra said.

'All of them,' Turnbull was grinning, glancing at the women as if to encourage them to join in. When he looked at me, I lowered my head.

'Allow me to buy his clothes,' George offered. 'Mr McAra?'

'No,' McAra shook his head. 'A debt is a debt and should be paid. All of them, Elliot.'

'Give me one last chance,' Gibbie pleaded. I thought of the happy, confident man who married Marie only a few weeks ago and compared him to this broken creature and I hated the very name of gambling.

'Give me one last chance,' Turnbull mocked. 'You've nothing left to put on the table.'

'He's got one thing left in his life,' McAra felt the quality of Gilbert's coat and threw it carelessly on the ground. 'He has the auburn-headed Marie.'

'What?' I could not help my exclamation of shock as a hundred memories returned.

'Well, Elliot? What about it?' McAra ruffled the pack of cards. 'You asked for one last chance, and I have granted it. All you need to do is put your wife where your mouth is.'

'Come on, Elliot, your luck must turn sometime.' Turnbull encouraged. 'It's only a woman.'

Charon looked from McAra to Gibbie. 'This is a respectable house. We will not take a woman as winnings.'

'I won't lose,' Gibbie said desperately.

'It will be a private game.' McAra said.

'Not in my hall.' Charon said. 'House rules or no rules.'

'Don't be a bloody idiot, Elliot,' George said. 'You can't gamble your wife. Think what you're doing, man! I'll lend you; no I'll give you a hundred sovereigns to tide you over.'

'I'll put down a thousand guineas as the value of Elliot's wife,' McAra said. 'If the house wins, Elliot will bring his wife to me, and I will pay the house the thousand.'

Charon considered for only a moment. 'Agreed.'

'Captain!' I stepped to George. 'You can't allow this. It's inhuman! It's like a slave market.'

'It would not be the first time a woman has exchanged hands across the gaming table,' George said.

'For goodness sake, Captain, do something.'

I saw the consternation on Captain Rogers' face. I also saw Turnbull frowning and guessed he was trying to work out where he had seen me before. I hoped to God that my disguise proved itself. If not, well I would cross that bridge later.

Gibbie ignored us. 'Deal the cards, Charon. My wife against all my evening's losses.'

'George,' I whispered, 'please do something.'

George nodded. 'Elliot, that's no way to treat a lady.' He pushed back his chair. 'You're no gentleman, damn it.'

'I am the Honourable Gilbert Elliot,' Gibbie tried to look dignified as he stood in his underwear in that hellish place. 'I am a better man than you, Captain Rogers.'

'You are a blackguard, a coward and no gentleman,' George goaded Gilbert, who stiffened and retaliated with a slap that knocked my captain's head back.

'Shall we say on Tuesday at dawn?' George said. 'Lieutenant Hepburn will act as my second. He will call on your man.'

'I will act for Elliot,' McAra lifted up Gibbie's coat and trousers. 'You may wear my new clothes, Elliot until after the meeting.'

It was only then that I realised what had happened. I had encouraged my Captain Rogers to fight a duel with Marie's husband. This whole thing was my fault and nobody else's. By interfering with Gibbie's life, I may have ended it, or that of George. I stared at George, unsure what to say or do. In return, he winked at me.

Chapter Eight

At that period, duels were reasonably common in Ireland and England although less so in Scotland. They were also illegal, so the seconds had to ensure complete secrecy before the two parties met, and find at least one escape route afterwards. Duels were affairs fought between gentlemen, generally with pistols at a set number of paces although the old-fashioned contests with swords were not unknown.

Talk of the duel ended that gambling session and all the players returned home. 'I could not think what else to do,' George said to me as we left Weir's Inn.

'You have put your life in jeopardy for my sake,' I said.

George adjusted his sword belt as we walked through the dark Grassmarket. 'It was not only for your sake, Dorothea. I have known Marie longer than I have known you, and I disapprove of Elliot's actions. What I said was correct. No gentleman would gamble his wife.'

'You are a good man, George.'

'I am only a man,' George said. 'And a gentleman, I hope. Or I strive to be, for the sake of my family line.' He grinned. 'God, that sounds pompous and pretentious.'

I looked away. When George mentioned his family line, I felt uncomfortable, as if somebody had walked across my grave. His company always buoyed me up although I knew our friendship could never develop into anything more profound. And then I had the desperate, longing hope that it could.

As we walked across the cobbles with the dark tenements around and the castle frowning down upon us from atop its rock, I looked sideways at George. I was growing used to his presence, his cheerfulness and resourcefulness. Although loath to admit it, I was becoming fond of this man. I shivered and again dared to hope. Perhaps, after so long, things might work out? Had I found somebody I could trust?

'We won't find a chaise at this time of night,' George broke into my train of thought.

'It's not a long walk to Thistle Street,' I said and wondered if George would take that as an invitation.

'I'll accompany you.'

'George,' I put my hand on his chest. It was as muscled as his forearm. 'You've done too much already, and now you could be killed.'

'I could also kill your friend Elliot and make Marie a widow.' George said.

We stopped walking and faced each other at the foot of the West Bow, the street that ascended in a crazy zig-zag toward the Lawnmarket. The night was cold and tainted with smoke from a thousand fires.

'That might be the best thing for Marie,' I said. 'Better no husband than a man who gambles her away.'

'He was drunk.' George said. 'He was frustrated, and he was scared. He's not a bad man, Dorothea, only a foolish man.'

I sighed. 'I hope Gibbie's learned his lesson. Will you kill him?'

George said nothing for what seemed a long time. Eventually, he spoke as if from far away. 'Killing is easy, Dorothea. Living with the knowledge that one has killed is not.'

I knew he had drifted away into his past. On an impulse, I took hold of his arm and squeezed tight. 'I wish you could withdraw from the duel.'

There was no fear in George's smile. 'I'm looking forward to it. I only wish it was not your friend. Now come on, step up and we'll get you home.'

I clung to his arm all the way back to Thistle Street and kissed him before he left. The night had taken an unexpected turn, and I felt sick for Marie. Yet I still watched George walk away. He looked so tall and confident in his scarlet uniform, and that is how I wished to remember him, not as a bleeding corpse with Gibbie's pistol ball through his head. Men could be so pig-headed! And now I had to see Marie.

Chapter Nine

'But Gibbie! He could kill you!' Marie said.

'He said I was no gentleman,' Gibbie had tactfully neglected to mention the real cause of the dispute. 'I had no choice but to challenge him, and Hector has agreed to be my second.'

'Hector McAra. I do not like that man!' Marie showed more sense than her husband.

I sat quietly in the corner of the room, wishing I was elsewhere, unsure if I should tell Marie what had happened and feeling utterly miserable.

'Captain Rogers is your particular friend,' Marie pointed to me. 'What right did he have to say such a horrible thing about my Gibbie?'

'Miss Flockhart was not present at the time,' Gilbert said. 'She cannot be held to blame for the actions of Captain Rogers.'

I looked from one to the other, wondering how Gilbert could possibly contemplate gambling away his lovely young wife. My opinion of men sunk even lower. I wanted to stand up and run from Tynebridge Hall and never return, yet to do so would be to leave Marie alone with this man who pretended to care for her while preparing to pass her onto Hector McAra. I could not see a way out.

'I hope you kill him, Gibbie!' Marie said fiercely.

'Not all duels are fatal,' I said, 'usually an exchange of shots is sufficient to satisfy honour.'

'He insulted me,' Gibbie was proving as pig-headed as George.

I opened my mouth to remind Gibbie what had happened, and closed it with the words unsaid.

'I know Captain Rogers is your friend, Dorothea,' Marie said, 'and I still hope that Gibbie kills him. Look, Gilbert, I have found you a book about duelling and how to act.'

'Thank you, Marie; you are the best and most considerate of wives.' Gibbie took the slim book with eager hands and opened it immediately. 'It says that I should stand sideways and keep my stomach drawn in to present the smallest possible target.'

Feeling like a spy or a traitor, I listened, prepared to pass on the intelligence to George. Being friendly to both camps was one of the most awkward things I have ever done. Simultaneously worrying about Marie and George was not easy. And Gibbie? I asked myself, was I concerned about Gibbie as well?

I was not. If Marie had not been my friend, I would have hoped that George killed him. Knowing what he had been prepared to do with Marie, any liking I ever had for Gilbert Elliot had shrivelled and died. The only reason I wished him to live was that Marie's life might be worse without him.

Gibbie opened the case of pistols that McAra had left with him. There were two entirely matched duelling pistols by Nicholas Noel Boutet of Versailles, both excellent examples of the gunmaker's art. He lifted one and sighted along the barrel, cocked the hammer and squeezed the trigger. The hammer fell with a soft click.

'Bang, you're dead,' Gibbie whispered.

I shivered, for if Gibbie succeeded, then my Captain Roger would be the loser and could be killed or severely wounded, and if Gibbie lost then my good friend Marie could be a widow after only a few weeks marriage.

As I had already said, maybe Gibbie's death would not be a bad thing. Maybe Marie would be better without Gilbert Elliot.

'These are superb weapons,' Gibbie said. 'McAra has been very good to me.'

A couple of days ago, McAra had been prepared to strip him stark and let him walk naked through the streets of Edinburgh.

'Boutet is the director of the French arms manufactory,' Gibbie said. 'See the balance these pistols have? One only has to lift them, and they point forward, and with so much weight in the barrel they won't jerk when I pull the trigger.'

Marie rolled her eyes at me. 'That's interesting, Gibbie.'

'They are blind rifled too,' Gibbie squinted up the barrel. 'That makes them more accurate.'

'I have to check on the servants,' Marie left the room. I wondered if she was upset and if I should follow her.

'I used to like your friend Captain Rogers,' Gibbie had not looked up when his wife left the room.

The surge of anger threatened to overcome me. 'I know what happened,' I struggled to keep my voice under control. 'I know that you had a bad run at cards. I know that you lost everything you had, down to your gold watch and the very clothes off your back. I know that you offered Marie, your wife, in an attempt to win everything back.'

Gibbie lifted one of the duelling pistols, and I swear that if it had been loaded, he would have shot me. All the colour drained from his face. 'Damn George Rogers,' he said. 'Damn him for a loose-tongued rogue.'

'You can damn George Rogers from Monday until Christmas,' I held Gibbie's gaze as I rose from my chair and stepped towards him. 'It was not George who told me these things. I heard from quite another source.'

'Then damn your source, whoever it was.' Gibbie dropped his pistol with a clatter. 'You can tell him...' He lifted the pistol and placed it neatly back inside the box. I saw his face alter and wondered if he was going to burst into tears or run out of the room. 'You can tell him nothing, Miss Flockhart. I can tell you that there will be no more gambling.'

Suddenly Gibbie's expression altered. 'I did gamble Marie, and nobody regrets it more than I do. If I could turn back the clock, I would.'

I was not sure whether to believe him or not. There had been too many lies, too much deceit, too much hurt in my life for me to accept such a rapid alteration. I stood still, trying to understand this man.

'If George Rogers kills me,' Gibbie had dropped all the bravado, 'then that ends things. I will be dead, and Marie can start afresh. If I kill him, then … then I don't know what will happen.'

I wondered if I should advise him to aim to miss.

'I do love her you know,' Gibbie spoke quietly. 'I love her so that it hurts, here,' he thumped his fist against his chest. 'Every day and every hour, it hurts, and I cannot explain why I acted as I did.' He looked at the pistols and then at me. 'It was as if some demon was inside me, ordering me to gamble, to stake everything I had. It was like a huge thrill of excitement staking the most precious thing I own.'

'You don't own her,' I said. 'She is your wife, not your possession.' My anger was bubbling again, and I wanted to hit him. I wanted to tear him with my nails and hurt him deeply for what he had done. Or was that a reflection of my hurt from ten years ago? I did not know, and I still do not know.

'I know,' Gibbie's voice was low. 'Please don't tell her.'

'Why not?' I asked. 'Does she not have the right to know what sort of a man her husband is? Does she not have a right to know what her man, who promised to love and cherish her, is capable?'

'Yes,' Gibbie said.

'Then why should I not tell her?' I took a single step closer to Gibbie. 'Are you afraid, Gilbert Elliot? Are you afraid of your wife finding out the truth about you?'

Gibbie could not hold my gaze. He looked at the carpet. 'I am afraid,' he said. 'I am afraid of the hurt it would cause her.'

I stopped the words that rushed to my mouth and halted my impulse to slap this man as hard as I could. Oh, I would have found that satisfying, but would it do anybody any good, except me? I doubted it.

'I have hurt Marie enough,' Gibbie said.

'You have that,' I was unwilling to allow him to wriggle free. I had heard smooth words before and knew they came quickly to a lying mouth and meant nothing.

'I don't want to cause her further pain.'

I knew I was panting with anger. I hated this man and all that he had done. 'I wish I could believe you,' I said.

'Please,' Gibbie looked up. 'Don't tell her. I'll put things right. I swear I shall.'

About to ask how I looked around as the door opened and Marie entered. She ran across to Gibbie, smiling, and put her arm through the crook of his elbow.

'Hello, husband,' she said.

'Hello, wife,' Gibbie answered.

I should have told her then, I know I should, but I was unable to break the spell. Happiness is such a fragile thing. It comes so softly and lasts such a short time, and often we don't recognise we have it until it is gone. I saw it then in Marie's eyes as she held Gibbie and I could not take it away. Caress your happiness, Marie, I thought. Hold it close, nurture it and savour it all you can for there are more bleak days than bright and more tears than laughter in this bitter world.

'I will leave you two alone,' I said. I could not stay any longer. Approaching Marie, I gave her a quick hug. 'May God go with you,' was all I could say.

I ran from Tynebridge Hall with all its memories and the two people who had such terrible secrets from each other, and I mounted Mercury once more. I did not ride home. I rode the short distance to Doctor Hetherington's house, told him about the impending duel and told him nothing else. He listened to my silence, and I am sure he understood. I remained there all night, and Doctor Hetherington slept in his box room while I occupied his bed.

'A human head is a diminutive target,' Captain Rogers thrust his cleaning rod into the long barrel of his duelling pistol. 'It is especially small from thirty paces away when one's nerves are stretched, and one's opponent is hoping to kill you.' His grin was unexpected.

'Are you enjoying this?' I was confused. 'This is Gibbie Elliot we're talking about here. You were a guest at his wedding a few weeks ago.'

'I know,' Captain Rogers peered into the barrel, shook his head, shoved the cleaning rod in and scrubbed a little. 'And it was you who wished to prevent the very dis-honourable Gibbie from gambling his wife.'

I could not argue with that. 'I wish there was some way you two could shake hands.'

George ignored my suggestion. 'We do not aim at the head. We aim at the widest possible target.' He slapped his hips. 'Hip to hip, lower belly and groin.'

I shuddered at the thought of a pistol ball ripping into George's groin, or the belly of Marie's husband. 'Oh, dear God. Why are men so bloody?'

'It's in our nature,' George said. 'If we were not so bloody, who would protect you against wild animals and wild Frenchmen?'

'I haven't been attacked by a wild animal in my life, and the wild Frenchmen are no more bloody and violent than British men.' I looked away, trying not to think of a lead ball tearing into George's vulnerable flesh, or of Marie crouching beside a fallen Gibbie.

'French women are equally bloody, or so I've heard.' George was finally satisfied with the state of his pistols and replaced them in their walnut case. Instruments of death created with care and packed in velvet. 'French women were the ones knitting and chatting as Madame Guillotine sliced off the aristocrat's heads.'

I had heard the stories.

'Our women, of course, are all sweetness and light,' George checked the powder horn and lead balls that also fitted into the case. 'Witness their behaviour when there is a hanging, and they gather in their thousands, or when they riot in the streets.' He grinned again. 'Maybe it should be women protecting men!' He winked and began to whistle *The British Grenadiers*.

'I wish you were not going through this.'

'I am a soldier,' George said. 'Until the French come, I have no other way of proving my martial valour.' He smiled. 'Come, come Dorothea. I am quite enjoying it all. How else can I prove my bravery to my chosen girl?'

I looked away at that, unsure how I felt to be George's chosen girl. I was not ready to be chosen, and I was not sure that I even wished such an accolade, or if George would choose me if he knew the truth. Even so, I cannot deny that the words did give me a particular pleasure and I looked sideways at his figure with that broad chest within the scarlet uniform and those splendidly shapely legs.

I recalled Mother Faa's words that a man in uniform would be important to me and thought that I could do so much worse than George. He had already proved himself a friend in need and now was about to give an example of his bravery. The thought that Gibbie could kill George killed brought me down to earth. Despite my friendship with Marie, I hoped that Gibbie Elliot would come off second best in the ensuing duel. Did I wish him killed? That depended on how genuine his final words had been. Did I trust his love for Marie?

No.

Did I believe Gibbie could, in his own words, 'put things right?'

No.

Marie would be better without him. His death would hurt her, but after a year or two the pain would ease, and she would be free to find a better man or no man at all. Yes, I hoped that George shot him.

Was that a terrible thing to hope?

I did not know. My history may have obscured my judgement as I struggled to decide what was best for Marie and what was best for me. I closed my eyes, knowing that all my wishes counted for nothing. Events would have to take their course, and I would have to react accordingly. Once more, fate would carry me along with it, as helpless as a twig in a river.

Chapter Ten

Christmas dawn 1803, low cloud glowered from the summit of Arthur's Seat and hovered a few yards above the ragged cliff-edge of Salisbury Crags. I stood with my feet in a muddy puddle as the two groups eyed each other across a hundred yards of the royal park.

'It's Christ's birthday,' I said. 'It's a strange day to pick to try and kill somebody.'

George pulled back the hammer of his pistol, aimed at a gnarled thorn tree and squeezed the trigger. The click was flat and sinister. 'Every day is a strange day to try and kill somebody.' He looked around. 'What do they call this place?'

'This is Hunter's Bog.' I looked across to the opposing party. 'It's the traditional place for Edinburgh's duels.' I could see Marie standing slightly apart from the group and wondered if I should go and talk to her. What was the etiquette in situations such as this? Could friends on opposing sides converse as their men were about to try and blast holes in each other? Should I try again to make peace?

Sheep on the slopes of Arthur's Seat bleated through the mist, and a sparrow-hawk hovered between the low sky and grey-green grass, searching for prey on the damp ground. Each voice echoed in the stillness, adding to the malignant atmosphere of the day.

'We should be in church, celebrating, not out here in the cold, planning ritual murder.'

'Tell that to your friend,' George replaced his pistol in its case. He sounded far calmer than I felt. 'If kings, princes and emperors can wage wars that kill their tens of thousands, why can't individuals decide disputes along the barrel of a pistol?' He grinned, with a flash of devilry in his eyes. 'When the world stops warfare, men may stop duelling.'

Ignoring his comments, I decided: 'This is madness,' lifted my skirt and nearly ran across to the Elliot camp. 'Marie! Marie! We must try and stop this folly.'

Marie's eyes were red-rimmed and her face bloated, tear-stained. 'What can we do, Dorothea? The men seem set on their course.'

'Gilbert!' I shook him by the arm. 'You are no warrior, and Captain Rogers is a trained soldier. He will pink you.'

'Only if I do not shoot him first.' Gibbie was hatless, and the wind had ruffled his blond hair, so he appeared more like a dishevelled schoolboy than a man set on killing or being killed. He was tenser than George, trembling as he examined his French pistols.

'Did your principal send you with an official apology, Miss Flockhart?' McAra was spruce and smart. He sipped from a small silver flask.

'I am acting on my own accord,' I said.

'Then please leave us in peace,' McAra said. 'You are distracting my man. Is this a ploy to unsettle him and give your champion a better chance of success?'

'It is not,' I said, noticing Marie's hand fly to her mouth.

'I hope not,' I had not noticed Turnbull standing at the edge of the Elliot group. He was like that, a man who slid into company unnoticed, created discord and left with a smile.

McAra turned his back to talk to Gibbie as Marie wiped tears from her face.

A dog cart jolted up, and Doctor Hetherington dismounted. 'This is arrant folly!' He announced. 'Two friends determined to blow each other's brains out on Christmas morning.' He doffed his hat and bowed to me. 'Good morning Miss Flockhart. I am surprised that you have any part in this foolishness.'

'Oh, Doctor, thank Goodness you are here. Can't you talk some sense into these men?'

'Sense?' Doctor Hetherington smoothed a hand across the nose of his horse. 'These men are full of notions of honour and position and pride. Sense is well down the list of requirements for a gentleman, I'm afraid.'

Lieutenant Hepburn was about twenty-five with steady grey eyes. He approached McAra with a formal bow. 'Is your man determined to go ahead, Mr McAra?'

'My man is ready.' McAra was equally formal. 'He will accept an apology in front of the same witnesses who saw the initial insult.'

'My man is not prepared to apologise under any circumstances,' Hepburn said.

'Very well then. Let us select the weapons.'

Both sides presented their cases of pistols and the seconds examined them. 'As the challenged party, my man has the right to choose.' Hepburn said. 'We will use the pistols we brought with us.'

'I have no objections.' McAra agreed. 'Provided my man has the first choice from the case.'

'Naturally,' Hepburn turned away.

George lifted one of his pistols and sighted along the barrel. He was not smiling as he looked directly at Gibbie and raised a hand. Gibbie returned the salute.

I watched as the seconds loaded the pistols and inspected each one. McAra nodded and replaced them in the case. Gibbie chose the weapon nearest to him, weighed it in his hand and took a deep breath. Despite the morning chill, there was a sheen of perspiration across his forehead.

'It is not too late to end this,' Doctor Hetherington said.

'It was too late the minute Rogers gave the insult.' McAra snapped shut the empty pistol case and handed it to Hepburn.

'It was too late the moment that Elliot decided to gamble with his wife.' George spoke loud enough for Marie to hear. 'No gentleman would do such a thing.'

'What?' Marie's face swivelled toward her husband. 'Gibbie? What does that mean?'

'It means that your darling husband was prepared to hand you over like a lump of meat,' George said at once.

'Would you order your man to stop trying to unsettle Mr Elliot?' Ignoring George, McAra spoke directly to Hepburn.

Hepburn gave a little bow and addressed George. 'Mr McAra is correct, Captain Rogers. The duel will continue without more words.'

George nodded and said nothing.

'No!' Marie stared at Gibbie. 'Say it is not true, Gibbie; tell me that Captain Rogers is mistaken.'

'It was not as simple as it sounds,' Gibbie tried to escape.

'Stand back to back,' McAra took charge. 'Take fifteen paces away from each other and then turn and fire.'

'Gibbie!' Marie screamed. 'Be careful!'

'Marie,' I put my arm around her and guided her away from the danger area as the two principals stood back to back. George looked splendid in his full regimentals while Gibbie wore a white shirt and dark breeches, bare-headed despite the chill.

'He could get killed,' Marie clung to me.

'Pull yourself together,' I held her tight, looking over my shoulder at George. He glanced back at me, winked, and then faced his front.

I saw the two men count the slow paces as Marie placed both hands over her mouth. The seconds stepped back out of the firing area, and Doctor Hetherington watched, shaking his head and holding his leather case, ready to rush forward and help whoever was injured. In the distance, at the opening of this shallow valley, McAra sat astride his horse, watching.

'Seven, eight.'

The voices droned on, monotonously counting the steps that could end in the death of them both. Even if one man killed the other and survived, he was then legally a murderer and could be pursued, arrested, tried for murder and hanged.

'Oh, Gibbie, take care, please take care,' Marie said.

I thought the same for George although I did not speak the words. One has to try and control one's emotions in public. I felt sick.

'Nine, ten.'

The protagonists were twenty paces apart now and still striding on, their boots splashing on the muddy ground, their faces set, white and determined. The sparrow-hawk hovered overhead, careless of the drama unfolding beneath.

'Bloody fools,' Doctor Hetherington shook his head. 'Bloody, pig-headed fools.'

I had not expected Gibbie to show such courage and despite the situation, I knew I was experiencing a thrill of admiration for both men, willing to put their lives at risk in such a manner.

'Eleven, twelve.'

Nearly there. In a few seconds, both men would turn and could face the final few seconds of their lives.

'Gibbie!' Marie's scream penetrated the tension. 'Please be careful!'

'Hush, Marie,' I gave her a little shake. 'You will distract them.'

'Thirteen, fourteen.'

Both men seemed to hesitate before the final step, and then they continued. 'Fifteen.'

They turned, both holding their pistol barrel-up in their right hand. There was no hesitation as the duellers stood still, right leg slightly in front, right arm extended and the pistol pointing straight at their target. Although they were only in that situation for a second or less, they seemed to stand for eternity. I saw that Gibbie had taken note of the words in Marie's book for his stomach was sucked well in to give as small a target as possible. Both men were slim; with the curve of hip and buttocks the most prominent part of them.

'Oh, God, George,' I prayed, 'take care.'

Both men fired simultaneously, with the slight puff of smoke from the lock followed by the orange muzzle flare and the longer smoke jet from the barrels. The sound was strangely muted rather than the sharp crack I had expected. It echoed from the slopes of Arthur's Seat, and the smoke hung white and acrid for a few seconds before it began to drift slowly away. Neither man stirred. They remained standing, arms extended, staring towards their opponent and then slowly, slowly, George slid to his right side as a scarlet patch spread across his right hip.

'That's it over,' Doctor Hetherington ran forward, speaking loudly. 'There, honour is even, you have both taken a shot, and nobody is dead.' I followed a few steps behind as the doctor relieved each man of his pistol. 'Now shake hands like gentlemen and forget this whole business. For God's sake, it's like something out of the Middle Ages, this duelling and fighting over empty words.'

I took the pistols from the doctor's hand. 'Captain Roger is wounded,' I said.

'It's nothing,' George lay prone on the ground with one hand over his hip. 'Elliot's bullet only nicked me.'

'Come, sir, over to my chariot and we'll have a look. Miss Flock-hart, dispose of these instruments of death at once in case these gentlemen wish another gamble with them. Come, sir.' Doctor Hetherington put an arm around the captain's shoulder. 'Lean on me, sir, and we'll soon attend to that. 'Elliot, go to your wife and explain your position. Seconds, make peace with each other.'

I could only admire Doctor Hetherington as he took control of the situation and gave orders to these gentlemen, who were of far higher social standing than a country surgeon could ever attain.

Propping George up on the back of his dog-cart, Doctor Hetherington sliced open his breeches at the hip. 'I may need your help here, Miss Flockhart. I take it you are not offended by the sight of a male leg? Of course, you are not; it was a damned stupid question. After all, a leg is only a leg, and the Good Lord provided most of us with two of them.' He looked at the wound. 'Right, off with them, sir. Miss Flockhart, your help here, please. Take the captain's boots off.'

I did as the doctor asked and within seconds George was lying on his side in the dog-cart with his boots and breeches at his feet.

'I said I might need your help, Miss Flockhart.' Doctor Hetherington frowned. 'Damn this pretence of shyness. A man is just a man. Come here, madam, and help your friend.'

I crouched at Captain Roger's side as the doctor examined the wound. The Captain's leg was muscular, covered with fine dark hairs and surprisingly shapely as it swelled into the bulge of his hip and buttocks.

'Hold that,' Doctor Hetherington cleaned the wound that stretched across the hip and handed me the bloody sponge. 'It's clean, Captain, a simple flesh wound that a few stitches will cure.'

Captain Rogers grinned at me. 'I'm afraid you are seeing more of me than we both expected, Dorothea.' He looked down at himself. 'Good shooting from Gibbie Elliot,' he approved. 'I have no idea where my shot went.'

'It does not matter where your shot went, so long as it was not inside Mr Elliot.' Doctor Hetherington lifted George's shirt tail. 'Hold that Miss Flockhart and keep it away from the wound.' He tutted. 'Come closer woman! Captain Rogers won't bite you for God's sake.'

So close to the half-naked captain, I could not help but look and admire. It was not conscious or intentional, but some animal instinct that I was not aware I still possessed. I was a woman, and George was a man. Indeed, George was very much a man.

'Now this will sting a little, Captain. Squeeze Miss Flockhart's hand if it helps.'

George's hand sought mine, but whether it was for comfort or some other reason I could not tell. 'On you go, Doctor,' he said. 'Do your worst.'

His hand was firm and warm around mine, and he was remarkably cheerful for a man who had just been shot. He seemed to be savouring the attention, and I wondered, with some shock, if he enjoyed me seeing him so exposed. I watched as the doctor pressed the two sides of George's wound together and sewed them with stitches of which I would have been proud. With three minutes Doctor Hetherington was finished. He bent to examine his work and patted George's backside.

'There now, Captain, that will leave a scar to fascinate the ladies, should you chose to allow them access to that portion of you.'

'Admirable,' Captain Rogers twisted to examine his wound. 'Although there will be few women indeed who will see it.'

'One already has,' Doctor Hetherington winked at me.

'You have a neat hand with the needle, Doctor.' I thought it best not to comment on what else I had seen.

'There was another lady present.' Covering himself, George wriggled around to sit on the hard seat.

'Mrs Elliot is long gone, Captain,' Doctor Hetherington said. 'The Elliot party departed as soon as you fools fired at each other. Lieutenant Hepburn is still here.'

I had forgotten about Hepburn and looked up. The three of us were alone in Hunter's Bog with the sheep and that questing sparrow-hawk.

'Thank you, Lieutenant,' George said, and I wondered if it was normal for Volunteer captains to give orders when they were naked from the waist down. Perhaps it was, in the military world. 'You better get back to the castle now.'

'Yes, sir.' Hepburn hesitated. 'Will you be all right? I can wait and help you.'

'If the authorities arrive, we'll all be in trouble,' George said, 'and I don't wish to be responsible for you. Get back to barracks, Hepburn. That's an order.'

'Yes, sir.'

We watched Hepburn march down the centre of Hunter's Bog toward Edinburgh. 'Could you cobble my trousers together please Doctor?' George touched his new wound. 'I don't wish to have them flapping around my hips.'

Dr Hetherington grunted. 'I'm not your blasted tailor, Captain, maybe Miss Flockhart would be better,' but he stitched the trousers back with as much skill as he had the captain's skin. 'Now don't use that leg too much for the next few days, Captain Rogers or the stitches could burst, and you could be in all sorts of bother. Let your regimental surgeon see it as well, and follow his advice.'

For a moment I watched these two men. They had come into my life very recently and yet I already liked both, for vastly different reasons. The doctor was compassionate, gentle even, and would be a man to approach for any medical or personal problem. He would be a dependable family doctor, I believed. However, Captain Rogers was a man of action with that intriguing scar on his chin and his swaggering walk. With all that, he was not arrogant and he lacked the cruelty that so many veteran soldiers seemed to possess. There was also something else, a seeming desire for danger or attention, I was not sure yet, and thought it would be at least amusing to investigate further.

I had proof of his bravery for he had stood up to a pistol at thirty paces without a single flinch. Now I saw that he retained his good humour even after an inexperienced civilian had bested him in a duel. Some men I had known would have cursed and shouted at such ill-fortune, while George merely accepted his defeat and the wound across his hip. I liked him rather more for both. I looked tactfully away as he struggled into his tight breeches, for he would undoubtedly reveal more than he intended. I smiled inwardly at my memories of his shapely leg with the gentle swell of his buttock so white and clean. Yes, I thought, I undoubtedly liked George Rogers, and for more than one reason. When I turned back he was fully dressed and with only the stitches in his white breeches as a reminder of recent events, that and the blood-stain already turning a rusty brown.

'I'll drive you up to the Castle,' Doctor Hetherington offered, 'if you can both squeeze into my cart.'

I also liked the doctor, I realised.

Chapter Eleven

Thistle Street seemed once more like a haven from the complications of the world. I listened to the slow ticking of the clock, looked around my drawing room and walked to the bookcase, where my books were old friends. Some were travel-worn, with stains from salt-water and spilt coffee, others I had bought since returning to Scotland. As well as Burns and various religious books, there was Wordsworth and Fielding, Homer and Tacitus, Smollet, Voltaire and Gilpin. Running my fingers across the spines, I selected a long-time favourite and retreated to my seat.

Opening Homer, I sat near the fire, trying to forget the outside world in the adventures of Odysseus. The familiar old words in the book blurred and merged as I attempted to concentrate. At that moment I did not care about romantic imagery or the wine-dark sea. I was seriously contemplating packing everything back up and returning to India. Despite the heat and the flies and the alien lifestyle, I had found peace there of a sort. I could lease a small bungalow and hire half a dozen servants whose company I would have preferred to these arrogant men whose pride was so much more important to them than their wives.

India. I closed my eyes and wondered what had made me return to Scotland. Since my return, I had experienced only trouble, except for the friendship of George and, to an extent, Doctor Hetherington. And Emily. Recalling my recent experiences in Hunters Bog, I shook my head at my thoughts and firmly pushed the images from my mind. Or most of them, for some, insisted on sliding back as a reminder.

'Oh, Captain Rogers,' I said, 'what have you done to me?' Knowing that there could be no future with George, I tried again to concentrate on Homer.

The knock on the door sounded like a harbinger of doom, and I felt suddenly sick.

'I hope that's not that Turnbull fellow,' Mrs Macfarlane bustled into the room. 'I'll give him a piece of my mind if it is.'

'I hope it's not,' I agreed as Mrs Macfarlane made her way to the door. I heard the light tones of a woman, and then Marie exploded into the room with her face crumpled and her hair an explosion under her loosely tied hat.

'Dorothea! You have to help me! They've arrested Gibbie.'

I stood up, hands outstretched. 'Oh, dear God. Sit down.' I ushered Marie into a chair. 'Now take a deep breath and tell me everything.'

It took me a good five minutes to get Marie calmed down and then she told me what had happened. The Elliot party had returned to Tynebridge Hall after the duel and Marie was asking searching questions about Gibbie's gambling habits when they heard a hammering at the door. Within a few moments, three sturdy men entered the house.

'What sort of men?' I asked.

'King's messengers,' Marie said. 'Sent by the court to arrest Gibbie for attempted murder and taking part in a duel.'

I nodded. 'I see. That was remarkably quick work. Who gave Gibbie away?'

'That's just it,' Marie said. 'It was Mr Turnbull who told the King's Messenger, Mr Turnbull who is Gibbie's friend.'

I was not as surprised as Marie was. 'Mr Turnbull is a most unpleasant individual. My Mrs Macfarlane has no time for him at all.' I knew that Mrs Macfarlane would be listening behind the door.

'I don't care what Mrs Macfarlane thinks,' Marie howled. 'I only want Gibbie back.'

I thought what best to do. Unfortunately, there was no doubt that Gibbie and George had broken the law, so the King's Messengers were well within their rights. 'I'll go and visit him,' I said. 'You stay home.' I could not imagine how Marie would act if she saw her husband in jail. Nature had not blessed her with the strongest of nerves, and the sight of Gibbie in chains could possibly unhinge her completely.

'No,' Marie shook her head. 'I'm not staying in Tynebridge Hall without Gibbie.'

'Where will you go?' I asked.

'The Campbells live at Flotterstone Manor,' Marie said. 'I will be safe there.'

'I'll take you there,' I steeled myself for yet another winter journey across Midlothian. Honestly, I did more travelling that season than I ever did in India. 'And tomorrow morning I will visit Gibbie.'

It was late when I returned, and I lay in bed a long time before I found sleep. Even then I tossed and turned in the throes of nightmares, and woke with a sore head and out of temper.

With Mrs Macfarlane out of the house on some mysterious message of her own, there was nobody to help me struggle with my boots, and dark green cloak and only the pier-glass witnessed me adjust my hat. I was less fashion-conscious than most women, but still, I preferred to look at least presentable when I ventured abroad. Sighing, I studied my appearance, decided it would do and waited for my hired chaise-and- driver to roll up to the door.

You may be aware of Edinburgh's ancient prison some called the Heart of Midlothian, and the locals knew as the Tolbooth. It is long gone now, and yet it is famous because Sir Walter Scott wrote about it in one of his interminable romances. In my day he was plain Walter Scott, you will recall that I saw him slicing turnips on Portobello beach the day I first met George. I never took to his books, however much money he made from them. There was always too much of the tartan about them, and praise for the outlaws and cattle thieves. To me, there is nothing romantic about thievery and law-breaking, while tartans and kilts belong in the Highlands, not all over the country. Anyway, somebody must suffer for a thief to gain, and despite what novelists claim, it is the poor folk at the bottom of the pyramid who are the most at risk. There is no honour among thieves and no gentleman outlaw who robs the rich to feed the poor. More importantly, the Tolbooth was in the High Street, and that was where Gibbie was locked up.

I could have walked from our house in Thistle Street to the Old Town, but I had no desire to struggle up the Earthen Mound or chance the stares and uncouth comments of the mob. At that period, remember, the Old Town was still in a state of transition, shared between the native people and the incoming Irish labourers. Most of the elite had flitted to the grander properties of the New Town although a few of the older gentry clung to the traditional ways and the houses in which their families had lived for generations. Year by year the respectable people were seeping away, and the ancient streets and buildings were becoming more rundown and no-doubt more picturesque. To me, picturesque means ruinous and although they may have been suitable for Sir Walter's novels or Wordsworth's poems they were not decent accommodation for any human being.

In the centre of the High Street was the Tolbooth, the infamous Heart of Midlothian and as I said, somewhere inside was Gibbie El-liot. A large part of me agreed that he deserved to be there, not because of his foolish duelling but because of the way he gambled with Marie. The Tolbooth was a dark building, tall, with the corners, nailed down with turrets and aeons of dirt griming the barred win-dows. It sat cheek-by-jowl with St Giles, the High Kirk that had once been a cathedral, and nearly blocked the roadway. It was not a place near which to linger, and it exuded an aura of evil from the wicked deeds that it had witnessed and the terrible people who the Law had locked inside the filthy walls. Murderers and rapists, assassins and torturers, body snatchers and habitual thieves had spent time here, and now naïve Gibbie Elliot was a guest, forlorn and foolish.

I halted the chaise fifty yards from the ugly building, paid the driver and asked him to wait.

'How long will you be, miss?' The driver was squat and unshaven, with sharp blue eyes.

'I do not know,' I said.

'In that case, I will move on,' the driver whipped up. 'I won't make a living waiting here.' He rolled away before I could protest, leaving me alone outside the city jail with two hard-faced City Guards watching me over their long-stemmed pipes.

'Good morning,' I decided that politeness was the best weapon to use with these old soldiers. Dressed in red uniforms and carrying lethal Leith axes, these men had been soldiers before they retired to the City Guard. They nodded in silent unison. I wondered how many years of service they had seen between them, how many battles and how much human suffering.

'I am looking for Gilbert Elliot.' I gave a little curtsey. 'The Honourable Gilbert Elliot.'

'He's inside.' The younger of the two guards said. I guessed he had passed his allotted three-score years and ten some time ago.

'May I speak to him?'

The guards looked at each other in slight confusion before the younger one nodded. 'You aren't hiding a false key are you?'

I guessed that was a joke and gave a laugh as false as the non-existent key.

'What's your name?' The old man's eyes were bayonet-sharp.

'Miss Dorothea Flockhart,' I nearly said too much.

'Why do you want to see Elliot?' The veteran was very direct with his questions.

'I am a friend of his wife,' I told the truth. 'She is worried about him.'

'Well, Miss Dorothea Flockhart, you take care in there and don't take heed of anything you see or hear.'

I gave a little curtsey. 'Thank you, Colonel.'

'It's Sergeant Bain,' the old man said.

I entered the Heart of Midlothian through the arched door and stopped to catch my breath. Guttering lanterns that hung on walls dark with age only slightly alleviated the stench of damp and despair. I could taste the misery in the air.

The interior was a maze of tiny stone cells, each with a quota of inhabitants, some sunk in depression, others entertained by gaudy women, or swearing over cards. Heavy chains around wrists and ankles secured all the prisoners to the weeping walls. Inside the front door, the turnkey sat on a massive chair nursing a staff and watching everybody who entered or left.

I gave my most polite curtsey. 'Excuse me, sir, I am looking for Gilbert Elliot.'

The turnkey looked me up and down, no-doubt wondering what a gentlewoman was doing in such an establishment. 'What do you want with him?'

'I'm a friend of his wife.'

'Are you carrying a weapon or anything to help him escape?' The turnkey's pouchy eyes scanned me. I shivered, wondering what he was thinking.

'No, sir,' I decided that politeness was best with petty officialdom.

'End door,' the turnkey said. 'Along the corridor.'

I took a deep breath and looked deeper into that terrible place. Honestly, the things we do for men, even for men we don't like or trust very much. According to the wisdom of my peers, I should have been sitting in comfort at home or parading along George Street trying to catch the eye of one of the handsome militia officers. But things were what they were. I reminded myself that I was visiting the Tolbooth for Marie's sake and not for Gibbie.

I bobbed in another little curtsey to the turnkey. 'Could you accompany me, sir?' I had no desire to walk alone into this den of blackguards although I doubted they were any worse than the gentlemen who sat at cards and claret in many of the elegant houses of the New Town.

Grunting, the turnkey rose from his chair and shambled in front of me along the stone corridor from which each cell door opened. Men and women moved aside as he passed.

'Here we are.' The turnkey unlocked a heavy door and pushed it open.

'Miss Flockhart!' Gibbie looked weary and streaked with grime as he looked up from the bench he shared with two ragged men. 'You should not have come.' He rattled as he stood and I saw the rusty chains that held him secure. 'Is Maria with you? Could Maria not come to see me?'

'You are shackled, sir,' I said.

'Miss Flockhart, Dorothea,' Gibbie sounded desperate. 'I am accused of duelling and attempted murder.'

'So I believe,' I said.

'I am guilty,' Gibbie said.

'You are,' I was in no mood to alleviate Gibbie's misery. 'Although I do not care about these crimes. I am more upset that you tried to gamble away Marie.'

Gibbie shook his head in instant denial. 'That is not true!'

'It is true, sir,' I said. 'I heard from a very reliable source.'

'I had no choice,' Gibbie said.

I said nothing. To leave Gibbie in *durance vile* and allow him to face a trial would be to risk his imprisonment, transportation or even the gallows. Worse, it would mean that Marie was alone in the world without even such a weak protector as this man. Once again I wondered if Marie would be better without him, and I decided that I could not make such a decision for her.

'Would Marie have gambled you in similar circumstances?' I forced Gibbie to think about what he had done. The other two prisoners in the cell sat in listless silence. No doubt they were more concerned with their impending fate rather than this over-dressed dandy.

'You must leave me here,' Gibbie did not give a direct answer. 'I am not worthy of Marie.'

'That is true,' I said. 'You are not.' I wondered if he was genuinely contrite. 'Perhaps the King's Messenger will relent and allow you to walk free. After all, you only gave Captain Rogers a minor flesh wound, and he is not making any complaint.'

The turnkey, who had been an interested observer to our meeting, laughed. 'That won't do at all,' he said. 'If the King's Messenger has got his man, that's all there is to it.' He pushed a soiled boot against Gibbie's chains. 'This young fellow is here until his trial, whenever that will be. Your witness has seen to that.'

'Is the witness so important?' I asked.

'Without a witness,' the turnkey said, 'the case would collapse. With a witness, your friend here is certain to be condemned. It's Van Diemen's land for him or the sideways look over his shoulder as the noose tightens.' He mimicked the facial expressions of a man being hanged and laughed as if the whole situation was highly amusing.

'Your friend Mr Turnbull put you here, Gibbie.' I looked around at the dismal, weeping stone walls. The atmosphere was choking, a mixture of all that was foul and all that was unpleasant.

'I trusted him,' Gibbie forced what might have been a smile. 'Perhaps the jury will take pity on a gentleman.'

The turnkey laughed again. 'You took part in a duel and shot at a holder of the king's commission in wartime. You have no excuse for doing Boney's job for him.'

'Gibbie,' I said. 'I would have much more sympathy for you if you had not tried to gamble away Marie, but she is upset.' I forced away my anger and tried to concentrate on what was best for Marie. 'She misses you.' I could say no more. In attempting to help Marie, I had spied on Gibbie in a gambling den and caused a duel between him and George. Now Gibbie sat in a filthy cell awaiting trial, and the fault was entirely mine.

'Excuse me,' I fled the Heart of Midlothian without another word. It seemed that whatever I did made things worse. I wished I had never returned to Scotland. I wished I had remained in India.

I do not know where I wandered that day. I remember a succession of dirty streets and tumbledown houses, narrow closes and filthy wynds where ragged women smoked long clay pipes and watched me through predatory eyes. Most of the denizens ignored me while others called out or shouted obscene insults. I turned a Nelsonian eye and walked on with my mind a tangle of guilt and anger, with old memories fighting new worries and bitter tears waiting to fall from my eyes. I do not know how long I walked through the morass of the Old Town or how many ancient, crazy closes I stumbled through. I only remember what happened when the sun was casting its final shadows, and a scattering of candles gleamed behind broken windows.

'Come in here, dearie; you look cold. A glass of fine Ferintosh will soon warm you up!'

'That's a grand cloak she has; it will fetch a pretty price at the pawn shop.'

I looked up, suddenly aware that I had blundered into some wynd off the West Bow, where three men stood at the entrance to a close, discussing me.

'She's lost, I reckon,' one man said.

'Isn't that a shame now?' There was no sympathy in the second man's voice.

'Where are you going, my dear?' The third man slipped clear of the close mouth and stepped behind me, blocking my retreat.

I increased my pace, hoping that the wynd led to the High Street. All I could see ahead was darkness and tall buildings.

'She thinks she's too good for the likes of us,' the first man stepped in front of me. 'Isn't that so?'

I ducked my head and said nothing, hoping they would go away. I felt the second man's hand grip my cloak. 'Ten shillings worth here, I'd say.'

'She'll have more than that on her.' The first man said.

'Leave me alone!' I did not know that I could scream so loudly. I had not brought my Joseph Manton with me as I had not intended wandering through these foul streets.

Somebody's hand closed around my mouth, and I was dragged backwards with my feet kicking and sliding on the greasy ground. I lashed out desperately, only to have somebody grab hold of my arm. The man holding me was powerful and stunk of cheap tobacco.

'Bring her in here, lads!' That was a female voice. I glanced up to see the most beautiful woman smiling at me. 'You can have your fun with her inside.'

I tried to scream again but that filthy hand prevented any sound except a stifled moan, and then I was being pulled through the entrance to the close and the woman stepped aside to allow the men to drag me into whatever horror awaited. There was darkness all around and the foulest stench imaginable.

'Halloa!' The voice was deep and welcome. 'What's going on there?'

'Who the devil's that?' the second man said. 'It's a blasted redcoat.'

'I'll take his head off his shoulders,' the third man pulled a lifepreserver from his sleeve.

'No,' the woman placed a hand on his arm. 'Let me handle this.' She raised her voice. 'It's just my sister. She's drunk as a lord. We're taking her home.'

'Let me see.' The voice sounded a second time, and I heard limping steps echo from the tall buildings on either side of the wynd. Captain Rogers had never been more welcome than at that minute.

'Knock her out,' the woman said. 'Stop her mouth.'

I saw the third man raise his life-preserver and then, mercifully, George limped in. 'You drop that cudgel my man, or I'll spit you clean.' He drew his sword with a thrill of steel. 'That woman is no more your sister than I am! Release her, sir. Release her, this instant!'

The third man said a word that I had seldom heard before and swung at Captain Rogers with his life-preserver.

'You devil!' The captain blocked the swing with his blade and stepped back. For a terrible moment I thought he was going to leave me alone, but instead, he twisted his sword and disarmed the life-preserver man. Then his strong hands were on me as my attackers fled.

'Are you all right Dorothea?'

'Thank you.' I took a deep breath as George helped me to my feet. ''You saved my life.'

'I doubt it.' George held me tight. 'They would have robbed you and left you.' He smiled. 'You should not be wandering around in this part of the city, you know.'

'I know that now.' I brushed myself down. It was strange how this wynd seemed so much safer when I stood beside George Rogers. 'Thank you for saving me,' I said again, as thundering feet signalled the arrival of two more redcoats.

'Are you all right, sir?' The privates had bayonets but no muskets.

'A group of men were attacking this lady,' George said. More soldiers arrived with a broad-chested sergeant at their head. 'Form them up, Sergeant.'

'Sir!' The sergeant threw an impressive salute and began shouting so loudly that he must have wakened every inhabitant of this wynd and any others in a hundred-yard circumference.

'You are a treasure, sir,' I said as George released me. I brushed down my clothes, 'a real treasure.'

'My pleasure,' George touched a hand to the brim of his shako and then grinned. 'I'd rather save you than perform guard duty or scour the streets for my men.'

'Do you have men missing?' I was beginning to recover.

'There are public houses a-plenty in this part of the city,' Captain Rogers said, 'and the duties of my men are not arduous or particularly time-consuming. They change guard and are on sentinel duty, plus two or three hours of drill a day. That's all, so they have plenty of time to visit the publics.'

'I see,' I said.

'Yes, soldiers and publics don't always mix well. My men tend to overstay their time, and I take out a picket to round them up before they get into trouble.'

'Would they get into trouble?'

Captain Rogers nodded. 'If they return drunk, or decide not to return at all, they could be court-martialled and end up at the flogging triangle. I don't wish that for my men.'

I shivered. 'You are a good man, Captain.' *And you are a compassionate man.* I had heard about military and naval commanders who enjoyed nothing better than having some poor devil flogged senseless. I was glad that George was not of that ilk. Indeed, if he had been, I would have turned on my heel and walked away. I can thole many things, but cruelty is not one of them.

'It makes sense,' George said. 'After two hundred lashes a man is useless for days. After five hundred he will never be the same soldier again, and the morale of the unit is shaken by having to witness such a scene.' He shook his head, 'Why, while I was in India...'

'I did not know you were in India,' I prompted. I looked again at the scar on his chin and thought of Serangipatam.

'I thought I had told you,' George said. 'When I left the Guards I went out East.' He grinned. 'We may have been close to each other without knowing it.' He looked up as his picket filled the wynd, with the sergeant glowering at them. 'I have to return to my duty now, Dorothea, but I don't wish to leave you in this part of the town, it's not safe.'

I nodded. 'I came here by mistake.' I wondered how much to admit and decided to tell him everything. It seemed that I had finally found a decent man, and one I could trust. 'I was in the Tolbooth visiting Gibbie Elliot.'

George pretended to wince and pressed a hand to his hip. 'The man who shot me? You should be ashamed of yourself.'

More soldiers were lining up along the close with a second, long-faced sergeant shouting at them. One or two looked a little worse for wear, and I guessed they had been sampling the hospitality of the local pubs.

'Sergeant!' George's sudden bark made me jump.

'Sir!' The sergeant could have been roaring at somebody on the opposite side of the city rather than speaking to an officer three paces away.

'Detail two reliable men to escort Miss Flockhart home.'

'Sir!' The shout was louder than ever. 'King and Mackie! You heard the officer! Take this lady safely home and return to barracks!' He lowered his voice to a bellow. 'And no stopping for refreshment you pair of damned blackguards!'

'Thank you,' I said, 'but I don't need an escort.'

'You clearly do,' George said. 'Or you would not be here. I'll be in touch.'

The two privates grinned shyly at me and touched their shakoes in simple salute. They were both in their late teens or early twenties, handsome enough young men in ill-fitting uniforms with the thin wrists of clerks. I could not see either of them giving Bonaparte's veterans much trouble.

'We'll see you safely home, Miss Flockhart', the taller man said.

'I feel much better with you two men as escort,' I agreed. 'Thank you.'

The young Volunteers proved to be entertaining companions, once they recovered from their shyness at being in the company of a lady. When I decided to find out more about their captain, they were more than willing to oblige.

'Is Captain Rogers a brave man?' I asked.

'As brave as they come, Miss,' the taller King said. He had slightly protruding teeth and the deepest of blue eyes that must have won him favour with a string of sweethearts. 'Why, when he was in India he practically won battles all by himself.'

'I heard he was in India,' I said. 'Was he not at Serangipatam?'

'Him and General Baird both miss,' the slightly smaller Mackie said. 'They were like blood brothers the two of them, both Edinburgh men marching to defeat Tippoo Sahib after what he did last time.'

I allowed the privates to heap praise on Captain Rogers 'Yet he is a Volunteer officer,' I said. 'And the Volunteers don't serve overseas.'

'He's a Volunteer officer now, miss,' King said. 'He was in the Guards first though and then joined John Company. That's what they call the Honourable East India Company, you see,' he was anxious to make sure I understood.

'I see.' That was something to tuck away for future reference. George had been in the Guards and then in India. He had not lied to me. I was slightly ashamed that I had doubted him, but when one's past contains little more than deceit and horror, one does not trust many people.

I was quite sorry when the privates left me at the door of my house and thanked them profusely. Unsure how much to give them, I parted with a shilling apiece, and they were seemingly well pleased with the bargain. I only hoped they did not stop by in some pub or other and land themselves in trouble. I closed the door, leaned my back against it and took a deep breath. I did not know what to do now.

I had got Gibbie in jail, and I could not think how to get him out. My interfering had made things worse. On the other hand, I now knew that George was an honest, brave man. I only wished that I could tell him the truth about me, but if I did, he would turn his back. He could do nothing else.

Chapter Twelve

'That man was back,' Mrs Macfarlane had heard my return.

I immediately knew who she meant. 'Mr Turnbull?'

'Yes.' Mrs Macfarlane glared at me. 'And you know what I think about him.'

'I do,' I said. At that moment everything was getting on top of me. With the blackmail threat and now Gibbie Elliot in jail, I could not cope with any more. Once more I contemplated escaping back to India.

I closed my eyes. No. I would not allow them to win.

'Mrs Macfarlane,' I said, and before I realised what I was doing, I was telling her about my troubles, or at least part of them. I told her about the blackmail without giving her the reason behind it, and I told her about Gibbie in the Tolbooth on the word of Turnbull. Mrs Macfarlane listened, nodding at all the right places.

'All right, Miss Flockhart,' Mrs Macfarlane said. 'You're in a bit of a pickle and that man Turnbull is at the centre of it all.'

'He's the horned beast,' I said.

'If you say so,' Mrs Macfarlane could not be expected to understand what I meant.

'I don't know what to do,' I admitted. 'Everything I try makes the situation worse.'

'You need Highland help,' Mrs Macfarlane said.

I must have stared at her with my mouth open.

'You are thinking of things the Lowland way if you don't mind me saying,' Mrs Macfarlane sat down without a by-your-leave. 'Now up by Loch Lomond side, the Macfarlanes have our own way of dealing with troublesome men, or troublesome women for that matter.'

'What do you mean?' I asked, wondering what sort of Highland rogue I had harboured in my house.

'You know that the moon is Macfarlane's lantern,' Mrs Macfarlane said.

'I have heard the expression,' I admitted.

'That means that the Macfarlanes work at night.' Mrs Macfarlane patted my arm. 'There is a Highland way of doing things, Miss Flockhart, and you need my man's help.'

Now, I have heard women talk about their husbands all my life, but never quite like that. When Mrs Macfarlane said 'my man', she was inferring a bond that was stronger than any marriage vows I had heard exchanged in any church. It was something fundamental, something spiritual, something of the soul, a binding that I knew Marie and Gibbie had not attained and maybe never would. Nor would I.

'What could Mr Macfarlane do?' I asked.

'Anything.' Mrs Macfarlane said, and I shivered at the stark simplicity of that single word.

I bowed to inevitability. I had attempted to solve matters by following what I thought were the correct paths, and things had got worse. Perhaps it was time to try the Highland way. 'What should I do, Mrs Macfarlane?'

'You will have to meet Macfarlane,' Mrs Macfarlane patted my arm again, 'and he will put things right.'

Looking into those bright, hard Highland eyes, I could not repress a shiver. The Highlanders had a reputation for bravery and daring that stretched back centuries. In very recent memory the Black Watch, the Royal Highland Regiment, had defeated Bonaparte's vaunted Invincibles in Egypt.

'What do you have in mind, Mrs Macfarlane?'

'Whatever is needed, Miss Flockhart,' Mrs Macfarlane said. 'Now, if you will excuse me, I have work to do.'

I did not hear Macfarlane arrive at the Thistle Street house. I only heard the low rumble of voices in the hall, and then Mrs Macfarlane was at my side.

'Macfarlane is here' she said.

'Bring him in.' I do not know what I expected, possibly some tall, dark-haired hero with a sword across his shoulder and a brace of silver-mounted pistols at the belt of his kilt. Macfarlane was not like that. He was middle-sized, middle-aged and almost respectable looking, with a neat beard and eyes calm with the peace of the hills.

He stepped in with his shoes making no sound on the floor and his shoulders nearly touching each side of the door jamb.

'Mrs Flockhart,' his bow was perfunctory. 'We have met before.'

'Have we?' I nodded as the memory returned. 'Yes, you had the whisky convoy in the Pentland Hills.'

'You gave us welcome hospitality,' Macfarlane reminded.

'Miss Flockhart needs our help,' Mrs Macfarlane explained the situation.

Macfarlane listened without visible emotion. 'You would prefer Turnbull's space to his company,' he said.

I had a chilling vision of this ordinary looking man suddenly producing a Highland dirk and plunging it into Turnbull's breast. 'What do you mean?' I asked in a sudden panic.

'It's all right, Mrs Flockhart.' Macfarlane may have read my mind. Highlanders can do such things if the mood is on them. 'I just mean we will take him away for a while so he can neither give evidence against your friend or demand money from you.' His smile was as quiet as a purring cat, and as dangerous as a hunting leopard. 'Mac-Gregor will help. He is a dependable man. You met him in the hills.'

I remembered the capable looking trio. 'Have you done such a thing before?'

'It's a way we have of getting rid of troublesome men and unwanted wives,' Macfarlane said.

Unsure what I was agreeing to, I knew I had little choice. 'What do I have to do?'

'All you have to do, Miss Flockhart, is receive Turnbull as you always do,' Macfarlane said. 'Leave the details to MacGregor and me.'

Despite the seriousness of the situation, one look at that quiet, confident Highland face reassured me that I was in the hands of an expert. I did not know how, but I knew that with Macfarlane involved, things were about to take a turn for the better.

'As you wish, Macfarlane.' Knowing about Highland pride, I hesitated before broaching the next subject. 'There will be a question of payment.'

'There will not,' Macfarlane straightened his back. His eyes challenged me to continue with that subject.

'Thank you, Mr Macfarlane.' He may have only been a sedan-chairman and a whisky smuggler, but I knew that Macfarlane was a better man than most I had met. I hardly heard him leave the room.

I lay back in my chair, tapping my fingers on the arm. I was unsure what Macfarlane had in mind, yet I knew he would be efficient. Now, I wished to find out more about George Rogers. It was time to take a step in that direction as well. I now knew he had told me only the truth about his military career, and he had never let me down in any situation. For the first time in years, I had a flicker of hope. If he was as decent a man as he appeared, then surely, God willing, he might understand my position and deception?

As it happened, I did not need to take any steps to contact him. Once again, Captain Rogers came to me.

The letter-carrier delivered the message the very next day. What was interesting was that it was sealed not with a simple wafer but a coat of arms, presumably the Rogers crest, with a heart and two unicorns in support. However, I did not waste much time in admiring the details.

The paper was so thick it creaked as I unfolded the letter and the copperplate writing was impeccable. It began with 'Dear Miss Dorothea' and ended with 'your devoted Captain George Rogers.' The message was short. 'I am looking forward to meeting you again. I do hope you can come along to the Regimental Ball at the Assembly Rooms so I can introduce you to my fellow officers. I have taken the liberty of hoping for at least three dances in advance.'

I do not know what I expected. I know that I had not wished for long paragraphs of devotion, or intertwined hearts. All the same, it was the first letter of its kind I had received for more than ten years, and I was not at all sure what to think. Had I indeed turned the corner? Was I ready for a sincere relationship with another man after all this time?

'Damn you,' I said, getting satisfaction from the oath. 'Damn you for ruining my life.'

I did not mean George Rogers. I remembered the white, predatory faces crowding down upon me, and I shivered. I had trusted and loved a man, once, and the results still made me cringe. I closed my eyes and tried to relegate the past to history and instead re-read the letter. I liked the phrase 'I am looking forward to meeting you again.'

And then the significance of the last sentence hit me.

Three dances! Any gentleman who asked for two or more dances was showing an interest in his partner. By telling me in advance, George was announcing his intentions, and if he kept his word, as a gentleman would, the whole assembly would be witness to our attachment. Rather than a desultory friendship, George was looking for something more permanent.

But was I the right woman for him?

I did not know. I hid the letter in the top drawer of my chest. It was safe there; Mrs Macfarlane was not one of those women who interfered in her employer's affairs, or not in that way.

I thought of my previous meetings with George. Had he been trying to entertain me with his description of his encounter with the French? Or was he trying to impress me? If the former, he had succeeded. If the latter, I had been more impressed by his actions immediately after the duel. He had accepted his wound with high good humour and no rancour against Gibbie, while many men would have cursed, demanded another shot and vowed vengeance. His appearance in that incident near the West Bow had been fortuitous, and his men certainly liked him; all these facts were very positive. I wondered anew if I had found a man I could trust. If only... The past exploded back into my mind.

And then I remembered Mother Faa's words about the uniformed gentleman and wondered if my life was about to change. I looked in the pier-glass, seeing the shadows under my eyes and the lines that no amount of powder and potions could efficiently erase and asked myself if I were ready to trust a man again, and indeed if I ever could.

Well, I told myself, my friendship with George Rogers had blossomed very quickly, and he seemed interested in me. I may allow myself to smile in future. I did not care if his war stories were genuine or not, I did know that he amused me and had never made any move that was hurtful. I tapped my reflection in the pier glass.

'Maybe you can put the past to rest, Dorothea.'

My reflection stared back at me, unsmiling. The shadows in my eyes did not shift. I wondered if my time had come. I wondered how George would react when I eventually told him the truth. Everything depended on that; once again my past was eroding my present and my future. Could I trust sufficiently trust George to let him know?

Chapter Thirteen

If you know Edinburgh, you will know the Assembly Rooms in George Street. Perhaps you have also been there. If not, then I will explain that they were built specifically to allow ladies such as me the opportunity of dancing with as many men as propriety would permit. The Assembly Rooms' elegance is unsurpassed even in Edinburgh, the most elegant city anywhere and their position right in the centre of the principal street of the New Town speaks volumes for their importance.

I know that some speak of Princes Street as something special. I do not agree. Oh, yes there are splendid views of the Castle, and now the gardens blossom where once the North Loch festered, but that is all there is to it. The architecture is mediocre, and at both east and west end the wind could blow one's gown above one's head and rip one's hat away. George Street is the place to see, be seen and meet the most refined of company, particularly in the early years of this 19th century.

I tried to look composed as the carriages growled along George Street to disgorge their human cargoes on the pavement outside the Assembly Rooms. Unfortunately, the weather was a trifle unkind, and a thin smirr of rain dampened the gowns of the ladies and glistened on shakoes and feather bonnets and the shoulders of magnificent scarlet uniforms. I allowed myself the luxury of enjoyment as

I joined the crowd, listening to the excited chatter of the younger people and the more restrained conversation of their elders.

A crowd of onlookers watched as the officers and their ladies strolled from their carriages into the Rooms. I saw Lady Pluscarden's mulberry coloured coach among the others and noticed the lady herself, sitting on a stool at the door of her coach, sipping from a glass of wine and watching the world pass. I wished to avoid that shrewd-eyed lady.

Fashions in Edinburgh followed the architectural trend, with an amalgamation of opposites that was a joy to the eye. One set of ladies wore the costumes of the classical revival, disregarding the long waist so that particular portion of a lady's body now seemingly stretched to the armpits, or the *oxters* as the colloquial would have it. As Emily once unkindly said to me:

'The petticoat is tied around the neck, and the arms put through the pocket holes.'

Colourful words perhaps, but apt, you must agree, as these shapeless dresses cocooned the ladies who wore such ridiculous costumes. I was not a follower of these supposedly-classical creations, as you will have guessed. We still wore the gown, as ladies had in the days of the Bourbons, but sensible women discarded the ugly hoops. Call me old-fashioned if you will, or call me traditional and you will be equally wrong, for neither is accurate. I am my own woman and will be tied by neither stricture or fashion unless they agree with what I think is correct.

Anyway, that is to jump a little, so forgive me while I return a few hours and a few hundred paces to Thistle Street. Before I left the house, Mrs Macfarlane had inspected me as if I were her daughter. 'Much better, Miss Flockhart,' she said as she stood back to admire. 'I much prefer the gown falling in straight loose folds.'

I had moved my feet, enjoying the feel of the muslin against my legs. 'I like this Empire gown,' I looked down at myself, wishing that I had rather more to display above the high waist. I knew men liked to admire those parts of a lady's person, so hoped that George

Rogers was not overly critical of my shape. I felt nearly as nervous as I had when first launched in the world, twelve years and more ago.

Mrs Macfarlane had read my mind, in her Highland way. 'You are fine as you are,' she said softly. 'Too much up there is worse than too little; it becomes heavy with age.' She had pressed her hands against her matronly breasts and laughed openly. She patted my bottom, 'and you are perfect there, Miss Flockhart. Not too much and not too little.' Her smile was full of mischief and knowledge. 'There is sufficient for a man to take hold of.'

I had coloured, not used to such frankness from a woman who could either be a servant or a friend. I was never sure how I should treat her.

'Take short steps,' Mrs Macfarlane advised. 'Put one foot in front of the other and when your handsome captain is watching, emphasise the swing of your hips. Not too much, you are a lady, after all, just sufficient to attract his attention.' She bent closer to me. 'Remember that he will be watching when you walk away.'

Now, as I looked around at the ladies sweeping into the Assembly Rooms, I could compare the fashions. While all the younger ladies and some of the older had adopted the modern, more straightforward style, some of the older had clung to the old vogues that they had known in their youth. Even some of the gentlemen dismounted from their carriages in a long coat and lace waistcoat, with tight stockings and a powdered wig. One elderly lady arrived by sedan-chair carried by two sturdy Highlandmen. I looked carefully but the chairmen were not Macfarlane and MacGregor.

I had agreed to meet George Rogers inside the building, which seemed a queer arrangement but perhaps he was returning from duty or some such. I walked as sedately as I could, with the feathers in my bonnet bobbing with every step, and avoiding anything unpleasant on the road, until I entered the building.

At that moment I was concerned with the non-appearance of George Rogers. I was also slightly alarmed that nearly every woman who wore the Empire style sported a white satin hat, with at least half having a blue velvet effect in front, with a crescent of steel beside a knot of small white feathers. I wished I had studied the current trend in hats with more attention. I was out of touch with fashion. Indeed, I had coiled myself into such a tight knot of worry for so long that I was out of touch with most everything.

I heard the minuet start in the ballroom next door and began to breathe hard with anxiety. I did like to be present at the beginning, to watch the others perform the slow dance that allowed them to display their gowns and grace and to take the measure of the company. I closed my eyes, hoping that George would not let me down. Perhaps there had been another invasion alarm? No, there were too many officers present for that.

I pressed my hand against my breast, feeling the fluttering of my heart. 'It's only a silly ball,' I told myself. 'It's not life and death. George has never let you down before. Think of something else. Think how you will act when the ball begins.'

'The characteristic of a country dance is that of gay simplicity. The steps should be few and easy, and the corresponding motion of the arms and body unaffected, modest and graceful.'

I hoped I had the modesty and grace to fit into this regimental society. There was undoubtedly sufficient gayness to be seen.

'Here you are,' George Rogers limped through the crowd like a Gulliver among Lilliputians, not in height but in bearing. Even officers of superior rank granted him passage. 'I do like your hat.'

I touched my bobbing feather. 'It seems quite out of fashion.' I had wanted to scold him for his lateness, but his natural smile chased away my anger. He bowed low to me and straightened up with a snap.

'Nonsense, it is most becoming.' George brushed aside my doubts with a handful of words. 'Shall we enter?'

'To the dance,' I caught his mood.

'My apologies for being late,' George eased my temper. 'Regimental duties, I'm afraid.'

'You are here now,' I forgave him at once and took his proffered arm.

George was so late that we had completely missed the opening minuet. Once again I contemplated mentioning the fact but forbore as such words might lead to ill humour or even a quarrel. A public disagreement with one's dance partner was undoubtedly not respectable. I bit my tongue and allowed George some peace. Besides, he had apologised, he was tall and elegant, and I enjoyed having such a handsome officer on my arm. Why was I thinking such thoughts? I shook my head. Nerves; it must be nerves.

The hall was already swirling with dancers when we stepped in, with the orchestra playing some tune I knew but could not name, and everybody present either enjoying themselves or attempting to catch the eye of somebody of the opposite sex. I looked around in sudden delight, for such occasions had once been the highlight of my life. When I was younger, I did not understand women who disliked such gatherings, for where else could one gather gossip and learn the latest styles of dress and manners? Now I was not so sure. Now I saw them as parades where men pursued women until the women trapped their victim, or where packs of men selected whatever women best suited them for breeding and perhaps wealth.

Cynicism does not create joy. I tried to push the thoughts away and concentrate on the ball. George claimed me for three dances in a row and proved himself as adept on the dance floor as he apparently already had on the battlefield. His recent wound barely troubled him at all, although I noticed him wince from time to time when the dance necessitated him putting weight on his injured hip. The scandalous part of me wondered what he would say if I offered to kiss it better.

I flushed and quickly pushed that thought away. I might return to it later, I decided.

'You once told me that you danced like a carthorse,' I reminded.

'I exaggerated a little,' George admitted. 'You seemed nervous at the time.'

'You were correct.' I tapped his shoulder with my fan. 'Who taught you to dance so well?' I allowed George to guide me to the side table where the silver punch bowls stood in formal ranks beside a formidable array of cups and glasses.

'The Regiment,' Rogers helped us both to a generous cupful. 'When we were in the Low Countries we had nothing else to do but dance.'

The punch was stronger than I expected. 'Did the French dance too?' I asked, trying not to splutter in a most unladylike manner.

'Only to certain tunes,' George smiled.

'I suppose that there were ladies present?' I experienced sudden unreasoning hatred for the women who had taught him.

'There were ladies present,' George Rogers blundered on. 'Could you imagine the scene if only the officers were dancing? Why, Miss Flockhart, I might have been partnered by Major Weir there,' he gestured to a pouchy middle-aged man who had carelessly managed to lose an arm somewhere in his career. 'Or Captain Buchanan.' The captain was a tall, thin fellow with large hands and a fearful facial scar that twisted his mouth into a permanent sneer.

These men gave me pause. As George had already made clear, war was not all glory and honour. I had a brief vision of my captain lying on some foreign field with a sabre slash across his face and his arm lying at his side. The image made me shiver and put me entirely out of humour.

'What sort of women?' I asked the question I did not wish him to answer in an attempt to chase the unwelcome images from my mind.

George sipped his punch. 'There were some delightful Dutch ladies with the most charming manners.' His wink caught me off-guard, and I wondered if he were teasing me, or attempting to make me jealous.

'Oh,' I opened my fan. 'Was there any lady in particular?' I nursed false anger. I wished to be elsewhere for a spell so that I could control my sudden concern. If Mother Faa was correct and this uniformed man was to be my husband, I had no desire for him to ride into danger. The presence of some foreign woman or other was of far less interest.

'Oh, there were many,' George had no idea of the turmoil inside my head.

'I see.' I have a temper. Sometimes it is useful, and sometimes it leads me to great trouble. Now I used it unwisely. By that age, I had no foolish and over-romantic notions about men. I knew that soldiers were no angels and, in common with most women of sense, I did not expect my future husband to be lacking in experience in the bedroom. It is a strange double standard that demands total abstinence from a woman yet nearly encourages men to do the exact opposite. I am fully aware that many married ladies are very respectable on the outside while harbouring a whole nest of lovers in secret; one look at the darkened carriages in the New Town when husbands are away will prove the truth of that. However, if people conduct such affairs in private, then no harm is done. I pretended to be out of humour to rid me of my fears for George's well-being, not out of concern for his fidelity.

'Well, I think you had better return to your Low Country women.' It was the only excuse I could think of as I turned my head, unable to take my gaze from the fearfully disfigured Captain Buchanan. My poor, brave George, putting himself in danger of such a fate!

Pinning up the train of my dress to show I was available for other men to ask to dance, I finished the contents of my punch glass at a single foolish swallow, turned with a flourish and walked away. I hoped George watched me as I swung my hips to show that I was as desirable as any Dutch woman. Thank you, Mrs Macfarlane, I thought, as I caught a glimpse of his gaze concentrating on that part of me that I swivelled the most.

I had no desire to hurt him, I only wanted time to think, and if I invoked jealousy in one or both of us, well, that was a natural way to encourage love. If the captain saw I was jealous of his previous acquaintances, he would realise how I regarded him and would surely reciprocate. I started as my invitation to dance attracted another man.

'I am Sir Lancelot Snodgrass,' the gentleman bowed before me. 'Would you care to join me on the floor?'

I raised my eyebrows at this somewhat unconventional introduction. 'Well, Sir Lancelot, I would be delighted to join you.' I curtseyed, hoping that George Rogers was watching. He had already exceeded the quota of dances required to announce his affection for me. Any more would be gluttony, yet I fervently hoped that George returned to feast with me.

You will remember that in the early years of this century, the respectable people frowned on skin-to-skin touching between the sexes during a dance. However, we could talk and mingle within certain perimeters.

I did not much like the look of Sir Lancelot but once one had pinned up one's dress, one was obliged to dance with any man that asked. To turn down any dance was the height of bad manners as well as signalling one's intention never to dance again that night.

'You are from Edinburgh?' Sir Lancelot had a deep voice that matched his deep-set eyes.

'Yes,' I said as we passed each other. I did not like the touch of Sir Lancelot's hand on mine even through my glove.

'So am I.' We circled each other with him trying to catch my eye and me trying just as hard to avoid his.

'That's interesting,' I said as we passed. I hoped that George was close by for I did not care one bit for Sir Lancelot's company.

'Perhaps we are close by,' Sir Lancelot panted in my ear. 'Where do you live?'

'Where do you live?' I countered for I had no desire to reveal my address to this man.

'In the New Town,' he said.

I did not believe him. The New Town had not yet expanded to its present size, and we were a small and compact community. I knew all the faces, if not all the names. 'That's interesting.' I hoped the dance would end soon so I could escape this man with his probing eyes and lying tongue. Some men made my flesh crawl.

'I am sure I know your face,' Sir Lancelot said.

'You could have seen me around,' I said. This dance seemed interminably long. I tried to keep in step with the rest. Where was George Rogers when I needed him?

'It was a long time ago,' Sir Lancelot said, 'and I am sure you were not Miss Flockhart then.'

I had not told this man my name. Something cold seemed to clamp around my heart. 'I fear you must be mistaken,' I tried to keep my tone light as I prayed for the music to stop so I could escape.

'I am never mistaken,' Sir Lancelot put his mouth close to my ear. 'A particular friend of mine told me to look out for you.'

'Oh?' I was in an agony of discomfort. Could I pretend a twisted ankle and limp from the dance floor? I wished I had not walked away from poor George. 'And who was this particular friend, pray?'

'Mr William Turnbull,' Sir Lancelot rolled out the name as if it was a prize sweetmeat. His gaze never left my face.

'Ah,' I tried to keep the sick dismay from my face.

'We're watching you,' Sir Lancelot said. We parted, circled and returned, with my dancing partner as attentive as ever Eve's snake had been.

'That must be an immense waste of time,' I tried to keep my tone light. If I had been a man, I could have provoked this odious man to a duel and cheerfully shot him. As a woman, I lacked that outlet.

'On the contrary, Miss Flockhart, we find you immensely entertaining.' The music stopped at last, and we curtseyed and bowed. 'Mr Turnbull informed me that you have many secrets.' Sir Lancelot touched my arm. 'I am intrigued to find out more. I wonder how much the good Captain Rogers knows.' Bowing again, he sauntered away. I noticed Lady Pluscarden watching from a seat in the corner and bobbed a curtsey.

I was shaking so much that I nearly fell into my seat.

'Here you are!' George's presence was most welcome. 'I thought I had lost you in the press.' He offered a glass of punch which I accepted with alacrity.

'That's better Miss Flockhart.' He pulled a chair to my side. 'I would like to say that I had no particular friends among the Dutch women.'

I had all-but-forgotten my pretended anger with George. 'Thank you for telling me that, George.' I still could not force a smile. 'I should not have acted as I did. The fault was mine, not yours, and I hope you can forgive me.'

'There is nothing to forgive,' George said at once, and I liked him all the better for it. 'I believe I was teasing you.' He smiled. 'The matter is closed.' He frowned. 'You look a little unsettled, Dorothea. Are you unwell?'

'I just had an encounter with a thoroughly unpleasant man,' I said.

'Oh?' George looked around the room with its colourful dresses, scarlet uniforms and scattering of civilian men. His tone hardened. 'Who was it?'

'A Sir Lancelot Snodgrass,' I said. 'A horrible creature.'

George raised his eyebrows. 'Pray point him out to me.'

'No, no,' I had no desire to involve my good captain in another duel. He had not proved himself the best of shots against Gibbie, and Sir Lancelot looked like a man who would delight in putting a pistol ball in anybody's head. 'Please forget it, George. He's gone now.' This evening was not progressing as I had hoped it would.

'I'll find him,' George rose on his last word and moved through the crowd. I followed, plucking at his sleeve until he took hold of me and guided me back to my seat. 'It would be better if you remained there.'

'Please, George, let it lie,' I wished I had controlled my tongue. *Hush your tongues*, Horace had said, and he never wrote a more accurate phrase.

I watched in an agony of suspense as George drifted from man to man. I wished I had said nothing. I wished I had kept my mouth shut rather than involving a man I more than liked in affairs he could not alter.

Another dance began, and the floor became a medley of men and women, laughing, talking and enjoying life as I sat there alone and anxious. I bit my lip, hoping that George did not find Sir Lancelot.

'Miss Flockhart!' I looked up. Sir Lancelot stood in front of me with a glass in his hand and George at his side.

'I found Sir Lancelot,' Captain Rogers said.

'So I see,' I waited, with my hands coiling and uncoiling on my lap. 'I rather wish you had not.'

'I can understand that,' Sir Lancelot gave a mocking little bow.

Trying to ignore Sir Lancelot, I faced George. Somehow, I knew that things were coming to a climax. What happened in the next few minutes would decide the future of our friendship. It would either deepen or end, and at that moment I desperately hoped that George would stand by me.

'Sir Lancelot informed me that you are not who you say you are,' George's voice was as cold as Arctic ice. 'Please tell me that he is mistaken.'

When I met George's eyes, I saw pain. He was a good man and a brave man, yet he was bound by tradition and honour to do what was best for his family line. I could not lie to him, I would not lie to him, and I refused to reveal more of the truth in front of Sir Lancelot. The music died, and I was aware of Lady Pluscarden watching from her perch.

I took a deep breath and prayed that George would understand. 'I am Dorothea Flockhart,' I said. 'Sir Lancelot is a man who mingles with unsavoury characters who are not gentlemen.' I stood up, fighting the trembling of my legs. 'You, Captain Rogers, know me well enough to know I am not given to telling untruths.'

'You hide your true self,' Sir Lancelot said. 'You tell the partial truth and leave out vital intelligence. Mr Turnbull and I have had long conversations about you.'

'Then, sir, neither you nor Mr Turnbull is a true gentleman,' I wished that George would come to my aid. *Please trust me George; I cannot reveal everything.*

Do you wish me to inform this brave soldier about your past?' Sir Lancelot said.

To my great relief, George spoke out at last. 'I am sure Miss Flockhart will tell me everything in due course.' I could have hugged him.

Sir Lancelot folded his arms and stared at me. 'I will wait here until she does.'

I was not sure which emotion was uppermost, indignation, anger or fear. 'I am not here to perform at your leisure, sir!' I managed to say.

'And yet, madam,' Sir Lancelot gave a neat little bow. 'I heard that you performed for the pleasure of others.'

I stared at him, speechless with humiliation and mounting hatred. How much did that man know? How much of my past life was bandied about by Turnbull and Sir Lancelot and their circle of friends? At that minute I wished I had remained in India, anonymous among the Indians who had proved true friends. I also wished I had brought my pistols, for I would willingly have pushed one against Sir Lancelot's forehead and blown his brains out across the assembled company. Perhaps respectable ladies should not harbour such thoughts, well, this lady did, and she had another idea where to press the muzzle of her pistol that would have appalled my more traditional companions.

I looked at Captain Rogers, hoping for support. He looked shocked. 'Tell me that it's not true, Miss Flockhart.'

I could not tell him that. My tongue seemed to swell within my suddenly dry mouth so I could not articulate a single word. The memories returned in a sequence of vivid flashes, each one imprinted in my mind. I saw their faces and heard their laughter. Man after man, laughing as they came to me. Only my anger prevented me from fainting; that and my intense hatred for Sir Lancelot Snodgrass.

'Miss Flockhart?' George Rogers' voice was hard as his eyes. I was the enemy now, as much as the French had ever been. 'Is that your real name?'

'It is what she calls herself now,' Sir Lancelot spoke lightly. 'I am so glad you came to me in person, Captain. It would have been ruinous for the reputation of your family if you had spent much more time with a woman of this type.'

'Captain...' I began. The words choked in my throat. 'George... You must trust me.'

I knew it was too late. Sir Lancelot's hints of impropriety or worse had already destroyed my credibility. A gentleman and an officer, a man who possessed the King's Commission, could not be seen with a woman whose reputation was less than perfect. George had already informed me of the history of his family and his brother who had eloped with a maidservant. The Rogers family could not afford any more scandal, George's career would end, and quite possibly his regiment would ostracise him. He would be cast adrift from all good society, a man shunned.

I could not allow that to happen. I would nurse my secrets and watch my future collapse.

'What is your real name, Madam?' George Rogers' voice cracked like the wrath of God. I saw the agony in his eyes and knew he had cared for me, as I had for him.

'I am Dorothea Flockhart,' I lifted my chin stubbornly.

'And now ask her how many men she has entertained,' Sir Lancelot was enjoying himself.

That was the moment of truth. If George supported me, there was hope. If he did not, then our friendship would die. I waited, hoping.

'Well, Madam?' George asked.

I could not plead, not with Sir Lancelot watching. I did not answer. It was up to George and the trust I hoped we had built up over the past weeks.

'Goodbye, madam.' Turning on his heel, Captain Rogers marched into the crowd. He did not turn around.

Sir Lancelot gave the most elegant of little bows. 'I am sure Mr Turnbull will be calling on you soon,' he said.

I was alone, sitting on my chair in that building I had entered with such high hopes only a few hours ago. It had taken one whiff of scandal, one suggestion of impropriety for a man I liked, and who I knew liked me, to walk out of my life. I knew I would not see him again. As the first of my tears fell, I saw Lady Pluscarden start and half rise from her chair. I left the Assembly Rooms before she could talk to me, and George Street welcomed me with a blast of air that was no colder than the thoughts that crammed into my brain.

Chapter Fourteen

I will not dwell on the remainder of that night. I will only say that I returned to Thistle Street in tears, with one shoe missing, and my hair a-tangle under my broken hat.

Mrs Macfarlane nodded. 'The night did not go well, then. Come with me, Miss Flockhart,' she brought me into the drawing room and poured me a large glass of claret. 'This may help.'

I stared at her, saying nothing as my mind turned somersaults.

'Where is the elegant Captain?'

I shook my head, holding the glass in shaking hands.

'Drink,' Mrs Macfarlane lifted my hand, so the glass pressed to my lips. 'Did he misuse you, Miss Flockhart?'

I shook my head again.

'There's been bad work though,' Mrs Macfarlane nearly poured the claret down my throat. 'Bad work.' She grunted. 'Will you be seeing Captain Rogers again, Miss Flockhart?'

'No,' I managed to say.

'And why not? A well set up lady like yourself! He should be proud to know you.'

'There are things you don't know, Mrs Macfarlane.'

'We all have a past, Miss Flockhart and we all do silly things in our youth.' Mrs Macfarlane poured out another glass of claret. 'Do you wish to talk about it?'

'I can't,' I said.

'Very well, then.' Mrs Macfarlane frowned. 'Was that Turnbull fellow involved?

I nodded.

'I thought so,' Mrs Macfarlane nodded slowly. 'It's high time he was put in his place.'

I agreed. Still numb from losing George in such a manner, I could take no more. Once more at the bottom of a deep dark well, I felt as if everybody I had ever known was kicking me, even George Rogers. I wanted to strike back.

'What should we do?'

Mrs Macfarlane smiled. We will discuss that tomorrow,' she said. 'Come on, let's get you to bed.'

'Yes Mrs Macfarlane,' I said as meekly as if she had been my mother. I did not expect to sleep.

I had looked at the clock a dozen times as it approached two in the afternoon. Each tick seemed to hang in the air before it sounded, and each quivering movement of the minute hand lasted ten times as long as it should do. I took a deep breath, stood up and walked the length of the drawing room. At last, I was fighting back. Finally, I was doing something, and I felt sick. Was that because of fragile nerves? Or fear? Or was it something else? I eyed the claret and whisky decanters and wondered if I should pour myself something. The clock ticked again, another second closer to two o'clock.

I must have jumped an inch in the air when the knock came at the door. I sat down, composed myself and attempted to look calm when Mrs Macfarlane ushered Mr Turnbull into the room.

'Here is Mr Turnbull for you, Miss Flockhart.' Mrs Macfarlane kept her expression neutral.

'Thank you, Mrs Macfarlane. You'll forgive me if I don't rise, Mr Turnbull' I said.

Turnbull gave a low bow as he entered. 'Miss Flockhart,' he purred. 'How good it is to see you once more.'

I faced him from my chair. 'I won't say the same for you.'

'You know my business here,' Turnbull continued as Mrs Macfarlane withdrew, leaving the door ajar.

'How much do you want this time?'

'Alas, I fear my fortunes have dipped a little,' Turnbull said. 'I have two gentlemen who most urgently require payment.' His smile was as broad as before.

'How much?'

'Only two hundred guineas should cover my present requirements,' Turnbull said. 'And think of the consequences if I don't pay.' He shrugged. 'You already have an example with the charming Captain Rogers. How many more friends would you lose and how much more damage could the truth do?'

I tried not to allow my hatred to warn him. 'There are always consequences.'

Mrs Macfarlane had deliberately left the door open. Now Macfarlane and MacGregor entered as quietly as if they were smuggling whisky past an Exciseman. Turnbull sneered at me, unconscious that Gaelic Nemesis was only a couple of feet behind him.

'I ask for only two hundred guineas, Miss Flockhart.' Turnbull repeated. 'That's not much to preserve you good name, is it?

Without saying a word, Macfarlane lifted a hessian sack and dropped it over Turnbull's head and shoulders. He held it tight as Turnbull began to roar, but the sacking muffle his noises, and Macfarlane's arms prevented him from moving. Macgregor cracked Turnbull over the head with a life-preserver, and they both caught Turnbull as he slumped.

It was easy and quick as that. I had not had time to move.

'That's better now, Turnbull. All nice and quiet,' Macfarlane said.

'Where are you taking him?' I asked, more numbed than shocked.

'It's best you don't know.' Macfarlane lifted Turnbull as if he were a sack of potatoes and balanced him over his shoulder. 'He won't bother you again.' He gave the man a hefty smack on the breech and smiled.

I followed them down to the hall where they had left their sedan chair. The hackney-sedan was a simple affair compared to the richly decorated chairs of the wealthy. This chair was of wood covered with canvas and black leather, with a door at the front. However, Macfarlane merely lifted the hinged roof and dropped Turnbull inside so he perched on the leather seat. Leaving the sack in place, they tied Turnbull's ankles together with strong twine and wrapped more around his body so he could not move a fraction. Finally, they tied a gag around his mouth on the outside of the sack.

'That'll stop him from shouting for help if he awakes,' MacGregor explained. 'People are used to us carrying ladies home, and the occasional man who has refreshed himself too much in a tavern. They might be too interested in a man yelling for help.'

'Thank you,' I said. 'You be careful.'

Macfarlane tapped the round badge of the Society of Chairmen that was the only decoration on his sedan. 'You see that?' he indicated the motto. 'Honesty is the best policy' it read, with a crown at the top. 'We're honest men, MacGregor and me. That badge proves it.'

'Honest as a royal duke,' MacGregor agreed. 'Or a belted earl.'

'This fellow won't give us any trouble,' Macfarlane said. He touched a hand to his forehead in a gesture that was anything but servile. 'Now you don't even think about this fellow again, Miss Flockhart. He won't be bothering you or anybody else for a long time.'

'Please,' I said, 'don't kill him.'

'We're not murderers,' Macfarlane said. 'This fellow will be safe. We'll allow him back into the world sometime.' He grinned. 'Just when depends on him.'

Closing the cab of the sedan chair, they secured it with a small padlock, winked at me and each took hold of the poles. 'Good day to you, Miss Flockhart,' Macfarlane said as they lifted the chair and walked away.

Carrying a sedan chair seemed such an innocent occupation, yet these two rogues were engaged in kidnap and also in ensuring that an official trial for attempted murder did not take place. Without a witness to speak against him, Gibbie Elliot could not face a judge.

I nodded. Macfarlane had killed two birds with one stone and surely had released Marie from a great deal of heartache. I wondered anew who had given Turnbull his intelligence about me, and if I should expect another visitor with similar demands. If so, I knew now how to rid myself of the blackmailer. I wondered why I did not feel any guilt or fear for Turnbull's likely fate. Was I so hardened now?

'Mrs Macfarlane!' I shouted.

'Yes, Miss Flockhart?' Mrs Macfarlane looked so innocent it was hard to believe that she had just arranged for her husband to transport a man from Edinburgh to God knows where.

'I am going out for a while,' I said. 'I might not be back until tomorrow.'

'Yes, Miss Flockhart,' Mrs Macfarlane said. 'Are you going to try and see the captain?'

'No,' I said. 'That bird has flown from the nest.'

'He might fly back,' Mrs Macfarlane said.

I remembered the darkness in George's eyes and I knew the answer. 'He won't' I said. 'He may wish to, but he won't.'

That episode of my life was over. That hope was gone.

I had hoped to hire Mercury again but instead found myself driving a slightly battered gig out of Edinburgh and south-west to Flotterstone Manor. I was fortunate with the weather, a crisp, cold day with the surrounding fields glinting with frost and the Pentland ridge sharp-edged against a dark blue sky. Flotterstone Manor nestled in a pass into the hills, snug under Turnhouse Hill with about eight acres of policies and some ancient outbuildings. The butler who answered the door was red-faced and cheerful.

'You'll want the mistress, then,' he said at once. 'In you come.' He opened the door wide.

Elizabeth Campbell greeted me with a smile and an immediate offer of a bed for the night. 'There's rain on the way,' she said.

'I've come with good news for Marie,' I looked around the immaculate room with its furniture in the most up-to-date French fashion. Trust Elizabeth to have everything perfect.

'Oh,' Elizabeth poured me a claret and handed over the glass. The red liquid was welcome after my cold drive. 'I'm afraid she is not here.'

I sipped at the claret, wondering which smuggling lugger brought it in and what stories of adventure and daring we would never learn. 'Will she be back soon?'

'I don't think so, Dorothea. One of Gilbert's friends came for her. A tall, red-headed, raw-boned fellow I don't remember meeting.'

'Hector McAra.' I said the name as if it were the words of doom.

'That's the man!' Elizabeth said. 'He said he was looking after Tynebridge Hall while Gibbie was away.'

I remembered Weir's Inn with the gold coins glinting under the chandeliers and McAra's cold smile as he raked in all of Gibbie's possessions, including Marie. I wondered at Marie's naivety in accompanying McAra. 'When was that?' I asked.

'Three days ago,' Elizabeth said, 'yes, that's right, three days.' She puckered up her face. 'I thought it rather odd that he should come for Marie but this entire situation is a bit of a quiz, is it not?'

I shivered. Marie had been alone with McAra for three days in Tynebridge Hall while Gibbie had been locked away in the Heart of Midlothian, chained helplessly to the wall. 'I have to go to her,' I said.

I did not know what I intended doing when I got there, but I knew I must do something. Did I plan to rescue Marie? If so, how?

'I'm sure Mr McAra will look after her,' Elizabeth said. 'He sounded like a gentleman.'

'I'm sorry, Elizabeth,' I said. 'I must go now.'

'You've only just arrived! At least stay to eat,' Elizabeth said as I withdrew from that bright room to face the darkening day outside.

Elizabeth was right in one thing. The weather had taken a turn for the worse during the few minutes I had been inside her house and the early evening brought the first of what promised to be a deluge of rain. I pulled my cloak tight, hauled my hat over my head and crouched in misery over the reins.

I worked out my route as I drove, negotiating the network of old roads that crisscrossed the ancient countryside. The rain increased as darkness dragged storm-clouds from the west, hammering at the body of the gig and lashing the puddles that spread across the surface of the road. It was about fifteen miles from Flotterstone to Crichton by the country roads, and each mile brought problems of slippery mud and deep puddles. I splashed and slowed and huddled deep under the flail of driving rain that soon turned to sleet that stung my face and hands.

Darkness comes early in a Scottish January, so I scratched a flint to light the gig-lamps as I approached the final few miles to Crichton. The yellow light pooled along the side of the road as I approached Tynebridge Hall.

The left-hand lantern flickered and then died. Pulling the horse to a halt, I dismounted and checked the oil. The reservoir was empty, and there was no spare in the boot of the gig. Cowering under the sting of the sleet, I pulled myself back into the driving seat and snapped the whip. I would have to continue with a single lamp.

We rolled on with the wind increasing, blasting the gig with pieces of twigs from the nearby trees and flattening the mane of my poor misused horse. I could not restrain my yelp as something crashed against my remaining lamp, nearly knocking it from its brackets and cracking the glass. Fortunately, the light still burned, so I was not driving blind. I continued, happier now that I was in familiar territory around Crichton and with the lamp hanging loose, now showing the muddy road, now the fields and woods at the side.

The lights of Tynebridge Hall showed intermittently through the madly thrashing trees, one second visible and the next gone as the branches swayed back and forward. My sole light showed the road leading to the hall. I eased the gig onto the approaches of the hump-back Royal Union Bridge and swore as my lantern flickered and finally died.

'Come on there!' I shouted to my horse, peering into the darkness ahead. Confident that I knew the lie of the road, I flicked the reins. 'Get along!'

I heard the rushing water as the River Tyne funnelled into the gorge beneath the bridge, and I pushed forward. For some reason I laughed, momentarily crazy as the gig rose up on the hump-backed bridge, and then I heard the terrible thunder as the water tore away the stone foundations of the ancient structure.

'Oh, dear God!' I hauled back on the reins. 'Stop! Stop!'

The horse gave a loud neigh as its hooves pawed empty air where the bridge should be. I felt the gig falter and then I was falling from my perch, forward into the dark. The cold water closed above my head, and I was struggling, carried forward in the current.

Chapter Fifteen

When I tried to scream for help, water rushed into my mouth, choking me, burning my chest as I swallowed in a mad attempt to drink the river away. The Tyne was terrifyingly cold and immensely powerful as it carried me down, battered me off a rock and tossed me head over heels along the course of the river. I struggled, trying to swim, trying to find a rock to cling to, trying to end my mad passage. I swallowed water, no longer thinking logically, not knowing what to do. I smashed into something substantial, realised it was the trunk of a tree trapped between two rocks, grabbed hold and clung on tight.

Gasping, I looked around, seeing only churning water and the darkness of rocks. I gagged, kicked with my feet and felt no bottom. My hands slipped on the wet wood as my strength gave out and I began to slide away. Was this death and the end of all my troubles? For a moment I was tempted to release my grip and allow the river to take me.

'Hold still!' I heard the voice. 'I'm coming for you!'

Water closed over my head. I clawed at the tree, feeling my fingernails bend and break. I could see nobody.

'Hold on!'

'I can't,' I tried to shout, and my grip eased away. I knew it was death and it did not matter. I let go and felt strong hands on my arms.

I struggled, kicking my feet and flailing my arms. 'Let me go,' I pleaded. 'Let me go.'

Something slapped me hard across the face, shocking me into stability. I gasped and tried to speak, only to swallow another mouthful of bitter cold water.

'Keep still!' That voice again, hard and commanding. This time I obeyed and felt somebody dragging me through the water. I could feel the river bed under my feet now and pushed on sliding stones.

'That's the way,' the voice encouraged. In the dark, I could not see who it was. It was a man for sure, a man with a white shirt. He pulled me out of the water and laid me face down on the banking. I retched, spewing water as he pummelled my ribs.

'You're killing me,' I said.

'Breathe!' my torturer ordered.

I tried to breathe, drawing great whooping dollops of air into my lungs, each one burning like liquid fire. I vomited again, getting rid of vast quantities of water with sounds and gestures that were anything but ladylike.

'That's the way, throw it all up.'

I gasped and heaved with my head splitting in pain and my throat and chest burning. 'Oh, dear God,' I said.

'That sounds healthy,' the man held me as I suffered. 'You're all right.'

'I don't feel all right,' I said.

'Better and better!' There was humour in the voice. 'Women never complain when they are ill, only when they are recovering.'

I wanted to slap this man who had saved my life.

'Come on.' I knew that voice. I wanted to find out who he was. He lifted me bodily in both arms and carried me along the bank of the river. I looked up.

'Doctor Hetherington,' I said.

'That's me,' the doctor agreed. 'Come now, and we'll get you somewhere dry and warm, or you'll end up with a pneumonic infection.'

'Doctor Hetherington,' I repeated. 'My horse?'

'You're more important than a horse,' the doctor said. 'We'll get you safe first.' He opened his front door with his foot and brought me inside. 'I seem to be in the habit of carrying you into my house.'

'Yes Doctor,' I said and was promptly sick over his floor.

'Let's get you out of these wet clothes to bed.' Doctor Hetherington sat me in one of the two chairs that stood on either side of his fire.

'No, no.' I shook my head. 'You can't. I must get to Tynebridge Hall and see Marie.'

'Not tonight,' the doctor said. 'Stay there until I can get the bed warmed up.' He poked the fire and added more coal. The flames shot up, orange-red and welcome.

'I must get to Marie.' I stood up, wavered and promptly fell. Doctor Hetherington picked me from the floor.

'Warm clothes and bed,' he said, 'and anything else can wait until morning.'

'No!' I fought him. I fought him with every ounce of my remaining strength as he stripped me naked and produced a large towel.

'Stand still!' His towelling was rough as first and gentled as I stopped struggling. He missed no part of me as I stood there, shivering in front of his fire, embarrassed beyond measure and not in the slightest afraid. 'You have many old scars, a few new bruises, cuts and abrasions but nothing's broken except two fingernails. Now, put this on.' He handed me a flannel nightshirt he had been warming over the back of his chair.

'That's yours,' I said.

'Yes.' Taking away the towel so for a moment I stood as naked as the day I was born, he draped the nightshirt over my head and pulled it down. It swamped me, being far too large yet very comfortable.

'There now,' for some reason Doctor Hetherington gave my hair a final rub with the towel and pulled it away from my eyes. 'You look very fetching. Now, get through the room and into bed with you.'

'You can't do this,' I said.

'In.' He lifted me as if I were a baby, carried me into his bedroom and rolled me between the covers. I had not seen him put the warming pan into the bed, but now he moved it away, leaving only the residual warmth.

'Marie,' I said.

'Go to sleep,' Doctor Hetherington said and tucked me up. I looked up at his battered face with that broken nose and wide mouth and knew he was by far the ugliest man I had ever seen, and I did not care.

I closed my eyes, still hearing the roar of the river, and then I drifted away to a place I had not been in for years. I felt my temperature rise and the visions returned. I felt hands on me, and I screamed, kicking out. I did not see the doctor. I saw that other man from ten years and more ago on that terrible day in the grounds of Tynebridge Hall. I heard the baying of hounds and the mocking laughter of the hunters. I remembered the fear and my screams as I ran through the thorns and brambles of the undergrowth.

I screamed out then, and thrashed on that bed, with the leering faces peering down at me, laughing as the dogs pinned me to the ground. I cowered, trying to cover my face, trying to cover my person, howling in fear and pain.

The doctor was there, watching over me. He could not help me. Nobody could help me as I writhed; screaming as the men and laughing women surrounded me. I fought them, oh, God how I fought them, slashing with my nails and kicking as they ripped the shreds of clothes from me. I remembered my screams; they were real in that night of horror; they were the only thing I could control. I remembered the terror. I still do and always will.

I came back to reality sodden with perspiration and with the covers a tangled mess around me. Doctor Hetherington was looking at me with concern in his eyes. 'Hello, Miss Flockhart.'

'Hello, Doctor Hetherington.' I replied automatically and looked down at myself. 'I'm naked.'

'You had a fever,' the doctor gently removed the damp cover and placed a blanket over me. 'I had to cool you down.'

I closed my eyes. I could not think clearly.

'Now we have to get your strength back.'

'What day is it?' I looked around. Weak sunlight seeped through the window, catching motes of dust as it alighted on the doctor's face. He looked tired and had not shaved for some days. The stubble emphasised the firm line of his jaw and his high cheekbones.

'Tuesday, I think,' Doctor Hetherington said. 'Perhaps Wednesday.'

'What day did I come here?'

'Saturday.' Doctor Hetherington put a hand on my forehead. 'Rest now. You need food and sleep.'

'I can't,' I said. 'Marie is in danger.'

'You've been in some danger yourself,' Doctor Hetherington said. 'You have old scars on your body and in your mind.'

'How do you know? What did I say?' I felt the colour rush to my face.

'Get some rest now.'

'I won't rest until I know what I said.' I tried to sit up.

'You seem to have been hunted by men and dogs,' Doctor Hetherington told me.

I nodded. Perhaps it was exhaustion made the tears flow unheeded from my eyes. Suddenly I felt a desperate need to tell somebody what had happened and this doctor already knew more about me than anybody else. He had indeed seen more of me than anybody else. I had the sudden realisation that I found it easier to talk to this ugly man than to anybody else.

'That's what happened, men and dogs.' I heard the rasp in my voice and began to talk, relieving myself of a burden I had carried for ten years. 'I was engaged to marry Lord Findhorn.'

Doctor Hetherington nodded. 'I did not know that you had such high connections.'

'I did,' I said. 'However, Lord Findhorn liked the cards.' His Lordship had been my first connection with a gambling man. 'Even so, I trusted him. He was older than me by ten years, and I fell for his smooth experience. I was not the first woman he had charmed.'

'How old were you?' Doctor Hetherington asked.

'Nineteen,' I said. 'I was a young nineteen and Findhorn wrapped me around his little finger.'

The doctor nodded. 'Men like Findhorn look for young women. They know exactly what to say and how to act to make themselves attractive to you.'

I remembered the smiles and the promises, the small gifts of jewellery and items of clothing. 'Findhorn proposed. He said we should get married somewhere romantic. I agreed, and he said he would make all the arrangements.'

'Did your parents not have a say in things?'

'They both died when I was young,' I said. 'A succession of elderly aunts cared for me. My final aunt was pleased to relinquish her responsibilities when Findhorn turned up.'

'He hunted you down,' Doctor Hetherington said.

I had not thought of that. 'Perhaps he did.'

'Did you get married?'

I was silent for a long time, listening to an array of small birds cheeping and chirping in the doctor's garden.

'We went through a wedding ceremony,' I remembered my happiness at having caught such a man as Lord Findhorn. I remembered looking at Findhorn as we stood in the courtyard of Crichton Castle as the tall and surprising debonair minister intoned the sacred words. I remembered my delight as Findhorn kissed me and the assembled guests had cheered and clapped.

'I had no friends there, except those I had met through Findhorn.'

'Why was that?' Doctor Hetherington asked.

'I knew few people,' I said. 'I had moved around from aunt to aunt and place to place.'

'Your life was difficult.' Doctor Hetherington said.

I did not reply to that. 'After the wedding ceremony, Lord Findhorn held the celebrations in Tynebridge Hall.'

'I understand,' Doctor Hetherington said.

'Do you?' I instantly regretted the edge of my voice. It was not the doctor's fault. 'His Lordship brought around a group of his friends and their women.'

I remember that while the men scared me, the women terrified me. Horrid women of the worst sort, with loud, abrasive voices and cheap finery, long nails and bold eyes, they had viewed me with a mixture of contempt and aggression as they vied for the attention of the men. Until that day I had believed I could control His Lordship, I had honestly thought that his affection for me would prove stronger than his love for the turn of a card. I had not learned that a gambler loses his mind, his senses and his soul the instant a dice is thrown or a pack of cards produced.

To let you understand, in my time men would gamble on anything, from the speed of a horse to a feat of endurance. Findhorn combined that passion with a lust for power over anybody, especially women.

'The carriages were lined up outside the hall, gleaming in the rain and with moonshine reflecting from the coachwork.' I could still see the horses tossing their manes and the coachmen sitting in patient groups, smoking their long pipes. I did not understand their mocking looks at me as I entered Tynebridge Hall in my wedding dress.

Doctor Hetherington sat in the corner of the room, listening to everything I said, his ugly, tired face concerned. I knew he understood as I unburdened my soul of ten years of torment.

'They gathered upstairs, the same room that Marie had her wedding breakfast, with the chandeliers swinging slowly above and the smoke from a dozen pipes spiralling. The men were loud, the women louder and I tried to catch His Lordship's attention. He ignored me. The cards called loudest of all.'

Doctor Hetherington nodded again. 'If speaking of this upsets you, Miss Flockhart, don't continue.'

They had placed the long oval table in the centre of the room and gathered around, yelling and shouting. The cards flicked back and forth, with gloating winners and swearing losers and sometimes His Lordship was in the former camp and sometimes in the latter. They had a break about midnight, and somebody began to sing. One of the women danced, leaping on top of the table to shake and gyrate as the men clapped and roared. Within a few moments, she was peeling off her clothes, and the men were grabbing at her, caressing and touching, stroking and slapping as she moved from one to the other, laughing. She enjoyed the attention and the hands as much as the men did.

'I think we should go now,' I whispered to His Lordship.

'The fun is just beginning,' he said and slid his hand up the length of the woman's leg. She pushed against him, and he ripped her skirt off.

'My Lord!' I said, and he laughed again. 'My husband.' He laughed at that, with his eyes wild and his mouth open.

'Husband,' he repeated, and his companions roared their amusement.

Doctor Hetherington lit his pipe and inhaled, watching me, allowing me to relive that night. His eyes were thoughtful. 'This Lord Findhorn laughed when you reminded him you were married?' He asked.

'Yes,' I said.

Doctor Hetherington nodded. 'Continue if you wish.'

'The woman danced for some time and then one of the men, Old Q I think, lifted her and carried her away. I did not watch, and I did not see her again. There were other women, other dancers. The cards came out once more, with higher stakes and loud cursing when men lost.' I closed my eyes, remembering.

'His Lordship gambled and lost, gambled and lost and eventually, he had nothing left. The men were roaring at him, and he pointed to me and said. 'You can have her.'

I shook my head, trying to make it into a joke. 'I am your wife!' I shouted.

They laughed again, and one pointed to the door where somebody lounged, watching. I looked, and the man sauntered across, smirking. It was the minister; or rather the man I had believed was the minister, a tall, red-haired fellow by the name of Duncan McAra.

'Please remind his Lordship,' I pleaded. 'You are a man of the cloth.'

'I am no more a minister than you,' the man said, and his laugh cut deeply into me.

Doctor Hetherington removed the pipe from his mouth. Leaning across to me, he touched my arm. 'Stop if you wish, Miss Flockhart. You don't have to say more.'

'Yes I do,' I said. 'Please, Doctor.'

Doctor Hetherington sat back again. 'I'm listening, Miss Flockhart.'

I told him what happened next. I could not believe that the whole thing had been a quiz, a lark, a trick and I was the victim of a piece of cruelty so horrible I still found it hard to believe.

'They grabbed me and threw me on the table as if I was a slab of meat. I struggled, screaming, and the men held me down and played the cards on my stomach, banging their hands on them and laughing.'

'Oh, dear God in heaven,' Doctor Hetherington shook his head. 'Oh, dear God. You were only nineteen.'

'His Lordship lost,' I said. 'I was handed over to the man who won that hand.' I felt the perspiration soaking through the sheet that covered me as I remembered that day. 'The false minister: Duncan McAra.'

I recalled his leering face with the red hair tied back in a neat queue and the perfect white teeth. 'You're mine,' he said and began to paw at me. I screamed and clawed at him, drawing blood from his face. He had squealed like a baby and recoiled, then slapped me so hard that I was dazed.

That made everybody laugh, so Duncan McAra slapped me again, knocking my head back and forward. 'I lost a tooth,' I opened my mouth wide and showed the doctor the gap.

'It's not noticeable.' Doctor Hetherington assured me.

I no longer cared if it was or not.

'One of the women shouted for a hunt, and before I knew what was happening, they were chanting 'hunt, hunt, hunt', with the woman encouraging the men and Findhorn as vocal as the rest.

They dragged me outside the house and into the grounds. They were laughing, baying like hounds and giggling, all at the same time, men and women together, including my Lord Findhorn and Duncan McAra.

I remember pleading to be released, begging them to stop as they spun me around and around until I was quite sick with dizziness, and then they pushed me away and told me to run. I did not know what was about to happen; I only knew it would be unpleasant and I ran.

'Now!' One of the women yelled. 'Now!'

I heard the hounds baying, and I screamed and ran and ran. I was dizzy with the spinning, and I staggered. I was never more scared than that night.

'Miss Flockhart,' Doctor Hetherington's hand was firm on my shoulder. 'Don't upset yourself.'

'I can't help it,' I said, as the tears flowed freely. 'I can't help it.'

I was crying freely now as the memories took control. 'I was only nineteen years old,' I said. 'I had no idea about life.'

Doctor Hetherington was beside me, holding me as I spoke. I gabbled out the words as I sought to release myself from the memories that had shackled me for so long.

'They released the hounds and hunted me down as if I were a fox. I ran into the woods. I remember the bushes and the thorns and the mud as I ran and ran and the hounds nipped and tore at my heels and then the laughter, the cruel, loud laughter. The teeth were not as painful as the mockery as Findhorn and McAra, and the others followed me, with the brazen laughter of the women screeching in my ears.

'Miss Flockhart.' Doctor Hetherington was kneeling at my side. 'You don't have to carry on now.'

For once, Doctor Hetherington was mistaken. I did have to carry on. I had to speak out the memories. 'The dogs pulled me down and worried me until the men came up, and the women with them. I lay in a ball among the thorns and the brambles, with the rain driving down on me and the lanterns bouncing yellow light through the trees. They surrounded me, the men and women and then His Lordship loomed over me.

'I gambled you and lost,' he said. 'Now Duncan owns you.'

'They held me down. The women held me down.'

The faces surrounded me, leering, mocking, joking, bloated white faces and thin, shaking faces, women with savage eyes and men full of lust. Lord Findhorn was grinning. 'We enjoyed the chase, and now you will entertain us further.' I hated that word, entertain. It should have been a happy word. When Turnbull had said that word at the Assembly Rooms, I had nearly fainted. I could not have admitted the experience to George Rogers for decent, dependable man that he was; he would never understand the sheer horror of such an ordeal. George enjoyed excitement; he revelled in danger; he could never have put himself in the place of a woman, helpless in the grip of such people. That was a barrier he could never breach.

I broke down then and stopped talking. I did not need to say more. Doctor Hetherington knew what would happen next and I could not speak.

'It's done now,' Doctor Hetherington took me in his arms. 'Oh, you poor wee soul. It's all done now.'

It was not of course. Experiences of that nature are never done. They are always there, lurking in the shadows of one's mind, waiting to return, waiting to revisit one with nightmares that are all the worse because they are true. I will never be free of these memories.

I felt safe in the doctor's arms. I felt safe as I cried, and I did not care that he saw me at my most vulnerable and at my worst. Somehow I knew that whatever else happened in the world, I had turned a corner, and things would never be the same again.

'They raped me.' I said. 'All of them, all the men as the women jeered and held me.'

The words were said. The memory I had blocked out for ten years was out and I relived every last, odious second. I spoke them to the doctor's battered face, and he listened with his arms around me. I did not tell him everything. Some things I held to myself; one was the final, terrible sorrow; the other was only my secret.

Chapter Sixteen

'I've never told anybody that before,' I sipped at my dish of tea, feeling utterly drained and so weak a puff of wind could blow me away.

'Thank you,' Doctor Hetherington said.

'Why are you thanking me?' I asked.

'Thank you for your trust,' Doctor Hetherington had aged considerably over the last few days.

With the fire bright in the grate and a weak winter sun illuminating the room, I felt better. Or perhaps I felt better because I had told somebody about my ordeal. I was not sure. I closed my eyes, more relaxed than I had been for many years, although the worry of Marie still tugged at my mind.

'You went to India shortly afterwards,' Doctor Hetherington said.

'Yes. When the men left me, I ran away.' I did not go into details.

'How?' Doctor Hetherington passed over a hunk of bread-and-cheese. There was no delicacy in his house. Everything was functional, battered and dependable, rather like the man himself.

'How?' I repeated the question, temporising as I considered my answer.

'You were nineteen, you were alone, and you must have been in a state of nervous distress.' Doctor Hetherington said. 'There is more.'

I could not escape those kind eyes. I knew that the doctor was trying to help, however uncomfortable I felt. 'There is more,' I said.

'You don't have to tell me,' Doctor Hetherington said. 'But it will help if you do.'

I did have to tell him. I had thought to keep that last horror to myself. I was wrong. I needed to reveal it to somebody so that no Turnbull or another of his ilk could bring it up in the future. I looked away, gathering my strength.

'What happened to the child?'

I started. That was a brutal question, asked in the doctor's most gentle voice. 'You know?' I stared at him in appalling confusion.

'I'm a doctor.' Doctor Hetherington said. 'There were signs.'

'Oh, God.' I began to shake. Automatically, I bit into my bread-and-cheese, chewing without taste as the darkness within my head cracked open.

Doctor Hetherington waited at my side.

'Yes.' I said. 'When I left Tynebridge Hall I did not know where to go. I had only my one remaining aunt, so I ran there and told her. She was scandalised and blamed me.' I felt the bitterness rise. 'She told me it was my fault; I must have provoked the gentlemen. So she sent me as far away as she could. She paid my passage to India in the hope of what? Of never seeing me again, no doubt, so I could not bring disgrace to the family.'

The bread-and-cheese was finished. I took the doctor's and started on that as he watched and listened. I had never met a man who listened to me before, and ten years of repressed bitterness and sorrow came out.

'There was no fault in you,' Doctor Hetherington began, but I interrupted him with my memories, and he closed his mouth, sat back in his chair and listened.

'Perhaps my aunt realised my condition; if so she did not say and I did not know until I was on the Indiaman bound east. I was nineteen, alone, scared and with a child, the father of whom I did not know.'

The memory of that voyage returned, the howl of the wind through the rigging, the swaying and creaking of the ship, the ranks of cannon on deck and the flying fish as we reached the tropics.

'There was one woman who befriended me.' She was a sergeant's wife, broad of face, of body and experience. Mrs Kelly, from County Clare and she saved my life if not my sanity. 'I lost the child. I lost my daughter one night of never-ending storms as we rounded the Cape of Good Hope.'

No woman who has lost a child needs to hear more than those few words. However, I did not think that any man would understand until I saw the empathetic pain in Doctor Hetherington's eyes.

'We buried her at sea, and that night I tried to follow her. Mrs Sergeant Kelly stopped me. She was a drunken, foul-mouthed woman with the kindest heart in the world.'

'Good people come in time of need,' Doctor Hetherington touched my arm and my heart. 'The best angels have dirty wings and clean souls.'

I was not crying. I was releasing myself and saying goodbye to the daughter I had never named or acknowledged. 'She is at peace now,' I said. Now I could mourn her. Now I had admitted her presence and her early death I could say goodbye.

'Yes, your daughter is at peace now.' Doctor Hetherington touched my arm, once. 'And you can also find rest.'

How had he known? I looked away, wondering if he could see inside my head. I did not talk in detail about India. There was no need. 'After eight years I came home,' I said.

Doctor Findhorn nodded. 'You did,' he said. 'Do you know why?'

'Perhaps,' I said, and left it at that. I had retained one item of information to myself. I had told the doctor more than anybody else. I had not told him everything.

Doctor Hetherington cut another slice of bread, smeared it with butter and added a generous hunk of cheese. 'You are a brave woman.'

'I don't feel brave,' I said.

'It was brave to return here.' The doctor said. 'What about Lord Findhorn?'

'I have not seen Findhorn from that day to this.'

Doctor Hetherington nodded. 'That will be a blessing.'

'Now Marie is in a similar situation,' I remembered why I had made that mad dash across Midlothian. 'Hector McAra is the son of Duncan McAra. I cannot allow history to repeat itself.'

'I will come with you to see her,' Doctor Hetherington said. 'Between the two of us, we should be able to help her.'

'You don't have to,' I said. 'It's not your fight.'

'Marie Elliot is my patient,' Doctor Hetherington said. He stood up and spoke quietly, 'and you are my friend, I hope.'

I needed a friend. I needed somebody on who I could rely, somebody who I could talk to and who would listen to me. 'I would like you to be a friend,' I wondered if I was merely looking for an anchor after George Rogers had left me. I did not think so. I hoped not. 'I would like you to be a friend,' I repeated.

The doctor held my gaze for a long second, smiled and looked away and yet in that time I saw an inexpressible yearning in his eyes, something I had never seen before. I did not know what it was.

'When shall we visit the Hall?' I asked.

'As soon as you are fit,' Doctor Hetherington said.

'Now,' I decided. I could not resist the impulse to touch the doctor's arm. 'Thank you, Doctor,' I said.

'That's what friends are for.'

I think we understood each other. I hoped Doctor Hetherington did not mind that I had eaten most of the bread in his house.

We stood looking at the wreckage of the Royal Union Bridge for five minutes before deciding that the river was impassable at that spot. The Tyne frothed through the gorge in a chaos of creamy brown water and surging foam, leaping over rocks and roaring over the tops of fallen trees. I remembered the gig plunging down the embankment that night and my fear in the water. I had wanted to drown. I had wanted to follow my daughter into the water.

'You saved my life,' I said.

The doctor pointed to the remains of the bridge. 'The Royal Union is broken,' he said.

He was correct. The old coat of arms had split in two under pressure of the water, so the unicorn pranced alone with its horn thrusting toward the gap. 'Oh, dear God,' I said, as I remembered the words of Mother Faa: 'Take care, Dorothea Flockhart, and be careful of the horned beast.'

I had thought that Turnbull was the horned beast. Perhaps Mother Faa had meant the unicorn and the bridge that collapsed. What else had she said? 'The horned beast that will bring death or happiness.' I had cheated death, thanks to Doctor Hetherington. Would happiness come through my admissions? I did not know.

A hundred yards downstream, the wreckage of the gig had been washed up and lay in a ragged line of splintered wood and torn leather. I was lucky to have escaped with only a soaking and a few minor scrapes and bumps.

'My poor horse,' I said.

'Your poor horse is at this minute grazing in the field of Jock Moffat, at my expense,' Doctor Hetherington said. 'He was out of the river before you were.'

'Thank you, Doctor. I am in your debt.'

'There are no debts between friends.' Doctor Hetherington's battered face suited this ancient, wild area. 'There is a footbridge quarter of a mile downstream if the river has not washed it away.'

After the torrential weather of my arrival, this day was crisp and calm, with the trees clutching at the sky and a few birds chattering among the branches. Underfoot, the first of the snowdrops were fighting through the mud, with a scattering of daffodil shoots showing yellow-tinged green. Spring was easing in, pushing aside winter's rearguard action and bringing the promise of new life.

'Come on, Doctor,' I lengthened my stride. 'I'm worried about Marie.'

The footbridge was of wood, three planks wide with a straightforward handrail of untrimmed logs. It shook as we walked across and within a few moments, we were in the policies of Tynebridge

Hall, where once-well-cared-for gravel walks were now neglected, and the wind had ravaged avenues of tall trees.

'This place needs looking after,' Doctor Hetherington said. 'I don't know who the owner is now, but he is neglecting his duties.'

'They won't welcome us,' I felt my heart-beat increase as it always did when I came to this place. I was glad of the doctor's company although for one moment I wished that George was here with his confident stride and his military experience. Feeling guilty at my lack of trust, I glanced sideways at Doctor Hetherington's battered, pugnacious, understanding face and reached out to him.

'I'm glad you're here, doctor.'

There were lights on in the Hall, and the sound of rough male laughter coming from the open windows. With my heart now pounding, I knew that if I hesitated, I would not be able to continue, so stalked to the front door and hammered the door knocker as if I were demanding entrance at the Pearly Gates.

I did not know the manservant who answered. 'We wish to speak to Marie Elliot,' I said at once. 'My name is Dorothea Flockhart, and this is Doctor Mungo Hetherington.'

The servant eyed me up and down as if I were not good enough to stand at his front door. 'Wait here,' he commanded.

'We'll wait inside,' I decided for him, pushing past.

The outer hall was a shambles, with furniture out of place and a picture hanging lop-sided on the wall. There were empty bottles in one corner, and the floorboards were dirty and scuffed.

'The servants need a good roasting,' Doctor Hetherington murmured. I agreed, silently, and stiffened as the inner door opened and Duncan McAra pushed through. In his shirt sleeves and the tight breeches that all men seemed to wear that season, he looked very casual.

'Good morning Miss Flockhart.' McAra sneered at me. 'How nice of you to visit.' His bow was low and, I thought, mocking.

'Good morning Mr McAra,' I responded with a curtsey. 'Doctor Hetherington and I are looking for Marie Elliot.'

'Alas, you have had a wasted journey, I fear,' McAra said. 'The fair Marie is no longer here.'

'Yet this is her home,' I was not prepared to let go as easily as that. 'Her husband leases it.'

'And I look after it for him,' McAra was as smooth as a silk sheet, 'until he returns from his present predicament. You do remember that he is in *durance vile* for duelling with your old paramour?' He shook his head. 'They were such naughty boys.'

I stiffened at the term paramour and tried to remain polite. 'Could you tell me where Marie is?'

'I believe she has returned to one of her friend's houses,' McAra said with a shrug. 'Elizabeth Campbell perhaps, or Emily Napier. I don't recall which.'

Other men were arriving in the inner hall, tall, leering men who reeked of wealth and vice. One stood in the shadows like a sinister statue. I fought the shake in my legs. 'Oh, I know she is not with Elizabeth Campbell,' I said.

'Mrs Napier then. Try there.' McAra said. 'Now if that is all, I must bid you farewell. We have things to do.'

'We have things to do,' one of the grinning mountebanks repeated and laughed.

'When did Mrs Elliot leave?' Doctor Hetherington asked.

'How the devil should I know, Doctor?' McAra shook his head. 'I am a gentleman, not a country saw-bones. I have better things to do than look after every stray woman that visits my house. Now go and mix some potions or whatever you do.'

'This is not your house,' I tried to control my temper. 'Gibbie Elliot leases this house.'

'Did you not hear about him?' McAra nearly laughed in my face. 'I won everything he has over the card table. Everything, all his money, all his possessions, his chariot and even his wife. I have taken over the lease of this house and all in it.'

'All in it!' the fools at the back repeated.

'And as for you, Doctor, your house is leased from the estate,' McAra said. 'I hold Elliot's lease now so I'd thank you to keep a civil tongue in your head or you'll find yourself evicted, bag and baggage, without notice.'

'Without notice!' the words were repeated. 'Go on, Hector, evict the saw-bones!'

'Come on, Miss Flockhart,' Doctor Hetherington said. 'We're getting nowhere here.'

'Yes, come on, Miss Flockhart,' McAra said. 'You're getting nowhere here.'

'I feel so frustrated,' I said as the front door banged shut and mocking laughter erupted from within, 'and now I've dragged you into this affair.'

'I dragged myself,' Doctor Hetherington said. 'I'm not sure if he can evict me. Elliot is the leaseholder at present, and I don't think that even he has that power.'

'Gibbie Elliot has a six-month lease,' I earned a curious look from the doctor for that piece of intelligence. 'The lease-holder has no power to evict without the permission of the property owner.'

'Whoever that is,' Doctor Hetherington said.

'Whoever that is,' I agreed.

We stood outside the Hall for a few moments while the sound of laughter inside increased.

'Let's look around,' I said. 'I'm not convinced that Marie left.'

Doctor Hetherington frowned. 'What do you mean? Hector McAra told us she had.'

'I know,' I said, 'and he is a gentleman isn't he?' I did not need to inject bitterness into my voice. It arrived without any conscious volition on my part. 'I know enough about gentlemen not to trust anything they say or do.'

Doctor Hetherington nodded. 'I understand,' he said.

As we walked around the house, I stared at the windows, wondering what was going on inside. 'If I had my way,' I said. 'I would burn the place down, so not a single stone, not one charred stick remained.'

'The owner may not approve,' Doctor Hetherington said.

'Would you do the same?' It was not a test. I genuinely wondered how the doctor thought.

Doctor Hetherington considered for a moment. 'Perhaps,' he said cautiously, 'if I could replace it with something better.'

We had reached the back of the building, where the windows of the guest bedrooms overlooked the policies. 'Look up there,' I said.

Doctor Hetherington followed my unladylike pointing finger. 'What am I looking for?'

'At this time of the day all the guest windows should be in darkness,' I said. 'But that one, at the very top, has a light burning. A candle perhaps.'

'Maybe a servant left a candle on.' Doctor Hetherington said.

'Did you see any servants?' I asked, 'save for that useless butler who answered the door? The place is a mess.'

'Trust a woman to notice that,' Doctor Hetherington said. 'I see I shall have to keep my house tidier in future.'

'I think that's Marie up there.' I appreciated the attempt at humour. 'I think she's locked in that room.'

'Why would McAra do that?' Doctor Hetherington asked. 'Or… Oh, good God in his heaven.'

I shivered. 'I think we can both guess.' I narrowed my eyes and stared up at the window, trying to peer through the small panes. 'I'm not leaving her here.'

Doctor Hetherington looked away. 'I rather thought that. What would you have me do?'

'I don't wish to involve you, Doctor,' I said. 'These are dangerous men.'

'What would you have me do?' The doctor repeated. He was obviously a stubborn man.

The idea came to me fully formed. 'First I need to borrow your dog cart,' I said. 'I have a couple of men I need to recruit.'

The doctor glanced at the sky. 'It will be dark in an hour.' He did not seem surprised at my sudden enthusiasm.

'We'll leave before dawn tomorrow,' I said, already relying on the doctor being a man of his word. 'First, I wish to look through the remains of my gig. There is something I would like to retrieve.'

The wreckage littered a quarter of a mile of the river bank, shattered pieces of wood and strips of leather and metal lying in forlorn memory of a once-useful vehicle.

'What are we looking for?' Doctor Hetherington asked.

'A long rectangular box,' I said. 'It's made of rosewood if that is any use.'

'No use at all,' the doctor said.

Concentrating on the rim of flotsam that marked the high flood mark, we searched by the dying light of the January day, lifting every piece of broken wood and looking under leaves and bushes. When the light faded, the good doctor brought a couple of lanterns and the yellow light pooled over the tangled undergrowth and reflected from the rippling brown water.

I saw the robin first, standing upright on a smooth surface, and immediately I know that it marked my box. 'Thank you,' I said as I lifted the box. The robin flew away, complaining that I had disturbed his perch.

'What is it?' Doctor Hetherington watched as I flicked open the catch.

'Two Joseph Manton pistols.' I showed him the pair in their nest of green. Both were sodden despite the box, but once I dried them off and cleaned them up, they would be functional. 'Do you have any gunpowder?'

'I have,' the doctor glanced at the pistols without interest. 'I own a fowling piece.'

'Good. My powder is damp.'

'That's not surprising. Why do you have the guns?' Doctor Hetherington showed no interest in my prize.

'After what happened, do you have to ask?' Lifting one pistol, I sighted along the barrel, seeing McAra's lean face. I cocked the piece and pressed the trigger, hearing the click as the hammer fell. In my mind's eye, I saw the lead ball fly from the barrel to strike McAra right in the centre of his forehead. And then it was not Hector McAra but Duncan, his father. That face metamorphosed into Lord Findhorn's and I shuddered and looked away.

'Miss Flockhart?' The doctor sounded concerned.

'I'm all right,' I lowered the pistol. 'And Doctor, please call me Dorothea.'

A slow smile spread across the doctor's face. 'I am Mungo.'

I curtsied, and the doctor bowed. We looked at each other and, to the pits of hell with propriety, I held out my hand. 'You're a good man, Doctor.'

His grip was firm and his smile genuine. We held each other's hand for longer than was necessary and I did not wish to let go.

We left an hour before dawn, moving without lights until we were clear of Crichton and then whipping up the horse and heading north toward Edinburgh. The road was dry, and lights glimmered in the farm-steadings that we passed. I could smell the freshness of spring in the air. In other circumstances, I would have enjoyed the day, but instead, I thought of Marie.

'Where are we headed?' Doctor Hetherington had not objected when I took the reins.

'Canonmills Bridge,' I said. 'There are a couple of sedan-chair carriers I know there.'

'Sedan-chair carriers? What are you planning?' Doctor Hetherington asked.

'I'm planning to rescue Marie,' I said.

'With a sedan chair?' Doctor Hetherington asked.

'Just with the carriers.' I did not explain further. I had already participated in an abduction; now I had further crimes in mind. I could be transported or hanged, and I did not give a damn. I only wished that Doctor Hetherington was not involved, but with a man as stubborn as he was proving to be, I knew that was not possible. On an impulse, I reached out and touched his shoulder. He was still there, solid as the rock on which Edinburgh Castle stood and about as ugly.

Chapter Seventeen

The last time I had disguised myself I had worn a red wig and clothes bought from a pawn shop. This time I altered some of the doctor's old clothes, or rather some of his older clothes for I doubted that he had added to his wardrobe for some years. I took in the waist and shortened the legs of a pair of grey breeches and adjusted the arms of a dark shirt and jacket. Although they were still far too large, they would do, and the extra space allowed me freedom of movement.

'Do you have a pier glass?' I asked the doctor.

'Oh, yes,' he gave a vague answer and brought me the small one he used for shaving.

'Do you have anything larger? I wish to see how I look in your clothes.'

Doctor Hetherington frowned. 'I'm sure I have somewhere,' he scratched his head. 'I don't have much use for such a thing.'

'I don't suppose you have,' I said. The doctor was as far removed from a dandy as it was possible to get.

It took Doctor Hetherington a good half hour to locate the larger mirror he had stored in the attic with other furniture he had probably never used. Dusting it with his sleeve, he brought it to me with a smile of triumph. 'Found it,' he said.

Thanking him, I propped the three-foot long mirror against the wall and turned this way and that to see how I looked. My top half was swamped and shapeless while below the waist, well, I could not help from being amused. Smoothing my hands down my flanks and over my hips, I revelled in the doctor's breeches. The freedom was tremendous after the restrictions of a skirt.

'Miss Flockhart,' Doctor Hetherington looked at my lower half and looked away again quickly. 'I am not sure it is decent.'

'Why doctor,' I could not hide my amusement. 'You have seen me naked.'

'When you were nak... in a state of undress,' the doctor said, 'you were my patient. When I see you in these breeches, I see you as a woman.'

I could not help my gasp of surprise as I looked away to hide my smile. It was many years since a man had last paid me such a compliment. It was many years since I had properly smiled. 'You're a tonic, doctor.' I wriggled my hips in deliberate provocation.

'And you are a tease, woman,' Doctor Hetherington growled.

'You are right, Mungo' I said. 'I do apologise. That was unforgivable.' I knew that he would forgive me.

When I looked at the doctor, he was even more thoughtful than usual.

'Your friends will be here soon,' Mungo changed the subject. 'I hope they know what you have planned for them.'

'So do I,' I said as I heard the doctor's gate creak, 'for here they are now.' Macfarlane and MacGregor walked up the path as silently as two ghosts.

'It's St Bride's night.' Macfarlane added a further coat of brick dust to his face to prevent any reflection from moonlight or candlelight. 'A good night to set to work. Now if you tell me where we are going, we'll be on our way.' We stood in Mungo's cramped hall, with the light from a single lantern casting long shadows.

'I'm coming with you,' I told him.

'You'd better not,' MacGregor said. 'We're used to being on the wrong side of the law while you're a lady.'

'It's my friend that we are rescuing,' I reminded. 'You are putting yourself in danger for me.'

'We've no love for the McAras of this world,' Macfarlane said.

'Give me ten minutes,' I looked at my two Highlanders. Rogues and vagabonds they may be, and criminals in the eyes of the law, but they were better and more honest men than the self-styled gentlemen who ruled the land. 'Somebody has to show you the way.'

The gun case was in the bedroom. I removed both pistols, loaded them and thrust them in my waistband, under the shirt. They were uncomfortable there, but having Joe Manton with me was reassuring.

When I returned, Mungo was hauling on a dark jacket. His face was as black as the Highlanders. 'I'll come along too.'

'I'm sure you are a fine doctor,' Macfarlane said. 'But this sort of thing takes different skills.'

'I'll come along too,' the doctor repeated.

I heard the determination in Doctor Hetherington's voice. 'You are a constant surprise, Mungo,' I said.

He smiled over at me, and I saw his eyes slide down to my hips and away again. I hoped I would not prove too much of a distraction for the good doctor, and shook my head. Let the poor man get what enjoyment he could from my state of dress; he deserved it.

A bright moon glossed the landscape as we crossed over the footbridge and into the policies of Tynebridge Hall.

'Here we are again,' I said to myself. 'Back here.' The trees seemed to be waiting for me, their boughs like arms, the knots in the bark like watchful eyes and their bulk like giants from folklore. All it needed was a howling wolf. I shook my head and started as a fox barked in the distance, the sound eerie in the dark.

'You say there are no resident servants,' Macfarlane broke into my sombre thoughts. 'That is good. Resident servants are careful while temporary servants are careless. They might leave a window open.'

'And if they don't?' Doctor Hetherington sounded nervous.

'You'll see.' Macfarlane touched the bag he wore across his shoulders.

More in hope than expectation, I brought them to the back door of the Hall. It was locked. Macfarlane pushed hard and pointed to the places of most resistance. 'It's bolted at the top, bottom and middle,' he said. 'We won't get in that way.'

We toured the house, searching for a suitable window with my frustration growing by the minute. 'Maybe we can't get in.'

'Calm yourself, Miss Flockhart,' Macfarlane touched my arm. 'Leave it to us.' He looked up as clouds obscured the moon. 'That's better; now we're harder to see.' Delving into the bag he wore at his waist, he produced a lantern and scratched a spark from a tinder-box. I saw that the lantern's lens was blackened, so only a thin beam of light shone out.

'All the lower windows are barred,' Doctor Hetherington sounded disappointed.

'It keeps the blackguards out,' I said, 'and the servants in.' I looked upward, contemplating climbing the sheer walls and was glad I wore breeches and not a trailing skirt. Honestly, life is so much easier for male than female house-breakers.

'We'll use this one,' Macfarlane stopped at a window. 'It's at an angle, nothing overlooks it, and it's quiet.'

'How about the bars?' Doctor Hetherington asked.

'Watch,' Macfarlane said. 'We'll take care of them.' Taking a length of thin rope from his bag, he coiled it around the two central bars, placed a short metal rod through the loop and began to twist. Within a few moments, the pressure made the bars creak against the surrounding mortar.

'Quiet now,' I hissed.

We all stopped when we saw light gleaming in a window on the next storey up. Macfarlane pushed us against the wall. There was the murmur of voices and a single laugh. The light flickered and vanished.

'Whenever you're ready,' I said.

Macfarlane nodded and continued until the iron bars shifted. 'That should do it.' Taking told of the bars, he began to pull them this way and that, loosening them further until he yanked one completely free.

'One.' MacGregor said and grabbed the next.

Within a few moments, a second bar joined the first.

'Two,' MacGregor said.

'Is that space enough?' Macfarlane tried to squeeze between the bars. 'No, we need another.' Looping the cord around another two bars, he repeated the original procedure and widened the gap as I watched. 'Right; that's us.' He placed the bars carefully on the ground.

'You've done this before,' I said.

Macfarlane grinned. 'Perhaps. Now there's just the window itself.' Taking a long dirk from under his arm, he scraped away the putty from the bottom window pane and eased away the glass. 'That was easy enough. The putty was brittle with age.'

'How easy it is when you know how,' Mungo said.

'We're nearly in.' Thrusting his hand through the hole, Macfarlane opened the catch and pushed up the lower half of the window.

'In we go,' Macfarlane entered first with the rest of us following. As soon as we were all in, MacGregor leaned outside and balanced the iron bars in place, then slotted a sheet of black paper where the pane of glass was missing. 'That might fool a casual observer,' he said.

I looked around. We were in the servant's store, a small room with bare floorboards and shelves on three walls.

'You're in charge now, Miss Flockhart,' Macfarlane said. 'Take us to your friend.'

I knew the interior of Tynebridge Hall as well as anyone did, in the light or the dark, so I led the way with perfect confidence. Twice I stopped as I heard voices ahead and once I pulled everyone into the shadows as footsteps echoed and a man stumbled from a room.

I did not recognise him and wondered how many strangers there were infesting this house.

Walking in front, with Macfarlane's thin beam of light guiding us, I was aware of the breeches around my legs. I found myself hoping that Mungo was watching and wondered what made me think that at this time. I glanced over my shoulder, caught Mungo's gaze, realised I did not care and emphasised the swing of my hips.

Go on then, Mungo. That's for you. I'm a woman, remember, not just a patient. Something had altered in me. Perhaps it was because I had finally acknowledged my experiences that night a decade ago or maybe because I was finally fighting back. And then we were climbing the stairs with Macfarlane's light bouncing ahead, the shadows receding and our steps brittle as the beat of my heart.

No lamps were burning in the topmost corridor, nothing except stygian darkness and a single wavering bar of light under one of the doors.

'That one,' I whispered and padded along the floorboards with my heart hammering and the darkness pressing down upon me. I tapped on the door. 'Marie?'

There was no reply. The door was locked.

'Marie?'

'Let me,' Macfarlane bent down and held his lantern to the lock. 'There's no key,' he said. 'I'll have to force it.'

I looked around; the darkness seemed to crowd around, watching us, hiding the evil. 'Hurry,' I said. 'And don't make any noise.' I had a dread of waking the house and having McAra and his friends discover us here. Whatever terrible things they were doing, we were also in the wrong; we had broken into the house and could be transported or possibly even hanged.

'MacGregor!' After a brief confabulation in Gaelic, the two Highlanders pressed against the door. I saw them strain, and then it burst open with a hideous noise. My Highlanders staggered inside the room, with MacGregor mouthing what I took to be Gaelic oaths.

'You'll wake the house!' Mungo said.

'Oh, dear God!' I stepped forward.

There was a short scream, instantly stifled as Macfarlane threw himself on a bed and put his huge hand over the occupant's mouth.

'Hush now! We've come to save you!'

I rushed in with Mungo at my back. He closed the door. A single guttering candle provided light, with all four of us crowding the room and a young girl staring at us with wide, terrified eyes.

Macfarlane looked at me in triumph. 'You were right, Miss Flockhart!'

I shook my head. 'No, I was not. That's not Marie!'

The girl on the bed could not have been more than sixteen, with a tangle of brown hair above a soft face and eyes puffy and red from crying.

'Who are you?' I asked, 'and where is Marie?'

Macfarlane removed his hand, and the girl immediately started to scream, which was not surprising, being wakened up in the wee small hours by a deluge of strangers.

Macfarlane quickly replaced his hand over her mouth. 'She's tied in.'

I saw the cords around the girl's ankles and wrists.

'What do you want us to do?' MacGregor asked me the question.

I had to make a quick decision. 'Oh, Dear God, I don't know.' I had expected to release a grateful Marie, not find a young stranger. Momentarily at a loss, I stared at Mungo. 'What shall we do?'

'Ask her,' Mungo was as sensible as ever. He knelt beside the girl and spoke in his calm bedside manner. 'Are you a prisoner here?'

The girl nodded, still terrified.

'Do you wish to be released?' It seemed a foolish question.

The girl nodded rapidly.

'Keep quiet then,' Macfarlane sliced her free.

The girl was shaking, staring at us. Reaching over, Mungo held her, making soothing sounds.

'We're friends,' I said. 'Are there any more prisoners here?'

She nodded. 'Yes.'

'Where?'

'I don't know.' She was sobbing.

'Have you seen a tall, auburn-haired woman of about twenty?' I asked.

'I don't know,' the girl shook her head.

'She's too scared to think,' Mungo said. 'It's all right, my dear. You're safe now.' He looked up at me. 'You won't get anything from her, Dorothea.'

'We'll try the other guest bedrooms,' I said.

'How about this young lassie?' Macfarlane sounded concerned.

'Bring her with us.' Mungo made the decision. 'We're not leaving her here.'

We moved along the corridor, opening the doors and peering in. Most were not locked, and the rooms were empty and in darkness. There were no other prisoners and no sign of Marie. I took a deep breath, unsure what to do next. I had been sure that Marie was up here.

'Listen,' Macfarlane took hold of my arm. 'Somebody is coming.'

We slipped into the nearest room as footsteps sounded. They were regular and heavy, the steps of a man. He was singing *Arthur McBride*:

> '*So gaily and gallant we went on our tramp*
> *And we met Sergeant Harper and Corporal Cramp*
> *And the little wee drummer who roused up the camp*
> *With his row-de-dow-dow in the morning.*'

Macfarlane clamped his hands over the girl's mouth as she began to make small whining noises. The footsteps hesitated and then continued, fading away as the man passed. The words of the song remained, so cheerful in this house of woe.

> '*Well now my fine fellows, if you will enlist,*
> *A guinea in gold I will slap in your first,*
> *And a crown in the bargain to kick up the dust*
> *And drink the King's health in the morning.*'

'Best we leave now,' MacGregor said.

'We have not found Marie yet,' I shook my head. 'I'm not leaving without her.'

'Dawn is not far away,' MacGregor said. 'Any servants will be up soon and then getting away from here will be much more difficult.'

'I'm not leaving without Marie,' I insisted.

'You'll get us all hanged,' MacGregor spoke with the voice of experience.

'You go,' I said. 'Take the girl to the doctor's house and look after her. I'll stay here. It is much easier for one person to hide than five.' I lowered my voice. 'I know this house.'

'You two take the girl,' Mungo backed me up. 'I will stay here with Miss Flockhart.'

While I blessed his loyalty, I had no intention of putting the doctor in any more danger. 'I'll be better alone.'

'I'm staying with you.'

Suddenly I knew that I wanted the company of this ugly, stubborn man. 'Thank you.'

'You two look after the girl,' Mungo said. 'Put her straight to bed and no...'

'We'll keep her safe,' Macfarlane held the doctor's gaze. 'We've both got daughters older than her; we know what to do with children.'

'Thank you, Macfarlane,' I touched his arm.

Mungo gave last-minute advice to Macfarlane, and then we waited until the Highlanders had taken the girl away. 'We'll take each room in the house,' I said, 'until we find Marie. Once McAra discovers that wee girl is missing he'll search everywhere for her.'

'Is there anywhere safe we can hide?' Mungo asked.

'I know this house well,' I said. 'All the nooks and crannies. McAra has been here a couple of weeks if that.'

Mungo looked at me. 'You are a quiz,' he said, without probing further. We stopped at the renewed sound of singing.

'If we were such fools as to take your advance,
It's right bloody slender would be our poor chance
For the King wouldn't scruple to send us to France
And get us all shot in the morning.'

'That man is drunk as half a dozen lords,' Mungo said.

'As long as he stays away from us.' *Us*. It is such a well-used word with such hidden meanings. 'Come on, Doctor.' I could not face the thoughts that filled my head. I could not tell even Mungo all the truth, and until I did, we were never a complete *us*, and our friendship was a sham on my part.

As the dawn light strengthened and the birds awoke, I led poor Mungo from room to room, searching for Marie. We did not find her. My frustration increased with every minute.

'They might have taken her somewhere else,' Mungo said, 'somewhere outside Tynebridge Hall.'

'I know that,' I snapped. 'And if Marie is still here I would hate to leave her behind. Go if you wish.'

'I do not wish,' Mungo said.

We searched the top floor first, touring each room, probing into beds and cupboards and finding nothing. Each time we heard footsteps or the murmur of a voice we slid into a dark corner and hushed ourselves into silence. Despite the anxiety, there was a thrill of excitement in hiding together, and I found myself anticipating the next scare and the slight touch of Mungo's hand on my arm, or the inadvertent brush of his leg against mine.

'Downstairs now,' Mungo said. 'There's nothing else up here.'

'Not yet; there's still the attic.' I thought of the dark, dingy space under the eaves and wondered if McAra had stuffed Marie up there with the mice and cobwebs.

'How do we get up?' Doctor Hetherington did not question my choice.

'There's a ladder in the north-western wing.' I remembered the wooden steps that ascended to the chilly dark.

'You do know this place well,' the doctor commented without enquiring more.

I led the way, listening for McAra and his cohorts. The ladder was as I remembered it, if slightly more dilapidated. Bare patches of wood showed through the varnish. 'I'll go first.'

I had never been scared of heights, and besides, if I was first, Mungo could admire that part of me that was immediately in his line of vision. I hoped to rescue Marie, but other sensations were creeping in as I bent forward slightly more than was necessary and emphasised my curves. The bolt of the attic hatch was stiff, and I needed Mungo's help to push it open, which necessitated the two of us balancing on the same rungs of the ladder and pressing close together. I did not object and, seemingly, neither did he.

The sound of the withdrawing bolt seemed to echo around that wing of the house, and we scrambled up the final few rungs and into the attic before somebody came to investigate.

'Come on Dorothea!' Mungo led the way and hauled me up.

'How far does this attic extend?' Doctor Hetherington peered into the darkness.

'The full breadth of the house,' I said.

'I wish we had brought a candle.'

I agreed. The darkness in the attic was oppressive. We waited for a few moments and then moved cautiously, feeling for the beams and careful not to put our weight on the lathe and plaster that was all that separated us from the rooms below. Even then I was grateful for the freedom that breeches offered compared to the constrictions of a long skirt.

'Marie is not up here,' I decided after fifteen minutes of muscle-cramping effort.

'I think you are correct.' Doctor Hetherington grabbed my arm. 'Listen!'

I listened. The sound of voices was quite distinct, the well-modulated tones of educated men punctuated by an occasional high pitched laugh. 'They are right beneath us,' I said.

One man was still singing *Arthur McBride*, the words clear:

> '*How now you young blackguards, if you say one more*
> *word*
> *I swear by the errins I'll draw out my sword*
> *And run through your bodies as my strength may afford*
> *So now, you young buggers, take warning.*'

Pinpricks of light permeated flaws in the plasterwork, with one steady glow filtering upwards.

We stopped, balancing on the beams, and l heard the words ghosting up from below.

'Did you hear a noise just now?' The speaker had the lazy drawl of one of the Lords of Creation and cared not a damn for anybody or anything. I knew that voice. *Oh, dear God, I knew that voice.*

'Not a thing, your Lordship,' another voice answered.

'I'm convinced I heard something.'

'Probably just the wind in the eaves.'

I stood still, trying hard not to breathe. The thought of these men discovering us was something I could not bear. Instinctively, I reached out to Mungo and curled my fingers around his. I swear I could hear the hammering of my heart. Mungo understood. He inched closer, pressing against me, hip to hip. The pistols were heavy at my waist, the steel muzzles cold against my skin.

'We'll take the women tomorrow,' that lazy, terrible drawl stated, with the words as plain as if he were standing at my side.

'It's like the old days,' another man said and followed the words with a high-pitched laugh that raised the hairs on the back of my neck.

I moved slightly to peer through the gap in the plaster, hoping to see the men who were talking. I had no need, for the voices had been clear, and I knew both speakers. The second had been McAra, yet it was the first man who caused chill perspiration to break out all over my body.

'Are you all right, Dorothea?' Mungo's concerned hand rubbed my arm. 'Dorothea?'

'Yes,' I said. 'Yes, I am all right thank you.' I was anything but all right. The owner of the first voice had been none other than Lord Findhorn, my one-time intended.

Chapter Eighteen

'Lord Findhorn!' Doctor Hetherington sounded as shocked as I felt when I told him the news. 'What the devil is he doing here?'

We remained in the attic with the dark now a comforting blanket and the knowledge of Findhorn's presence a sick weight in my stomach. 'I don't know.' I said. 'I don't know.' I wished I was anywhere but Tynebridge Hall. I wished Lord Findhorn was dead and buried and I could finally relinquish my dread.

'Do you wish to leave now?' Mungo could have read my mind.

I fought the desire to run. I had spent ten years running and hiding. 'I won't leave Marie alone here with Findhorn and McAra,' I controlled my panic and tried to reason. 'These men said *women*, plural, so that young girl we rescued was not the only one.'

'The girl did say there were others,' Mungo agreed.

We heard the men beneath us moving and the loud, arrogant voices that brought nausea to my throat. Braying laughter echoed throughout the house.

'Come on,' I said. 'Marie's not up here. We have to find her.'

We descended from the attic into that sinister house, with grey dawn seeping through the windows and the knowledge that the men would be prowling around like predatory wolves. I was scared, I was more than scared, and I was more determined than I had ever been in my life. I looked behind me, where Mungo's life-battered face was set, and knew I wanted no other man as my companion. George Rogers had been a good, brave man, but he entered into things for the fun and the excitement. Mungo, I knew, was as scared as I was, and was helping me for my sake, and because he also wished to help Marie. That took a different sort of courage. I could not voice my feelings for him, although I knew what they were. It was another impossible situation.

I led Mungo down the servants' stairs with their bare functionality and plastered walls, to the first floor, where portraits lined a long central corridor, and the floorboards creaked beneath our feet. We moved quickly now, taking more chances as we checked each room. The furniture stood like skeletal memories of family life, some covered in dust sheets, others waiting for happier times, the laughter of children and the love of husband and wife. At present, there was only fear and tension and the chill knowledge of impending horror.

'Voices,' Mungo pushed me inside a recessed doorway. The key was in the lock and mercifully turned with ease. We bundled inside and closed the door as quietly as we could.

There was no smiling now, no flirting on my part as I leaned against the panelled wall with the terrible memories racing through my mind and my heart thundering against my chest. When Mungo put his hand on my arm, I could feel his strength as well as his fear.

The voices increased, mingling words with the foulest of oaths.

'Gone away, by God!'

The roar could hardly have been louder.

'They've found that the girl has escaped,' Mungo said.

'Stay still,' I felt myself shaking with fear. I did not know what Lord Findhorn would do if he found us. 'For God's sake stay still.' My hand gripped the doctor's so tightly I swear I could feel his bones creaking.

'It's all right,' he murmured, again and again. 'It will be all right.'

I touched the pistols, praying that Joe would not let me down. From my position against the wall, I could see out of the window to the policies. I heard the blare of a hunting horn and the loud baying of dogs. 'God help us,' I said. 'They've released the hounds.'

'View halloo!' Somebody shouted, and others took up the cry. I slipped to the window and peered out. There were half a dozen men there, all crying and yelling as they followed the hounds.

'Please God that Macfarlane is away safely,' I said.

'I think your Highlander is among the least likely to get caught,' Mungo said. 'And with all these men out of the house, we have more chance of finding Marie.'

I could not fault his logic, although I had to force my fear-paralysed limbs to move out of that room and into the corridor out-side. We worked even faster now, opening doors and peering inside and moving on to the next. Some rooms were as I remembered them from a decade before; others were more dilapidated, with worn fur-niture and fittings in need of repair. We did not find Marie. Twice I stumbled, and each time Mungo was there to catch me. He seemed to anticipate my actions. I thanked him the first time. I did not thank him the second, there was no need, and he understood.

I had come to rely on his understanding.

Eventually, we reached the room where Marie had married Gib-bie. It was a ghost of its former self with empty bottles strewn across the Axminster carpet and half the crystal of the twin chandelier broken and lying on the ground. Dog hairs polluted the couch and chairs, and a whip lay abandoned on the table. I swear there was blood on the lash and I shuddered to think what use Findhorn had put it and who had been on the wrong end. Please, God, it had not been Marie. We negotiated the stairs to the ground floor. The main halls were empty of people; there was not a single servant, nothing save the sort of mess that drunken bachelors leave behind.

'Nothing here,' Mungo had a supporting hand on my arm. 'Come on Dorothea.'

Only the basement remained, and the outbuildings. Our steps echoed in that empty house as we ran down the stone steps to the basement, home of the servants' quarters, the kitchen, pantry and the storerooms. Mungo heard the muted sounds before I did and motioned for me to listen.

'What was that?'

We stopped. 'It's like a scraping,' I said. It echoed in the empty house, a ghostly sound, reverberating without form.

'Down here,' Mungo took the lead, through a heavy door and into a succession of wine cellars, each one darker than the last. 'There must be a lantern in here somewhere.' Feeling along the wall, he found a shelf with a candle in a brass candleholder and a tinderbox. Scraping a spark, he set flame to the wick, so a wavering light guided us past the crumbling walls.

'I don't know this part of the house,' I said. 'I've never had to come here.'

At the very end of the cellars was a low door, closed with two external bolts. The scraping came from within, magnified by the silence.

Mungo drew back the bolts and extended the candle.

'Marie?' I called, tentatively, hoping to God that there was no mastiff or other creature inside.

The sound increased. Mungo put his hand on my arm, 'stay here,' he said, crouched and entered first. Although the chamber may once have been a wine cellar, it had been modified, with chains fastened to the wall and Marie lying on her side, naked as a new-born baby and covered in filth. She whimpered when she saw our light.

'Oh sweet God!' Mungo spoke quietly. 'What manner of men are these?'

'The worst kind,' I said. 'The worst kind in the world. Marie, it's all right. We've come to take you away.'

Marie closed her eyes and cowered away when we brought the candle closer.

'Marie! It's me!' I crouched at her side. 'It's Dorothea Flockhart and Doctor Hetherington.'

Marie looked up at me, blinking through red-rimmed eyes. I removed the dirty rag that acted as a gag.

'Dorothea!' Her face crumpled.

'Come on now.' I held her tight as Mungo examined the chains. 'We'll get you out of here.'

Only a simple pin fastened the chains and Mungo pulled out in seconds. Marie began to rub at the rough red marks around her ankles and wrists.

'Here,' removing his jacket, Mungo draped it over Marie's shoulders. The tails extended to her thighs, covering her modesty. 'It's not perfect, but it's better than nothing.'

'You remember Doctor Hetherington,' I said as Marie stared at him.

She nodded, cowering away. Her left eye was swollen and bruised, her lip puffy and her body scarred and filthy. I could only imagine what ordeals Lord Findhorn and his friends had put her through.

'You're safe with us,' I tried to sound more confident than I felt for we were still deep in Tynebridge Hall with Lord Findhorn and his cronies running loose and the full extent of the policies between us and even moderate safety.

Marie was softly sobbing as Mungo lifted her to her feet. 'Can you walk?' His voice was gentle.

'I'll try, Doctor.' Marie sounded like a little child.

'Come on then.' With the candle pooling its yellow light in front, we left those terrible cellars to return to the ground floor.

'We're not far from the window we entered by,' I said. Had that only been the previous night? It seemed as if we had been wandering around Tynebridge Hall for a week at least, with the fear of capture fraying our nerves every second.

'Over here.' Once again, Mungo took charge, leading us to the room with the broken bars. The prospect of freedom made me dizzy, and I sucked in huge draughts of fresh air. Mungo slipped outside first and reached back to guide the still dazed Marie through the gap. It was now late afternoon with the light fading and a fresh breeze carrying a light rain. An owl hooted mournfully, to be answered quickly by its mate.

The grounds immediately outside the hall were clear, with about fifty yards of unkempt grass to cover before we reached the shelter of the surrounding woodland.

'Maybe we should wait until full dark,' I said, and instantly changed my mind. 'No, Marie has had enough. Run for the footbridge.'

Mungo glanced at Marie. 'You're right. Marie can't take much more. Now, remember that Findhorn and his men are out there. Be very careful.'

I nodded, suddenly wordless.

'Ready? I'll take Marie; you look after yourself,' Mungo said. 'On the count of three. One, two, *three.*'

We ran across the open patch as if we were racing for a prize. I have never been so glad to wear male attire as I lifted my legs and threw myself forward. I heard Mungo gasping for breath and Marie's little whimpers of fear as our feet thudded on the damp grass. I heard that owl call again, and the distant barking of a dog and then we were among the shelter of the trees, and all I could hear was our breathing and the rustle of branches and twigs in the breeze.

'This way.' Grabbing Marie's hand, I headed for the footbridge, with Mungo in the rear.

Snowdrops probed white underfoot as the owl call floated through the gathering dark. I again heard the staccato barking of dogs, and Marie grabbed my arm. 'Dorothea!'

'I hear them,' I said. 'Keep going! Once we're across the bridge, we'll be safe.' Or I hoped we would be safe. The River Tyne had achieved some magical properties in my mind as if Findhorn and his devil's legion could not cross running water.

I heard Marie squeal and felt her hesitate. 'Ow! My foot! Dorothea!' She was limping, favouring her left foot and looking at me with panicked eyes.

I looked down; she had stepped on a sharp branch which had stuck in her sole. 'Doctor!' I pleaded.

We stopped, gasping for air, with the trees looming sinister in the gathering dark. Mungo knelt at Marie's side and lifted her foot. 'Let me see.' His voice was gentle, a bedside manner out here with dogs and predators hunting us. 'You have a twig deep in your foot,' Mungo said. 'I won't take it out here, or you'll lose a lot of blood.'

'Oh, Lord!' Marie's eyes were huge as she looked at me. 'Don't leave me!'

'We won't,' Mungo said. Stooping, he put his shoulder under Marie's middle and straightened up. Clasping one arm around the back of her knees, Mungo stepped on.

With Mungo encumbered, we moved slower, following the network of overgrown paths toward the footbridge. However well one knows a place in daylight, it is always different in the dark and when a rising wind is creaking through the surrounding trees and weeds have long-since choked the paths, nothing seems certain. I lost my way twice in the next ten minutes and each time suffered a rapid attack of nerves until I found the correct path.

'How are you two doing?'

'We're all right,' Mungo said, although I could tell by his laboured breathing that he found carrying Marie a burden. She was only twenty but a full grown woman with plentiful curves.

We staggered on. I heard the hounds sounding, and the malignant call of a hunting horn, and then I saw the yellow glitter of lanterns through the trees.

'There they are!' That was McAra's voice, choked with excitement, and again there was the long blast of the hunting horn. 'I saw them! They're heading for the footbridge!'

'Run, oh, please run,' Marie pleaded as we tried to increase our speed along the path.

I heard Mungo's rasping breath and the rushing water of the Tyne. I saw the bridge ahead with early moonlight gleaming on the simple handrail and trees overhanging the river. Our River Jordan, with the Promised Land on the far side, the brown churning Tyne separating Hell from safety, and the bridge was the straight and narrow thread to sanctuary.

'One last effort,' Mungo said, and promptly tripped over a root that stretched under the path. He staggered, tried to recover and fell face first, spilling Marie in front of him. Marie screamed and rolled, with Mungo's coat rucking up to her shoulders, so she lay white and vulnerable, face down on the muddy ground.

'Marie!' I hesitated, not sure who needed my help most, and then the dogs exploded from the dark trees and surrounded us, baying, teeth gleaming white as they nipped and bit at our legs and feet.

'Marie!' I shouted again, just as Mungo rose.

'Dorothea!' He pushed me toward the bridge, only twenty yards ahead. 'Run! Save yourself!'

'But Marie!'

'I'll get Marie! Go! For God's own sake, run!'

And then it was too late. McAra thrust through the undergrowth and blew a long blast of his hunting horn. Others crowded behind him, with Lord Findhorn last, his face bloated, his nose red-veined.

'You,' he said, looking at me, his chest heaving with exertion. 'I've caught you at last.' His smile was slow. 'Oh, what fun we will have with you, my lady Dorothea.'

'If you hurt her,' Mungo flicked his coat down to cover Marie's nakedness, 'I'll see you in the highest court in the land. If you put one finger on either of these women...'

Lord Findhorn's laugh broke into Mungo's words. 'You'll do what, Doctor? What possible power do you think you could have over me, a peer of the realm? My friends and I control the judges and the legal systems while you?' He laughed again. 'You are a poor country surgeon, a bone-setter with neither family nor connections.'

'I am an honest man, and that counts for much,' Mungo faced him, signalling behind his back that I should run.

I would not. I would not leave Mungo and Marie alone with these monsters.

Findhorn's laugh was echoed by the men who collected in a jeering crowd at his back. 'You are a fool if you believe that.' I saw Sir Lancelot Snodgrass there, with McAra and others I did not know.

I said nothing. I am not sure if fear choked me or if it was anger. I only knew that I wished to kill my Lord Findhorn. There was no indecision there. I remembered how he had treated me when I was Marie's age, and all the hatred and anger returned, chasing away any fear I still heard. The pistols pressed against my stomach.

I stood still, staring at this man who had deceived me, hunted me and raped me, staring at this man who had ruined my life. I was as calm as I had ever been and the image was as clear as midsummer: *I was standing over him with a pistol in my hand, and he cowered before me.* I had kept my pistols concealed ever since I left Mungo's house. Now I slid my hand under Mungo's shirt and touched a walnut butt.

'Bring them back to the house,' Lord Findhorn ordered. 'We still have two women to hunt tomorrow.'

I had never seen Mungo angry before, but now I did. He was stocky rather than tall, and more compassionate than any man I had ever met, but when Findhorn's grinning cohorts came forward, he landed the most beautiful punch I ever saw. I had stepped to try and shield Marie when Sir Lancelot approached Mungo. Mungo's fist felled him, so he crumpled into an untidy heap on the ground.

'Run! Dorothea!' Mungo ordered. 'I'll hold them off.'

But I did not run. I would not leave Marie alone with these terrible people, and I would not allow Mungo to fight for me. Drawing the right-hand pistol from under my cloak, I aimed it directly at Lord Findhorn and pressed the trigger. There was a small puff of smoke from the lock but nothing else.

'Your powder is damp,' Findhorn sounded more amused than alarmed. 'Best check that sort of thing when it rains.'

Screaming in as much fear as fury, I threw the pistol at his Lordship and then jumped at him, clawing at his eyes with hooked nails. Now, God knows that I am a quiet, demure woman, despite my occasional bouts of temper, yet for that instant, I was as savage as any

Amazon from the mythical past. However, His Lordship had vast experience in striking women, and his back-handed slap knocked me to the ground. I lay there for a moment, dazed, and then Findhorn's minions surged all over us, and our resistance ended.

I saw two men grapple with Mungo. He punched out again as somebody knocked him over the head with the butt of a whip and three men began to attack him as he fell. They were grunting with effort as they kicked him, with Findhorn smiling.

'McAra,' Findhorn sounded calm. 'Take these three into the house and please ensure they don't get out this time.'

I kicked and scratched and struggled as they dragged me back to Tynebridge Hall. I may as well have walked meekly for all the good it did. With Mungo semi-conscious and limp, the men surrounded me and within a few moments, we were back in the cellars. The feel of manacles around my wrists was terrifying.

'Sleep well.' The drunken man who had sung *Arthur McBride* fondled my breasts. 'We'll see you tomorrow.'

Sir Lancelot laughed. 'Good-bye, Miss Flockhart.'

Lord Findhorn lifted a lantern high, so the light played on us. 'I was very pleased when I heard you were back, Dorothea. I should have kept the information to myself rather than telling Turnbull,' he shrugged. 'He had his reasons for speaking to you, wherever he is.'

'I'll kill you yet, Findhorn.' I no longer pretended anything except loathing.

Findhorn slapped me again, backhanded. 'I don't think so, Dorothea. I have your little pistol. You may remember the rules of our little game? We will remind you tomorrow, you and your young friend.'

He shifted the lantern, so it shone directly on Marie. 'You, Mrs Elliot, you are mine now, so I expect you to do as I tell you. And Doctor, we'll find something amusing to do with you, later.'

Mungo struggled to sit up. Blood seeped from an ugly cut on his head. 'I'm warning you, Findhorn. Don't hurt these women.'

'You're warning me?' Findhorn stepped closer and kicked Mungo in the stomach. 'You are in no condition to warn anybody.'

'No condition to warn anybody,' Sir Lancelot echoed, with the others nodding and grinning agreement.

When Findhorn withdrew, we lay in silence for a few moments.

'Sorry Marie,' I said at length. 'And I'm sorry Doctor, for getting you into this.'

'You did not get me into anything,' Mungo said. 'I chose to come, and I chose to stay, remember?'

I pulled the chains in frustration. I had only been secured for a few moments, and already the iron was chafing at my wrists and ankles.

'What will happen tomorrow?' I think it was the first time I had heard Mungo sound uncertain.

I glanced at Marie, who was slumped in misery and thankfully not listening. 'Findhorn and McAra will set Marie and me free in the grounds. After a few moments they'll release the hounds, and then they'll follow and hunt us down.' I tried to sound calm although my mind and body were silently screaming with fear. 'I don't know what they have planned for you, Mungo.'

'I doubt it will be pleasant,' Mungo yanked fruitlessly at his chains. 'I wish I could have helped you more.'

'You did more for me than any man ever has,' I said truthfully.

'You mean more to me than any woman ever has,' Mungo's words were so soft I had to strain to hear them.

I did not know what to say. In a few hours, I would be dead or wishing for death, for Findhorn would have no mercy. 'You are a good man, Mungo,' I refined the phrase when I realised I was repeating what I had said to George Rogers. 'You are the best man I have ever met.'

If circumstances had been different, I would have allowed my feelings for Mungo to grow. I knew that any relationship was impossible, and then I snorted. *Good God, what did it matter? There was no future.* 'I think I could have loved you, Mungo.'

The silence lasted a long time. 'I have loved you since the first time we met, Dorothea.'

I closed my eyes. I did not wish to hear more.

The door opened, and a beam of light landed between us.

Chapter Nineteen

'I don't know what to do with you two,' Macfarlane's Highland accent was one of the most beautiful things I have ever heard in my life. 'We leave you for a few moments and look at the pickle you get yourselves into. Is this little girl the missing Marie?'

'It is,' I must have sounded dazed as I wondered if I had said too much to Mungo. 'And where did you spring from?'

'Oh, we were near the footbridge when you were captured,' Macfarlane said. 'We followed McAra and the others. Who is that ugly, red-faced fellow?'

'Lord Findhorn,' I said.

'No friend of yours, I would reckon,' Macfarlane said.

'You would reckon correctly,' I agreed.

'Let's get you out of here,' Macfarlane unfastened my chains and moved on to Marie while MacGregor worked on Mungo.

I took a deep breath. 'I'm not going anywhere.'

They stared at me, as one would expect them to do. With my mind still reeling from all that had happened and Mungo's statement, I would have been sensible to return to his house to consider what to do next. I did not wish that. I wanted to strike back at Findhorn. I wished to hurt him as he had hurt me, point a pistol at his head and blow his brains out.

'We can have you in the doctor's house in quarter of an hour,' Macfarlane said.

'No.' I shook my head. 'I'm here, and now I am free I am going to retaliate.' My language was infinitely milder than my intentions.

'Dorothea! No!' Marie held the doctor's coat tightly around her, although none of the men present was in any way interested in her nakedness underneath. 'Run away now! Please!'

'If you three could take Marie somewhere safe,' I continued. 'Just leave me here. As a good friend of mine said once, the time for running has stopped.' To be honest, I had no idea what I was going to do, but the sight of Findhorn had put iron in my soul. I had been pushed around for too long. I had run away to India and had returned to try and rebuild my life, only to fall into the same situation, with the same people.

'I'll stay with you,' Mungo said, and I blessed him without words.

'And me,' Macfarlane said. 'MacGregor will look after the young lassie.' His grin was pure mischief. 'He's got five daughters, so he knows what to do.'

MacGregor laughed openly, showing gaps in his teeth. 'I have five daughters and three sons,' he said, 'and one more on the way.'

It was not the right time to offer congratulations although I promised myself that I would hansel the new arrival as handsomely as I could. I was building up quite a catalogue of debts in Tynebridge Hall, and I would honour them all.

'What do you have in mind?' Mungo asked.

'Let's get Marie away safely first,' I said, 'and then we'll work out what best to do.'

A couple of hours before, we had crept around Tynebridge Hall as a trio of scared fugitives. Now I felt like Nimrod. The memories of the evening when Findhorn and his cohorts hunted me had always been present. They had strengthened after I saw him.

I had tried to fire one pistol and thrown it at Findhorn. I still had its mate. 'Do you have any gunpowder, MacGregor?'

'Here's my powder horn.' It was flattened cow horn, plugged with a piece of leather and decorated with interlaced Celtic designs.

'It's beautiful, thank you.'

'It was my grandfather's great-grandfather's.' MacGregor spoke with pride. 'He carried it at Inverlochy when the great Montrose broke the pride of the Campbells.'

'And now it will serve to break the pride of Findhorn,' I said. And his head, I thought. I was aware of Mungo watching me, his face concerned.

I unloaded my Joe Manton and withdrew the powder charge, replacing it with dry powder from Macfarlane's horn.

'You've done that before,' Macfarlane said.

'I had to carry a gun in India,' I knew I was giving too much away, 'in case of snakes and badmashes and the like.' I felt Mungo's eyes on me and wondered what he was thinking. I blocked the thought. I had other things to do before I could consider Doctor Hetherington.

'I've never met a woman like you,' Mungo cut through my mental defences without effort.

'I've never met a man like you.' Despite my intentions, I was equally honest. Mungo could do that to me. Before I left Scotland the only men I had known had been of Lord Findhorn's type, loud, arrogant and grasping. They had been men handsome and successful on the outside and ugly as the devil's tail on the inside. In India, there had been hard-drinking military men from the King's and Company's armies, or Company servants, prematurely aged men vastly overburdened with responsibility. Only since I returned had I met men that I could allow myself to trust and genuinely like, and two of them were Macfarlane and George Rogers. The third and last was Doctor Mungo Hetherington.

Once again I remembered Mother Faa's prediction that I would marry a man in uniform. Yet, if I had a choice between Mungo and Captain Rogers, which one would I choose? I pondered; there was no doubt that George was the more dashing, a handsome, well-set-up man with lands and no-doubt a vast fortune. On the other hand, Mungo Hetherington had proved utterly reliable in all circumstances; there was no doubting his bravery. I knew that he liked me, and he claimed he loved me. He could also be trusted. On at least two occasions he had me at a terrible disadvantage, naked and vulnerable and he had been nothing other than a perfect gentleman in the real sense of the word. Mungo was a gentle man.

There was one part of me, one tiny, treasonous segment that was slightly disappointed that Mungo had not been somewhat more forward. It was that part of me that had tried to entice him with my tight breeches and the swaying of my hips. Now that I recalled these incidents I felt slightly ashamed of my behaviour, for there could be no future between us except for friendship. The doctor had made it plain that he was from an inferior social standing and I had my secret. The attraction was there, and we had both declared our feelings. Or had we only claimed our love because we thought we were going to die and we could be reckless with our emotions?

I did not know.

I realised that I had been looking directly at Mungo as the thoughts had raced through my mind. What must the poor man think of me?

'I'm sorry,' Mungo said. 'I've been staring at you.' He lowered his voice. 'If our circumstances were otherwise,' he said.

I was not sure what that meant and answered without thought. 'Things are what they are.'

We looked away simultaneously. Macfarlane studied the wall as if he had never before seen such fascinating stonework.

I checked the workings of my pistol and replaced it under my cloak. 'Shall we go?'

'What do you intend to do with that thing?' Mungo was abrupt. I knew the question had been on his mind for some time.

I said nothing, not for any desire to appear secretive and mysterious but merely because I did not know the answer. I retained my image of Findhorn cowering away as I shot him in the head.

We moved on at last. I led with Mungo next and Macfarlane padding in the rear. He may have been a middle-aged man with more grey than black in his beard and a spreading waistline, but I would rather have him on my side than any swish young gallant. Macfarlane carried the lantern, whose light flicked and pooled ahead of me.

I heard somebody singing *Arthur McBride* and stopped abruptly, stepping into the shadow of a recessed doorway. I did not know the man who walked towards us. He was young, with a confident gait and clothes that would cost five year's income for a working man.

> '*Well we beat that bold drummer as flat as a shoe,*
> *And we made a football of his row-de-dow-dow*'

Without conscious thought, I waited until he was past, produced my pistol and rammed the muzzle against the back of his head. The man gave a loud squawk and jumped in the air.

'One word, I said, 'and I'll blow your brains all over the wall.' Honestly, I don't know where I got these words. Until that night, I had no idea I could be so bloodthirsty.

If the man had not moved, I don't know what I would have done, but Macfarlane clamped a huge hand over his mouth and dragged him into the nearest room.

'Close the door!' I hissed as Mungo hesitated.

Now only Macfarlane's lantern gave us light as I ordered my prisoner against the far wall.

'You're that woman!' he said, foolishly, when Macfarlane removed his hand. 'We captured you.'

'And now we've captured you back,' I said. 'How many of you are in the house?'

'That's for me to know and you to find out,' the man said. Indeed I was not sure if he was a man yet, more a youth with the smoothest of skin on his face and soft childish lips. I doubt he had needed to lift a razor in his life.

'Oh, we'll find out,' Macfarlane glanced at me and winked. 'We'll cut off your fingers one by one and make you eat them,' he continued with a list of horrors that made me shudder and wonder in which Gothic romance he had found them. Certainly, I doubted that my middle-aged housekeeper's husband could do such things. And then I remembered the skill with which he had abducted Turnbull and wondered anew.

'He means it.' Mungo gave his short but significant contribution to the conversation.

'Six!' the youth's resistance broke.

'Name them,' I demanded.

The youth's eyes swivelled from me, a woman with a darkened face wearing man's clothes and carrying a pistol, to Macfarlane with his lurid threats and Highland accent, to Mungo, with the flow of blood now dark and encrusted from the crown of his head to his chin. We must have looked a desperate crew.

He hesitated, so I pushed the pistol against his back and twisted. 'What's your name?'

'John.' The youth said. 'I am the Honourable John Lindsay.'

'Well then Honourable John, now you can tell me who your companions are.'

'They'll kill me.'

I gasped as Macfarlane took over. Without a word, he ripped the honourable John's breeches down to his ankles, revealing that he wore nothing beneath. John yelped and tried to cover himself.

'Against the wall,' Macfarlane said. 'Facing outward.'

The Honourable John squealed like a pig as Macfarlane slammed him against the wall and produced his dirk. Lantern light played along the length of the blade as Macfarlane placed it against John's smooth belly.

'Lord Findhorn!' The Honourable John nearly screamed the word.

'And who else?' Macfarlane tapped the blade of his dirk on a very personal place that made me wince and the Honourable John crouch to protect himself.

'Hector MacAra,' John said, and now he had started he seemed unable to stop. 'And the Honourable Peter Hain, Sir Lancelot Snodgrass and Sir Martin Marshall.'

'That's five,' Macfarlane tapped the knife, and again, harder than before.

'And me!' Honourable John said.

'Thank you,' I looked at Macfarlane, not sure what to do next.

'Off with them!' Macfarlane took over, throwing the Honourable John onto the ground with a single movement and ripping off his boots and breeches. I watched as John wriggled there, naked from the waist downward.

Using his dirk, Macfarlane ripped John's breeches into long strips and tied his ankles and wrists together, leaving the last fragment to fasten across his mouth as a gag.

'That will keep you quiet,' Macfarlane said. 'If you move, I will come back for you and...' he gave some threats that would have made Bonaparte run screaming in fear and which reduced the Honourable John to a blubbering wreck. Men in that condition are anything but impressive, but a small, unpleasant part of me found some satisfaction in the procedure. John would have been one of the hunters; now he was a broken and unhappy little boy. Hopefully, he learned from the experience and would never subject a woman to anything similar.

'Men are never happy without their breeches,' Macfarlane said. 'I hope you are not offended by what you saw.'

'Not in the least,' I said. 'But we should have asked young Johnny where his colleagues were,' I was belatedly sensible.

Macfarlane shrugged. 'Maybe I should go back.'

'No, we'll keep moving,' I decided.

'What do you intend to do with them?' Mungo asked. 'Tie them up and leave them?'

'I intend teaching them to leave us alone.' I decided that as I spoke. I was determined not to be a victim again. Thrusting Joe Manton inside my shirt, I rubbed my hand across the butt. It felt warm and smooth and reassuring.

I had a small glow of triumph as I moved around the Hall. I knew my enemy and how many there were, and I wanted revenge. Oh, I knew that is probably a sin, but I was not dealing with honourable, respectable men but with the very opposite.

Somebody was singing, the words loud and coarse. I nodded to Macfarlane and loosened the pistol inside my cloak.

'Come on,' I said, once more feeling my heartbeat race.

Macfarlane gave a small smile. 'Was your mother from the Gaeltachd?'

Two men were approaching, one about twenty-five and already drunk, the other Sir Lancelot Snodgrass. We allowed them to pass us and then pounced. I thrust my pistol into the neck of the younger and Macfarlane simply grabbed Sir Lancelot and smacked his head against the wall. Taken by surprise, the men hardly resisted as Mungo opened the nearest door and we hustled them inside. We did not need to ask the number of men, so we contented ourselves by asking the name of the younger and where their companions were.

'What the devil?' Sir Lancelot clasped a hand to his head. 'Do you know who I am?'

'Yes, Snodgrass,' Macfarlane said.

'How did you escape?' Sir Lancelot was slack-mouthed as he stared at me. Unable to resist the temptation, I gave him a back-handed slap that drew blood from his mouth.

'That's for Marie,' I said. Only Mungo's worried look prevented me from landing another.

'You filthy whore,' Sir Lancelot added a choice selection of epithets that should have curled my hair.

'I wonder how you look with your breeches off,' I said when he had run out of insults.

'What do you mean? I am Sir Lancelot Snodgrass, and I demand you release me.'

Macfarlane's laugh ended Sir Lancelot's tirade. 'Shall I cut them off, Miss Flockhart?'

'Yes, please,' I watched with as much pleasure as satisfaction as Macfarlane ripped his blade down Sir Lancelot's breeches from hip to ankle. The cloth parted, with Sir Lancelot goggling and swearing.

I looked and forced a harsh laugh. 'No wonder you need your friends to support you,' I said.

The younger man, Sir Martin Marshall, stared open-mouthed and obeyed as Macfarlane flourished the dirk ordered him to remove his breeches.

'So that's two more.' Five minutes later I looked back at the men, naked from the waist down and bound hand and foot. Their nakedness did not interest me. 'You're right Macfarlane; they're nothing without their breeches.' I shook my head. 'Nothing to see and nothing to boast of.'

'There are three left,' Macfarlane said.

I nodded. 'Let's find them.' I was glad that Sir Lancelot was out of the way. Now I wanted McAra and Findhorn. The rest were nonentities; they mattered less than the chaff in a riverside mill.

We scooped up the Honourable Peter Hain as he sat on the stairs and bundled him into an empty room. He struggled, kicking at me and using the most commonplace language, so I thrust Joe Manton inside his mouth and cocked the hammer. His eyes widened in horror.

'Down to the cellar with him,' I said. 'Chain him where we were chained.'

'McAra and Lord Findhorn will find him there,' Mungo warned.

'That's the idea,' I said. 'When Findhorn and McAra come for us, we'll take them instead.'

'You can't do this,' Hain said when I withdrew my pistol and dried the barrel on his shirt. 'You don't know who I am.'

Macfarlane laughed and fastened the chains around his ankles and wrists. 'You sit still, your Honourableness, and behave.'

I stared at the Honourable Peter Hain. Half naked and chained to the wall; he still looked as trustworthy as a viper. I could not help but despise these men. 'We'll use him as bait.' I heard the malice in my voice.

I knew that Mungo had been watching me. I hoped he understood that I was cleansing myself of the horror I had endured here.

'Dorothea,' Mungo put a hand on my shoulder. 'Be careful.'

'I will,' I said. Mungo was not advising me to take care of myself. He was urging me not to cause too much damage to Findhorn and his men. Every time I captured one, I felt the desire to hurt, to rip, to savage and even to kill. I was sure that Mungo read my feelings.

With Hain sitting against the wall all nicely chained up, we withdrew to the shadows and closed the shutter of Macfarlane's lantern.

'Now we wait.' I said. 'Now we wait for Findhorn.' I pulled back the hammer of my pistol and felt my excitement rise, and my fear. I fought the tears and remembered the nineteen-year-old girl I had been and the lost decade of my life. The image returned, Findhorn kneeling at my mercy. I could see his fear and taste the blood in the air as I pulled the trigger. I wanted that. Oh, God forgive me, but I wanted to kill that man.

A few hours ago the dark had been threatening. Now it was our friend. I remembered one time in Bengal, waiting in the night with a tethered goat. The animal, like Hain, was bait, and rather than two predatory lordlings, we waited for a leopard. The method was the same, the prey equally dangerous and the thrill of the hunt similar, except in this instance I could not keep the tears from my eyes or the feeling of sick hatred from corroding my soul.

The darkness folded around us, once again thick with menace, still except for the shuffling and mewling of Hain. I hoped he was suffering. I hoped that he suffered one-tenth of what I had experienced, I hoped he endured a fraction of the agony of fear which he and his type had put Marie and that little girl through.

I uncocked Joe Manton and cocked it again. I rubbed my hand over the butt. I took a deep breath, held it and released slowly. I uncocked the pistol. Mungo's hand crept to my arm. I shook it off. I did not want Mungo. I wanted Findhorn. I wanted him kneeling at my feet, crying for mercy as I blew out his brains.

'Where are you, little girls?' I recognised Findhorn's voice and stifled my fear. I was not proud of how I felt. I wished it were otherwise. I uncocked my pistol and cocked it again. I felt the perspiration coat my forehead and soak Mungo's shirt on my back.

'We're coming, Dorothea!' My name sounded obscene in Findhorn's mouth. 'Oh, Dorothea!'

I was never more grateful for Mungo's touch on my arm. I could feel myself trembling. I wanted to kill, to run, to cry, to curl into a ball and escape. I wanted to be anywhere except here, but most of all I wanted to kill Findhorn.

Mungo was close, his arm around me. I shook him off. I wanted him, and I wanted space. The past crowded into my head, chasing away the present. I was no longer Miss Flockhart, I was a nineteen-year-old girl again, full of hopes and dreams and love.

I grabbed that love and held it close. The love was real; only the object had altered.

'Oh, Dorothea, we want you!' laughter followed the cruel taunts.

Mungo reached across again. This time I allowed his touch.

Lantern light bobbed through the network of cellars, now glossing across a rack of wine bottles, now splashing on the stone slabs, or shining on the groined ceiling. Findhorn said something and McAra laughed. Unable to stop myself, I cocked the pistol, the sound metallic and loud in the dark.

'What was that? Who's there?' The lantern light swung around, bouncing from corner to corner. I remained still and silent. The light shone on Findhorn. Even in his white trousers and white shirt he looked the nemesis of an angel, a man with the soul of a devil and the bloated, pale face of the truly dissipated. He carried a lantern in his left hand and a long cane in his right.

'Probably a rat,' Lord Findhorn's voice raised the small hairs on the back of my neck.

'We could use the rats,' McAra said. 'Have the women hunt them, like ratting dogs.' He went into obscene details as they strolled past.

'My Lord!' Hain's voice cut through the darkness. 'They're waiting for you!'

'Damn it!' I had never heard Mungo swear before. 'He must have got the gag off.'

'Get me free!' Hain shouted.

'Now!' I gave the order without thinking and ran toward the lantern light. I expected the vicious swing of Findhorn's cane and ducked away, hearing the high-pitched whistle as it missed me by inches.

'Stand there!' I thrust my pistol into the lamplight so Findhorn could see it. 'Or I'll blow your head off.' Dick Turpin could not have said it better.

Unfortunately, Lord Findhorn was less than impressed. 'Is your powder still damp, Dorothea?' Lifting his cane, he slashed at me again. I stepped back, and he promptly threw the lantern in my direction. I ducked; it soared over my head to crash against the wall and fall to the floor, where it lay in a flickering circle of oil-fed light. Findhorn stepped backwards.

'Lord Findhorn! Show yourself! Face me, you coward!'

Findhorn had vanished in the dark. A second later McAra also extinguished his lantern and plunged the cellar into blackness. I stepped to the wall and stood still, holding my pistol ready, my finger on the trigger, waiting while the memories overcame the present.

The silence was deafening, overwhelming, like a physical force pressing down on me. I knew Findhorn and McAra were close by and my hatred and fear rose in equal measure, replacing all my love. I remembered waiting for the leopard and the *shikari* whispering the golden rule.

'*Keep still and keep quiet. Patience.*'

I had patience. For the past ten years, while most of me wanted only to avoid trouble and never see Findhorn or his type of man again, another small part knew that we would meet again. I had not planned this encounter, yet deep down I wanted it.

I had always wanted to kill Findhorn for the pain and horror he had caused me.

It was no dream, no vague possibility but a deep part of my being. That realisation shook me. I had considered myself to be a pacific, civilised and relatively educated woman, yet here I was admitting to animal feelings of revenge. I wanted retribution, no, more than that, I wanted to cleanse myself of the terror and agony, mental and physical, of that evening more than ten years ago.

All I had to do was wait, and Findhorn would move. He would make a mistake, and I could shoot him. I remembered Captain Rogers' words; *a human head is a diminutive target.* The widest target was hip to hip, the belly, the thighs and the groin. There would be an undoubted, savage satisfaction in shooting him there and watching him writhe in agony. I wanted him to suffer. I waited with my pistol cocked, and my mouth stretched into a smile although there was not a trace of humour in me.

'Can somebody get me free? Help me, my Lord!'

I had forgotten about Hain, who was shouting and rattling his chains. I tried to ignore him, listening for Findhorn's footsteps in the dark.

Something rattled of the wall nearby and rolled on the ground. A bottle? Who was throwing bottles? I flinched as something crashed near my head, and a splinter of smashed glass flicked my arm. Fighting my fear, I remained still. Findhorn or maybe McAra was trying to locate me.

'My Lord!' Hain was bellowing again. There were quick footsteps beside me, and somebody grabbed my arm. I jerked it free and swung sideways with the pistol, without any contact. A light flared a few feet away, and I saw McAra's pale face and staring blue eyes, and then the light died, and we were alone and wrestling desperately in the dark. I knew I was fighting for my life.

Bony fingers seized my throat, squeezing and without thinking I rammed up my knee, catching him shrewdly in the groin. He jerked forward, retching and somebody else arrived. I recognised the scent of heather and peat as Macfarlane grabbed hold of McAra and threw him to the ground. I could not forget McAra's sneering, pallid face and kicked out, catching him on the chest. The feeling of contact was pleasurable, so I kicked again. McAra yelped as I made contact with something soft.

'He's mine,' Macfarlane sounded as calm as if he was sitting in the drawing room in Thistle Street.

The light died, and I heard Macfarlane drag McAra away. There was a single loud cry and then silence.

I heard the scurry of footsteps running past. 'Who's that?'

'Not me!' Macfarlane said.

'Nor me!'Mungo had been standing only a few feet away.

'It's Findhorn,' I said. He's running!' I followed, listening for Findhorn's feet. The sound was sharp on the stone flags and echoed from the stone walls and the stone ceiling. 'Come back, you coward!'

Findhorn did not stop. He strode through the cellar and up the stairs, and I was a few steps behind all the way. I would not give up; I wanted that man more than anything I had wanted in my life. Nearly. *I wanted my baby back.*

Findhorn sprinted up the stairs from the cellar and onto the ground floor. I heard his gasping breath and knew his life of dissipation and drink had made him unfit. Still holding the pistol, I chased him. He glanced at me over his shoulder with his bloated face full of hatred. I heard somebody following behind me but did not stop.

'I'm coming for you, Findhorn,' I shouted.

He ducked through a double door and slammed it behind him.

I don't know what possessed me that night. I think it may have been the culmination of ten years of nightmares and fear, ten years of starting at every shadow and cringing every time I heard drawling tones that reminded me of Findhorn and his cronies. I do know that I had altered from the hunted to the hunter and the lust to kill was on me. I was the predator; I was Nimrod the mighty hunter, I was the nineteen-year-old girl returning to right the wrong. Was it some feminine instinct to destroy the man who had robbed me of my youth and happiness? Or was it more fundamental, a basic human desire for revenge? I don't know, and my attempts at self-analysis always end up with me twisting myself inside-out without reaching any conclusion.

I did not care what it was. I only knew that I must hunt down Findhorn.

Without hesitation, I kicked open that door and rushed into the room. Findhorn stood at a gun cabinet, struggling with the lock. He turned to face me, his eyes burning with hatred. The only time that I ever saw anything similar was when a wounded leopard turned pm us outside the village in Bengal, and it turned on us. Its eyes were like that, savage, untamed, a beast at bay.

The leopard had been pursuing its natural bent in hunting the villagers' goats. Perhaps Findhorn saw women as his natural prey, soft creatures to be hunted, tormented and used for his warped pleasure. Well, now one of his victims had turned the tables.

'Stand there,' I aimed my pistol at Findhorn's belly. In my mind's eye, I saw him falling, writhing in pain.

Findhorn must have read the determination on my face. Swearing, he threw his cane at me; it rattled against the wall behind my head. Some instinct had told me he would miss and I had not flinched. Findhorn ducked and ran out of a connecting door. I did not fire. I had only a single barrel, and I did not wish to miss. I followed, avoiding the chairs he strewed in his wake in his attempt to delay me.

Once more I heard somebody behind me. The doctor, perhaps? Or was it Macfarlane? I did not care. I only wished to end this.

'Dorothea! Be careful!' That was Mungo's voice. I was too intent on my prey to listen, yet I was glad he was there.

Findhorn ran into the corridor and stopped between two portraits. On his left was a smiling woman with a brood of children around her knees. On his right was a fine-featured man in a military uniform set against a background of battle and siege. In between these respectable people stood the poltroon.

I took deliberate aim at his groin, and he squealed and ran. I watched and followed.

'You coward!' I yelled. 'Running from a woman. You blackguard.'

The insults would not sting him. Men such as Findhorn were thick-skinned; they lived in their own world of self-indulgence, far from the real men's life of duty and honour, wife and family. I walked in his wake as he drew back the bolts of the side door and lunged into the night. Floating amongst drifting clouds, the moon was nearly full, Macfarlane's lantern providing ghostly light that gleamed on the boughs of trees and reflected on Findhorn's white clothes and the foul creature inside them.

I heard his gasping as he blundered across the grass and into the tangle of trees. I knew how he felt, for I had been in his position. I was there now, in my mind. I had never been away from that day, for time and distance do not remove memories. They always remain, sharp and searing to taunt and twist and torture.

'Run, Findhorn,' I called. 'Run you, scoundrel. I will catch you.'

I will catch you, however long it takes; I will always be here, Findhorn.

I followed My Lord Findhorn, seeing the twinkle of white breeches tight across his buttocks and the white flapping of his loose shirt. Lifting a stone, I threw it after him. 'Run, Findhorn, run!'

There were footsteps behind me. Mungo and Macfarlane I guessed. I did not look back. They were not part of this drama. Findhorn and I must finish this together; close the circle he had started ten years before when I had been a confused young woman who had dreamed of matrimony with a charming older Lord. I closed my mind to the future as I inverted my past.

I had no difficulty in walking between the trees, following Findhorn's blundering passage and the gleam of moonlight on his white clothes. I could see myself in his running form, feel his panic and blanked my elation. I knew I was wrong to enjoy this; I knew I was becoming as bad as the creature I hunted. I did not care.

'Run, Findhorn,' I pitched my voice to carry through the trees. 'I don't need a pack of dogs and half a dozen men to hunt you down. I know where you are you blackguard, you filthy, disgusting copy of a man, you bloated *thing.*'

The trees seemed to part before me, branches swaying as Findhorn staggered on. I heard him desperately swear as he snagged his shirt on a tangle of hawthorn, ripped himself free and ran on. I passed the shredded fragments of shirt without a smile. I knew where he was headed. This path led to a bramble patch, and although it was winter, the thorns remained, dry and tangled and sharp.

'Run, Findhorn, run!'

I saw his face as he peered over his shoulder at me, and then he plunged down a slope and into the massed ambush of brambles. I watched and said nothing as he yelled, dragging himself through the chest high bushes that hooked and tore at his breeches and shirt. I heard the ripping of material and heard Findhorn gasp with frustration and pain.

'Run, Findhorn, run!' Lifting a piece of rotted wood, I threw it at him, catching him on the back.

He squealed and pressed on, with the thorns tangling around his legs and waist, hooking into him, tearing his breeches, drawing blood with every step. I saw the flash of white flesh as the bramble thorns tore into his white breeches, I saw him rip himself free, so his breeches shredded from waist to calves.

I watched as Findhorn got himself more entangled and then I walked around the gulley and over to the far side, where Findhorn would have to emerge. Above me, the moon reached its zenith, a silver ball in a sky speckled with stars. It was serene up there, uncaring as Findhorn and I played out our little drama far beneath. If there are men on the moon, then our antics may have amused them that night. If there are not, then only the silver orb observed us, and nobody could see the thoughts inside my head.

I waited for Findhorn at the top of the slope as he struggled out with his shirt in shreds and blood from a score of scratches seeping through the remains of his breeches. He was gasping, his shoulders heaving as he neared me.

'Good evening my Lord,' I said.

When Findhorn looked up the expression of dismay on his face was as intense as anything I have ever seen. He stood with his chest heaving and brambles tangled around his legs and thighs. I aimed my pistol at his belly and pulled back the hammer.

He turned away, cowering from the threat of the muzzle. I watched without sympathy, noticing the blood on the bulge of his exposed buttocks, the deep scratches that ran from shoulders to waist and the trembling of his entire body.

'How does it feel to be the quarry, Findhorn? How does it feel to be in the same position as you put me and others? How many others? Do you even know? Face me, you coward, or I'll shoot you in the spine.'

He turned, shaking. I saw the gleam of tears in his eyes, and I did not care. I extended my arm, aiming at his belly. 'I hear that if I shoot you there, you will die slowly,' I said. 'You will suffer, but not as much as you have made me and others suffer for years.'

I heard people around me. I knew they were there although they were outside my world. I think I was mad in those minutes, as the insanity that for years had been knocking at the door of my mind finally entered. I stood there forever and for a half-second, as my mind wandered from the terrifying past when this man and his cronies had raped me to the terrible present when I was on the cusp of becoming a murderess.

Findhorn was sobbing. He sank to his knees, begging forgiveness that I would not grant. 'You seek grace at a graceless face,' I misquoted the old Border Ballad, 'but there is none for your men and you.'

Findhorn broke and turned away into that confusion of thorns so the brambles wrapped around him. He tried to run, and fell face first over a bush with his torn breeches exposing flabby white buttocks, ripped and bloody. I extended my hand and aimed. Could anything be more humiliating for a man than to be shot in that position by a woman? Perhaps, but I wished to see his face. I wanted to see him grovel and plead. I wished to see his fear as he had seen mine.

'Get up,' I said. 'Get up, or by God, I'll shoot you as you are.'

Findhorn struggled to his feet, wincing and crying as the thorns ripped at tender flesh.

'Face me,' I ordered. 'Turn around and face me.'

He did so, and I saw the tears on his white face. I aimed the pistol at the centre of his forehead and thumbed back the hammer. Findhorn dropped to his knees amidst the brambles.

'Please,' he said. 'Please don't kill me.'

The circle was almost complete. All I had to do was squeeze the trigger to put a lead ball in Findhorn's head. I could imagine the sound, the kick of the pistol against my hand, the spurt of orange flame. I could imagine the back of Findhorn's head exploding in a mess of blood and bones and brains.

'Please, please,' Findhorn was sobbing, great tears rolling down his bloated face. 'No, please.'

I felt my lips stretch into a smile that exposed my teeth. There was no mirth in my expression as I put pressure on the trigger of Joe Manton.

'No! Please, don't!' Findhorn was grovelling, face down in the thorns, a broken, near-naked thing in the guise of a man. I looked at the pathetic wreck.

'I can't do it,' I lowered the pistol. 'Oh God help me, I can't do it.'

'You don't have to.' Mungo was at my side. 'You have won. You have broken your tormentor and removed the evil memory.' He took the pistol from me and uncocked it. 'This man and his friends no longer have power over you. You are in charge of your life and your mind.'

I watched Findhorn lying sobbing in the thorns. Near naked and torn, he no longer looked dangerous. He only looked pitiful. Whatever he had been, he had never been a man. The circle had been closed, the cards turned, and I felt empty.

Chapter Twenty

We were alone. Macfarlane and MacGregor had temporarily taken charge of Findhorn, and his cronies and Mungo had given Marie and the young girl something to make them sleep. I leaned back in Mungo's chair and allowed the warmth of the fire soak into my battered body. Opposite me, Mungo nursed his glass. I watched the firelight play with the red claret.

'Well, Mungo,' I said. 'We've had some wild times.' I waited for him to say something although in truth I did not know what he could say.

'We have, Dorothea,' he said. 'And if things were different,' he paused and repeated, 'if things were only different.'

I prompted him. 'If things were only different, Mungo, what?'

The smile lit up his ugly, battered face. 'If I had money or the hope of making it, I would be looking for a woman very like you.'

I felt my heart-beat increase. 'And if you had money, Mungo, and you found a woman very like me, what on earth would you do with her?'

'I would ask her to marry me,' Mungo said. 'You know that I love you.'

It was the answer I hoped he would give, and now I must crush him, for the sake of his future happiness. 'A woman like me could never agree to marry you,' I fought the catch in my voice.

'I am aware of that,' Mungo spoke slowly. He drank his glass of claret and poured another, offering to do the same for me. He looked competent there, this stocky, caring, dependable man.

'You know my history,' I looked directly into his face. 'What respectable man would ever want to marry a woman who was forced by a gang of other men?' I forced out the word, being deliberately brutal. 'Who would wish to live with that knowledge?'

Mungo's chin lifted in what might have been defiance. 'I know your history,' he said, 'and I have seen you recover from the depths to fight back against a life that used you badly.'

I looked away. *No respectable man would want anything to do with a woman such as me.*

'If I had money, I would be proud to have a wife like you,' Mungo said. 'Any man would. But, alas I have none, and I will not expect any woman to immure herself in the depths of the countryside as a poor doctor's wife.'

I ignored the financial references. They were irrelevant. I had to be even more brutal to shake this man's dreams. 'I was raped,' I reminded. 'Many times, by four or five men, and I lost my daughter.'

I waited for the disgust and the withdrawal, the polite protestations of friendship that would fade as soon as we parted. In other words, I waited for the reaction I expected from the type of men with whom I had mixed all my life.

'I know,' Mungo said. 'And I feel deep sympathy for you, Dorothea. It was not your fault, and there was nothing you could do to prevent it.'

I nodded. 'It still happened,' I said. 'I was violated. I was contaminated.'

'They attacked you,' Mungo said. 'I wish you could find a man who deserves you.'

'I have found a man like that.' I said, suddenly forceful as I met Mungo's gaze. I finished my claret and passed over the empty glass for a refill. I needed French courage more than I had when I faced Findhorn.

'Ah, the bold Captain Rogers,' Mungo nodded. 'He is a good man.' I hoped I heard jealousy in his voice. Trying to push Mungo away was cruel-hard. I did not wish to hurt him.

A blackbird called outside, the notes as melancholic as a sunset, the call as beautiful as any orchestra and more poignant than the most exquisite piece of literature. I did not reveal my final secret to this pig-headed, ugly and utterly beautiful man. I could not tell him that ever since I had arrived back in Scotland, I had been living a lie. As soon as he knew, our friendship would end, and I did not want that. I wished to savour what we had as long as I could, although it was a house of deceiving cards built on sand. I had dealt some of my hand, and he had countered; now I only held the joker.

'That's unusual,' Mungo glanced out of the window. 'There is a coach drawing up outside the house.'

I looked. Lady Pluscarden's mulberry coach slid to a silent halt on the road, with the two footmen as handsome as ever as they opened the door and the driver bending to talk to his horses.

My heart began to patter again.

'What on earth does Lady Pluscarden want with me?' Mungo shook his head.

'Maybe she has heard how good a physician you are.' I tried to sound amusing.

The second that Lady Pluscarden emerged, one footman closed the coach door, and the other approached the house. I saw Her Ladyship's gaze rest on him for a second and shook my head. She must have been at least seventy yet was still full of fun and mischief.

'Doctor Hetherington!' Lady Pluscarden met his bow with a shake of her head. 'Oh, stand up man; I've no time for that nonsense today. I come bearing tidings of great joy, rather like the three wise men except there is only one of me and I'm neither wise nor a man.'

I stood up, curtsied despite Lady Pluscarden's words and watched as she sat in Mungo's seat.

'Indeed I am only a stupid old woman,' she eyed Mungo up and down. 'You have a comfortable house, Doctor.'

'It is a poor place for you to visit, Your Ladyship.'

'That's surely great nonsense, sir.' Lady Pluscarden used her favourite phrase. 'Now, sir and lady, what's all this I hear about you, eh? What's been happening here?'

'I'm sure there's nothing you wish to hear, Your Ladyship,' I said.

'If I didn't wish to hear, do you think I would have asked? And you should be ashamed, lady, hiding away as you have. Miss Flockhart indeed! I've never heard the like!'

I felt Mungo's eyes on me and could not control my blush of embarrassment.

'We'll come to that later, lady! Now, Doctor, where are your patients hiding?' Lady Pluscarden stamped her foot on the table. 'Tell me, sir! I will not be denied! There are too many secrets in this house.'

'One patient is in my bedroom and the other in the box room next door,' Mungo said. 'There is no secret there, Your Ladyship.'

'Let me see.' Rising abruptly, Lady Pluscarden strode to both rooms. 'Ah, yes, two little angels recovering from their ordeal. I heard some of what happened from Mrs Macfarlane.'

'Mrs Macfarlane?' I stared at Lady Pluscarden.

'Don't look so surprised, lady! I've known Isabel Macfarlane all her life.' Lady Pluscarden nodded to Mungo. 'Miss Flockhart, as she calls herself, is in a state of fragile nerves, Doctor. Pour us both some claret and tell me all.'

'Yes, your Ladyship.' With an apologetic look at me, Mungo hastened to obey as Lady Pluscarden settled herself down in his chair. She listened as Mungo told my story and, being the honest man that he was, he left nothing out. As he finished, Lady Pluscarden nodded.

'Good, well done Doctor and you lady. Now, what are you going to do with your prisoners? And with that rascal Turnbull?'

I shrugged. 'I had not thought that far, your Ladyship, and as for Turnbull, I don't know where he is.'

'He's tied securely in Hoolet's Wa's in the Pentland Hills,' this surprising old woman said. 'Safe, if not warm.' She pursed her lips.

'As for your prisoners, Macfarlane and I will take them to town. We'll leave them naked at the Tolbooth with a placard around their chests stating what they have done.' Lady Pluscarden smiled at me. 'It's all right, lady, I won't mention your name and nobody will dare question me. I know all the judges, intimately in most cases.' Her smile was pure mischief. 'They'll reputations will be ruined and they won't ever be in a position to bother you again.'

There was a sound from the bedroom and Marie's voice sounded.

'About time that young woman awoke.' Lady Pluscarden raised her voice. 'Robert!'

The tallest of her footmen entered.

'Robert! Bring in our passenger. Quickly now!' Lady Pluscarden watched Robert scamper away, winked at me and proffered her glass for a refill. I heard the coach door open and close again and footsteps in Mungo's small entrance-hall.

Gibbie Elliot had lost weight and looked ten years older. He gave me a wan smile. 'Where is Marie?' He asked.

'I'll take you,' Mungo said at once. 'It's good to see you again, Elliot.' He led Gibbie though, and I heard Marie's wild cry of delight. Mungo returned, smiling.

'Without any accuser,' Lady Pluscarden explained, 'the procurator fiscal had no reason to hold him. Gilbert is free, and if he tries to gamble again,' she fixed me with a hard eye, 'he'll have me to answer to.'

'How do you know Mrs Macfarlane?' I could not stop the question.

'She's my sister,' Lady Pluscarden said. 'We are not all born into lands, lady. Some of us marry greatly.'

'I had no idea,' I stared at this powerful lady who had just admitted to being low-born.

Lady Pluscarden finished her claret and smiled when Mungo handed her the bottle. 'Thank you, Doctor Hetherington. I concealed my past because it amused me. Others conceal their past for quite the wrong reason.' She looked at me, raised her eyebrows and smiled.

I knew Mungo was waiting for me to say something. I heard low voices from the bedroom next door. Marie laughed. If she could forgive Gibbie, perhaps Mungo would forgive me?

Lady Pluscarden eyed me over the rim of her glass. 'You are very quiet, my Lady.'

Mungo raised his eyebrows. 'My Lady?' He was smiling.

Thank you, Lady Pluscarden, I thought, before facing Mungo. I had to tell him sometime. 'When I was in India, Lord Tynebridge died, and with no males in the family, I fell heir to the title. I am Lady Tynebridge.'

Mungo gave a small nod. 'Yes, your Ladyship. I know.'

'You know?' I stared at him. 'How do you know?'

'I knew Lord Tynebridge and when he died all the talk was of the new heir, a woman in India, and then a year later, you turn up with your knowledge of Tynebridge Hall.' His smile was slow. 'It was not hard to put the pieces together.'

'Why did you not tell me?' I was quite indignant.

'Why did you not tell me?' Mungo returned.

'I thought my elevated rank would put you off,' I said. 'I was not sure how people would react to me.'

'Why Flockhart?' Mungo asked. 'Why choose that name?'

'It is my mother's name. I am legally entitled to use it if I wish.'

Mungo nodded, his eyes concerned. 'Why hide who you are at all?'

'I was ashamed,' I said at last. 'I was ashamed of what had happened to me.'

'You have overcome that now,' Mungo said. 'You have nothing of which to be ashamed. Now you start again, my Lady.'

'My Lady,' I repeated in misery. 'I knew you would withdraw from my company if I told you.'

Mungo frowned. 'You are my lady,' he said. 'I have already told you that. I don't care if you have a title or not. I believe Robert Burns said: rank is but the guinea stamp, the man's the gowd for a' that.' He smiled, 'in your case, the woman's the gowd, and pure gold at that.'

'Oh.' I stared at him, unheeding of Lady Pluscarden or anything else. I suddenly remembered precisely what Mother Faa had said. She had said that there would be a man in my future and he would wear a uniform. That had been accurate. George Rogers had worn a uniform. Mother Faa had not said I would marry that man. I had misconstrued her meaning. I pushed George to the past and smiled at Mungo.

'I'd rather you called me Dorothea.' I said. 'A while ago you said you wished I could find a man who deserves me. Well, I have.'

Mungo nodded. 'I am sure Captain Rogers...'

'No,' I shook my head. 'Not the gallant captain. I mean the loyal Doctor Hetherington if he will have me.'

Mungo stared at me with his mouth slightly open. 'Have you?'

I saw Lady Pluscarden's nod of approval as I waited for Mungo's reply.

'I would be honoured, my Lady Dorothea,' Mungo stepped across and kissed me, just once.

'Lovely,' Lady Pluscarden craned her neck to examine Mungo as he bent over me. She had the last word. 'You have found a good man with a broad chest and a shapely rump; you will never be short of entertainment, Lady Tynebridge.'

Historical Note

Much of the historical detail in this book is accurate, or as accurate as it can be. In 1803 there were fears that Bonaparte may invade and the coast east of Edinburgh held encampments of militia. Edinburgh was like an armed camp with thousands of men enrolled in Volunteer and Militia formations in expectation of the French landing. There were Field Days at Portobello beach, where the Royal Navy simulated a French invasion, and the local Volunteers and militia fended them off. Walter, later Sir Walter, Scott, the novelist, was only one of the prominent men involved in the Volunteer movement.

There were some invasion scares, including one in early 1804 when an over-zealous watchman believed that a fire in Northumberland was a sign that the French landed. He set light to a signal beacon, and the Volunteers from across the Borders mustered to repel a non-existent invasion. I used that incident although pushed it forward a few months.

Alexander McKellar was a real person and famous on Bruntsfield Links. He ran an Edinburgh pub, but not the Golf Hotel, which still stands. Women played golf at Bruntsfield from at least the middle of the 18th century.

Whisky smuggling was rife at the time, with Highlanders making illicit whisky, often known as Ferintosh, and carrying it into the urban centres. There were also local men and women involved in the trade.

Crichton Church and Crichton Castle exist. However, the church was in bad shape in 1803 and not until the 1820s was it restored to anything like its present condition. Tynebridge Hall is not real and nor was the Royal Union Bridge. The details and geography of Edinburgh and Midlothian were much as described.

The incident where Dorothea drove her gig over the Royal Union Bridge was inspired by a newspaper article of 2nd November 1808:

> *On the morning of Wednesday 26th a most dreadful accident happened to the London mail in crossing a bridge nine miles on the Glasgow side of Moffat. The centre arch of the bridge had previously fallen and the night being very tempestuous, the lamps were blown out in consequence of which the circumstances could not be observed by the coachman who proceeded unknowing the danger. The horses were precipitated over the ruins into the river carrying with them the coach by which dreadful accident two persons were killed and another so bruised that scant hopes are entertained for his recovery. The coachman and guard were saved but much bruised and three horses were drowned.*

> *Mr Clapperton the surgeon is to be much praised for his ready assistance and the exertions of Mr John Giddes, one of Mr Rae's servants are deserving of notice who at the risk of his life went into the river with a rope fastened to his body and saved the life of a lady, one of the passengers and some of the mail bags which must otherwise have been carried down the stream.*

Helen Susan Swift
Scotland
March 2018

Dear reader,

We hope you enjoyed reading *A Turn of Cards*. Please take a moment to leave a review, even if it's a short one. Your opinion is important to us.

Discover more books by Helen Susan Swift at
https://www.nextchapter.pub/authors/helen-susan-swift

Want to know when one of our books is free or discounted for Kindle? Join the newsletter at http://eepurl.com/bqqB3H

Best regards,

Helen Susan Swift and the Next Chapter Team

You might also like:

The Name of Love (Lowland Romance Book 4) by Helen Susan Swift

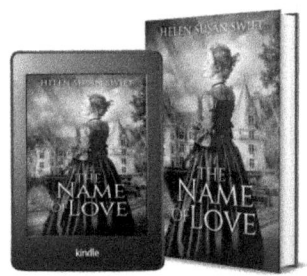

To read first chapter for free, head to:
https://www.nextchapter.pub/books/the-name-of-love

Lightning Source UK Ltd.
Milton Keynes UK
UKHW021503110920
369713UK00011B/460